Martha Gellhorn was born in 1908 in St. Louis and educated at the John Burroughs School and Bryn Mawr College. After her junior year in college, she worked briefly as a proofreader on the *New Republic* and as a cub reporter on the Hearst *Times Union* in Albany before spending four years in Europe, free-lancing and writing her first novel. Returning to the U.S. in 1934, she wrote reports on the living conditions of the unemployed, which were admired by Eleanor Roosevelt; when she fictionalized her findings in *The Trouble I've Seen* (1936), the book carried a preface by H. G. Wells, praising her "lucidity and penetration." Not long after this success (her picture appeared on the cover of the *Saturday Review of Literature*), she became a war correspondent in Madrid; in the following nine years, she reported war as it spread over the world from England to China. In 1966, her reports on civilian suffering in South Vietnam caused her to be barred from that country. Since 1934, she has published eleven books of fiction. Her nonfiction work is a selection of war reports, *The Face of War* (1959, expanded to include Vietnam and the Six-Day War 1967, expanded to include Central America 1986, final version 1988); and a selection from six decades of peacetime reporting, *The View From the Ground* (1988). Journeys in China, the Caribbean, Africa, and Russia are described in *Travels with Myself and Another* (1978). Martha Gellhorn now lives in Wales and London.

POINT OF NO RETURN

(originally published as *The Wine of Astonishment*)

Martha Gellhorn

with a new Afterword by the author

PLUME AMERICAN WOMEN WRITERS
SERIES EDITOR: MICHELE SLUNG

A PLUME BOOK

NEW AMERICAN LIBRARY

A DIVISION OF PENGUIN BOOKS USA INC., NEW YORK
PUBLISHED IN CANADA BY
PENGUIN BOOKS CANADA LIMITED, MARKHAM, ONTARIO

TO JAMES GAVIN

and to the men he commanded

in World War II

PUBLISHER'S NOTE

NAL BOOKS ARE AVAILABLE AT QUANTITY DISCOUNTS WHEN USED TO PROMOTE PRODUCTS OR SERVICES. FOR INFORMATION PLEASE WRITE TO PREMIUM MARKETING DIVISION, NEW AMERICAN LIBRARY, 1633 BROADWAY, NEW YORK, NEW YORK 10019.

 PLUME TRADEMARK REG. U.S. PAT. OFF. AND FOREIGN COUNTRIES
REGISTERED TRADEMARK—MARCA REGISTRADA
HECHO EN DRESDEN, TN USA

SIGNET, SIGNET CLASSIC, MENTOR, ONYX, PLUME, MERIDIAN and NAL BOOKS are published *in the United States* by New American Library, a division of Penguin Books USA Inc.,
1633 Broadway, New York, New York 10019,
in Canada by Penguin Books Canada Limited,
2801 John Street, Markham, Ontario L3R 1B4

Library of Congress Cataloging-in-Publication Data

Gellhorn, Martha, 1908–
  [Wine of astonishment]
  Point of no return / Martha Gellhorn; with a new afterword by the author.
      p.   cm. — (Plume American women writers)
  "Originally published as The wine of astonishment."
  ISBN 0-452-26223-2
  I. Title.   II. Series.
PS3513.E46W56   1989
813'.52—dc19   88-27237
                                                        CIP

First Plume Printing, July, 1989

1 2 3 4 5 6 7 8 9

PRINTED IN THE UNITED STATES OF AMERICA

> *1* <

THE FARMHOUSE was quiet, the soggy patch of field and the near forest were quiet under the flannel sky. It had not stopped raining.

Lieutenant Colonel John Dawson Smithers looked at the wet mud on his boots and trouser legs, at the bacon can filled with cigarette butts, the broken horsehair armchair, the rusted kerosene stove, and thought: this war has gone to hell. Where is everybody? It doesn't have to be so cold in here.

"Hammer!" Lieutenant Colonel Smithers shouted, and nothing happened. No orderly, no staff, no nothing; just a bunch of black mean-looking pine trees, and this rain out of a faucet, and time to wait in.

He decided he would read; the unlucky man who preceded him in this rathole had left behind a picture of Rita Hayworth, all teeth and bosom, tacked to the wall, and a two-

months-old copy of Life. Lieutenant Colonel Smithers began
to study some handsome colored photographs of insect-eating
tropical plants. It was hard to keep his mind on what these
flowers were up to. If Bill Gaylord was around, they could
talk over the situation; it relieved you even if the talk got
nowhere.

Very bad business, Bill, Lieutenant Colonel Smithers remarked in silence. You ought to see them at Regiment. Sour.
Sour and full of secrets. The 256th and 258th must be getting
the stuff kicked out of them. You taken a good look at those
trees? They're amputated, is what. Tree bursts like hail.
Nobody's moving. Can't move. I guess we'll be going in
tomorrow or maybe the day after. I don't like it, Bill. I don't
like the way people look around here. I wish we were back
on our little old front in Belgium. Why don't they tell me
something so I can get busy? Doc Weber says we'll have
more trench foot than we can count, let alone anything else.
Nothing will push through that mud. I saw a tank up there
at Regiment: when it turned it left a wake like a boat, I
swear it was.

"Hammer!" Lieutenant Colonel Smithers shouted again. It
was giving him the shakes to sit here and think about that
forest, and do nothing and have nothing to do.

Pfc Hammer entered the room in haste and without knocking, as was his custom. Every day was Christmas for Hammer,
as far as Lieutenant Colonel Smithers could see; the boy
didn't have enough brains to look on the dark side of things.
That pink and white face, those always delighted blue eyes,
turned to Lieutenant Colonel Smithers with an expression
of joyful and intimate obedience.

"I called twice," Lieutenant Colonel Smithers said.

"Yes sir. I was helping carry some radio equipment. I'm sorry, sir."

Radio equipment, Lieutenant Colonel Smithers thought, and imagined Pfc Hammer gently rolling a pair of red plastic PX dice.

"Is there any coffee?"

"Yes sir. I'll take your raincoat to dry."

Bert Hammer walked quietly down the hall to the farmhouse kitchen which was now the Battalion message center. When the old man was like this, worrying, he would blow up if you made one extra noise.

"Fellows," Pfc Hammer said to the kneeling group in the message center, "I got to leave the door open a crack so I can hear the old man. Keep your voices down."

Maybe the old man would make him jump around all afternoon just because he was in a bad humor. They had built a crackling fire in the kitchen stove, and Sergeant Follingsby invented a hot toddy, made from lemon crystals and some cognac the new switchboard operator kept in his canteen, and he was eight hundred francs ahead and everybody was having a fine time, if only the Colonel would take it easy and leave a guy in peace. Why can't he have some fun like the rest of us when he gets a chance, Bert Hammer thought. We're out of the line, aren't we? That ought to make any sensible person happy.

Lieutenant Colonel Smithers abandoned the insect-eating tropical plants. It was no use. Instead of savage plant mouths, snapping shut, he saw that road of sliding mud which disappeared into the black tunnel of the forest. He felt this waiting, like a cold uneasy sickness in his stomach; and anxiety like a closing weight over his eyes.

[3]

I got to put my mind on something else, Lieutenant Colonel Smithers decided. He listened to the steady rain and the distant noise of the guns and heard himself repeating, over and over, silently: this is bad, this is no good at all.

"It took a while, sir," Pfc Hammer said. He held a canteen cup full of pale cool coffee. "The stove was out."

"How about Crewe?"

"Yes sir. I forgot to tell you. A message came that he smashed his hip; he's gone to the rear."

"Allright, Hammer."

The coffee was undrinkable. If you were going to lose your jeep and driver, in a road accident, it was better to lose them here and now; there wouldn't be much use for jeeps in the Hürtgen forest. He was sorry about Crewe though. This reminded Lieutenant Colonel Smithers that they had reached Bittelheim at 0200 hours this morning and that Crewe had run into a truck at 0300 hours; and that he himself had had very little sleep. Crewe brought to mind the lost half of the baggage train which Crewe had been detailed to look for; Lieutenant Loring should have tracked that down by now. Which recalled the fact that, baggage train or not, they were short of warm clothing and overshoes and Lieutenant Hermann was away on a stealing mission, ordered to use his own discretion in the procurement of same. And Captain Martinelli had said that most of their radio equipment was drowned out on that lousy drive last night from Belgium, so he would be checking it now with Lieutenant Hooper. Waines ought to be back soon with the mail; they had to find that. Nothing was worse for the men than hanging around, wet and aimless, and no letters from home and no Stars and Stripes to gab about. The exec would be asleep, having been up all night and all morning. But where was Lieutenant William Gaylord, who might just as well be here to pass the time of day?

We need action, Lieutenant Colonel Smithers thought, yet he did not believe that; his outfit was too experienced for heroes. But the fierce boredom of war drove you; anything was better than waiting; you had to move, you had to do something; and action was their job and you hoped that if you pushed and didn't stop you could get this over, get out of it, get free, escape from waiting in all the worst places of the world for nothing except more fighting. Or a decent rest would be good; the whole Division out of the line, with days ahead, and mobile showers, clean clothes, sleep, hot food, liquor, mail, movies, girls . . . Anything at all would do, except this hour to hour hanging on, with time like a rock in your brain. Lieutenant Colonel Smithers put his hand up to his face; he had felt the nerve that started jumping just below his right eye. It did that, now, more and more often; it frightened him; a twitching man was suspect, he had a weakness.

There must be some place in Europe where you could pass the month of November without going bats. No matter how foul Europe was, and that was plenty, it couldn't rain everywhere all the time. He had heard that Cannes France and Capri Italy were good, though it seemed the Airforce had taken them over. The Infantry, on the whole, went no place you would care to remember. Nobody would choose Bittelheim Germany as a winter resort. London would be nice now, for a short leave. Some people said Rome was allright, plenty to buy, willing women, no rain. When you got right down to it, November would be best at home.

Slowly, like floating in sunwarmed water, Lieutenant Colonel Smithers drifted into the old daydream. If I were home now, he thought: this was the way the dream always began.

There were never many ducks on the Chattahoochie, a wide brown river flowing between untidy trees, but this year the great wedges, instead of flying farther south, descended with their soft roar of wings, and he was waiting. Hidden under the trees, in his boat, he raised his gun; they were braking in the air, swirling, and he fired twice, so fast that it sounded like one report; and two birds fell like stones. Then he reached into the big pocket of his khaki bush jacket (as pictured in Esquire for use on safaris) and pulled out more shells, loaded, and fired again; I bet I led them six feet, he thought; and two birds again splashed into the water. His dog, who in life was ugly, loving, and incompetent, leaped from the boat and swam for the birds, sure and sharp as a torpedo; returned; swam out again; returned to be hauled over the side and shake himself, and stand brown, gleaming and beautiful in the sun that sifted down through the trees.

It was time to go now, the smooth sunset hour, so he picked up the birds, whistled the dog to follow (and forgot the boat) and walked up the bank and across a field to the road. His sand-colored Buick convertible was waiting there with the top down: a sportsman's car. This car was new; he had bought it in his mind when the Division was fighting near St. Lô. His family's shapeless Dodge sedan was no car for a man who lived as he did. The soil of Georgia looked dark red in this light and the pine trees stood out triangular and almost black against the gold of the evening sky, and the air smelled of wood smoke and the water smell of rotting leaves, clean and delicious like a land at peace.

He stopped before his house and ignored it. He would leave the ducks in the kitchen and mix himself a bourbon highball to drink while taking his bath. Quickly, Lieutenant Colonel Smithers thought: Mom and Dad are visiting Suzanne and her 4-F husband in Chattanooga. Somehow, his parents were always away with his sister when he returned on these frequent visits to La Harpe. He did not see the bathroom but only smelled the soap which was like that shaving lotion he had bought in Paris. He did not consider who would cook his supper and he avoided thinking about the dining room; but he ate, with slow pleasure, a splendid meal: fried chicken and garden peas and new potatoes, biscuits with honey, and crunchy pecan pie.

Now he was dressed for the evening in his new double breasted pin stripe grey flannel suit, blue shirt and tie, brown suede brogues, and driving out Highway 29 to the Topple Inn. The girl beside him pretended she had to move closer because the wind was mussing her hair. Her hair was a floating mist of gold; her face was vague; around her throat she wore a delicate string of pearls. And he knew what she wanted: indulgently, triumphantly, he put his arm around her and drew her close. It'll be much better on the way home, he thought, when we're parked and I can use both hands. "Johnny," she sighed, snuggling against him, "I belong to you."

She was Mary Jane Cotterell who had replaced Elise Rathbone—for variety's sake—sometime in Belgium. Elise was a brunette but equally available. He'd been going slow with Mary Jane in his mind, because in a way Elise had been too easy. Mary Jane was a small, fragile sort of girl; she'd have little breasts, she'd . . .

Lieutenant Colonel Smithers got up and went to the cracked window and looked out on the soupy rain. He had never had a date with Mary Jane Cotterell in his life, nor with Elise Rathbone either, and never would have. Mary Jane's father was a millionaire; she lived in a house with white pillars two storeys high, behind a wide lawn covered in ivy. She went north to a finishing school and didn't think anybody in La Harpe was good enough for her except the Beakes and the Rathbones of course, also millionaires, and good family too. Miss Cotterell wouldn't settle for plain low-class millionaires, Lieutenant Colonel Smithers thought. And above all, she wouldn't be caught dead going to the Topple Inn with Johnny Smithers who worked as a salesman for the Meredith agency, and lived over by the mills where no one lived who was anybody, and whose family went to the wrong church and didn't keep servants. If I were home, Lieutenant Colonel Smithers told himself, I'd be coming in from work and I'd be listening to everything that went bad all day in the house and I'd be fixing some damn thing that was broke and eating as fast as I could and getting out. Bittelheim is what you've got; you'll never be a Lieutenant Colonel in La Harpe. The room felt even colder now.

The knock on the door was very welcome and he was delighted to see Sergeant-Major Postalozzi, so he said, "Where've you been all afternoon, anyhow?"

"Down at the crossroads, sir. The replacements have got here."

"Does Captain Waines know?"

"Yes sir. Him and Major Hardcastle are there now."

[8]

"How do they look?"

"Pretty good, sir." They looked like drowned rats, they looked like orphans, they looked dead on their feet. They were huddled under those ugly pine trees, wet and pooped, not belonging anywhere, not knowing what was going to happen to them or what kind of outfit they'd come to.

"Okay." He could check them later, which would be an agreeable change from this room, but he had to give the Company commanders time to line things up.

"We picked out a new driver for you, sir."

"What's his name?"

"Levy, sir."

"*What?*"

"Levy, sir."

"Whose idea was that?"

Sergeant Postalozzi said nothing. His grey face, with the flapping bulldog cheeks, said nothing.

Lieutenant Colonel Smithers could hear the rain, smearing and slurring against the window, and a scurry of mice or probably rats in the floorboards. This damned mudhole, he thought, I haven't got a Jew in my Battalion.

"Where is he?"

"Outside, sir."

"What's he look like?" I know what he looks like, a greasy little kike with those eyes they've got.

"Pretty good, sir," said Sergeant Postalozzi.

"Send him in."

Lieutenant Colonel Smithers knew the Jew boy was standing inside the door, waiting. Let him wait, he thought, and turned a page slowly. Then the silence embarrassed him and he said, "Over here, soldier."

"Yes sir."

The man stood with his back to the window. His overcoat hung about him, mushy and smelling of wet wool and the nights it had been slept in. It looked short because the man was so tall. His helmet liner had flattened his hair in a band across his forehead. He had not shaved for several days and his eyes were heavy and sad with fatigue. His face was correctly expressionless. Except in the movies, Lieutenant Colonel Smithers had never seen such a handsome man. And in the movies, as everyone knew, they tricked it all; the guys didn't really look like that. If Postalozzi was trying to be funny, he'd find out what happened to funny sergeants. Probably Postalozzi was just being dumb. *Levy*.

"What's your name?"

"Levy, sir."

Lieutenant Colonel Smithers had an angered feeling that someone was making a fool of him.

"New overseas?"

"No, sir."

"When did you come?"

"October 1943, sir. Italy."

"What Division?"

"Eighteenth Division, sir."

Combat infantry, Lieutenant Colonel Smithers noted with amazement.

"Why aren't you with the 18th now?"

"I got hit, sir. When I broke out of the hospital, they shipped me back to England."

"Just arrived from England?"

"No, sir. I was a replacement in the 90th."

"You certainly move around. What happened there?"

"I got hit again, sir."

"Spent a lot of time in hospitals, haven't you?" Lieutenant Colonel Smithers said. It was bad luck having a man near you who got hit all the time. He had never been wounded. On the ship coming to England he told himself, "Johnny, you're not going to get killed *and* you're not going to get hit, hear?"

Jacob Levy held the sombre conviction that his third wound would be the last. In his experience, as long as an infantryman could walk, he was sent back to a combat Division. Unless he went nuts and they sent him to the places for warwearies.

"Ever been a jeep driver?"

"All the time, sir."

"Okay," said Lieutenant Colonel Smithers who was confused by this interview. "Sergeant Postalozzi'll show you where the Motor Sergeant is."

"Yes sir." Pfc Levy saluted and left. The door did not bang, as it usually did, when he closed it.

Jacob Levy went down the narrow dark hall of the farmhouse and found the message center. In all the farmhouses he had known the officers parked in the front and the enlisted men at the back; the message center was their usual waiting and meeting place. The soldiers, kneeling in a circle on the floor, looked up, saw that this big man was a newcomer and not an officer, and went on with their game. Obviously this was no time for him to ask questions; they were busy. He had not been in any room as warm as this for two weeks. You didn't have to go looking for a sergeant; a sergeant always came after you by himself. No hurry, Jacob Levy thought, and squatted on his heels, with his back against the damp grey wall. It seemed to him that he had been bumping around in that truck with those other sad characters, for days. If there weren't so many people here, and all of them strangers, he'd make himself comfortable and try to get a little sleep. But if he stretched out, as if he owned the joint, they'd think he was horning in on their place. He would wait, which was what you did most of the time anyhow.

Aside from everything else about a wound, the changing around got you down. This was the third C.O., not counting all the majors, captains, lieutenants, sergeants. Always new ones and then he had to find out what they were like and then he had to figure out how to satisfy them. He did not want to be popular or promoted; he wanted to be left alone. This was the principal difference, to his mind, between being a Jew and being a Gentile. They left the Gentiles alone until the guy proved he was out of line but a Jew had to earn being left alone. There was nothing new in this and nothing to get sore about, but if you didn't get hit and could stay in the same outfit it was less trouble.

This southern Colonel would have to be satisfied quick because he was all set not to leave a man alone. He looked like an average Colonel, young, twenty-eight or so, probably pretty stuck on himself with that build and that wavy brown hair and those silver oak leaves, not too bad, just southern.

One of the players had backed out of the game and was counting his money with an air of innocent wonderment. They're sure taking kids in this army, Jacob Levy thought. This one didn't look as if he'd started shaving yet. Jacob Levy said, "Are we in Germany here, Mac?"

"We was in Belgium yesterday," Pfc Hammer said. "I know that."

"Germany," Sergeant Follingsby said. He was stoking the stove. "I don't know exactly where at. Aachen's someplace around here, I heard Lieutenant Hooper say."

"Thanks." So now it was Germany and it was no different. In the trucks they'd come through villages that you couldn't hardly tell from France or Belgium or even Italy. What made these crazy European people stay in these godawful little towns? The only difference in Italy was there'd be more children and more women washing their laundry in a horse trough. Who'd want to live in the filthy dumps, no roofs, no windows, smashed to hell, wars all the time? Why hadn't they got up and left a couple of hundred years ago? And the way they went on fighting about their countries you'd imagine they really had something to fight for.

Jacob Levy closed his eyes and began to think about the place where he was going when the war was over, if he didn't get that third wound. For a long time he planned simply to go home. He had never considered whether he liked his city, his house or his life; they were what he had and all he knew. But in the last hospital, perhaps because he doubted the chance of ever getting home at all, he began to dream of a new place and an unknown life. St. Louis was allright; he never had any trouble there. He knew a lot of people, maybe you could call them friends; he'd played football at Soldan High and that sort of fixed things up for him; Poppa's store would be his, just the way it was Poppa's, a family business; they'd lived in the house on Enright and Clarendon since he was born and comparing it with the holes he'd seen in Italy and France, he knew how good a house it was. His folks weren't the nagging kind, always asking questions; he could do what he wanted, with his own front door key and the use of the car whenever he asked for it. There was everything to go back to. He did not want to go back.

For a time, not knowing where to fix his hope made him sick the way the pain in his side made him sick. But it was hard to plan a life if you didn't know how to do anything, except the stuff the army taught you and helping Poppa in the store. Even helping Poppa wasn't knowing anything; he only knew what anybody could do, mixing sodas and wrapping packages and finding the things people asked for and saying how much they cost.

Then, slowly, and yet like revelation, Jacob Levy found what he wanted.

Every summer the family took a trip in the car for two weeks, to a different place. Poppa used to say he wanted to go to Europe some year. If Poppa only knew; they were lucky they'd stayed in America. These holidays were blurred together: Lake Michigan, New York City, Miami Beach, the Ozarks. But there was one summer which Jacob Levy started to remember, in the last hospital, as if he were living again under that same sun. Softened by time, gentle, safe, the memory of a stream in the Smokies came back to him. He knew it as well as Enright Avenue, though he had only been there once, in the summer of 1936, when they were driving to Charleston. And, thinking of this quiet place, he knew that he had never liked cities, and had never truly wanted the life he was born to. There were too many people around in cities; they expected something of you or they were waiting to criticize you. They sort of looked at you; they talked too much; they were always in a hurry. Momma and Poppa could come and visit him or maybe he'd go and see them once in a while. But where he wanted to live was by his stream.

The stream was so cold it hurt your hands to cup up the water. It was bright and clear like ice, but it ran over smooth brown rocks and little patches of gravel and sand, so standing above it you might think the water was brown. There was an old wood bridge for wagons, but nothing ever came that way. The boards of the bridge were grey like elephant hide, and thick, and warm in the sun. Lying on the bridge, you had the world to yourself; the water made a rushing sound so loud you couldn't hear anything else. There were ferns, like the ones in the florists', growing down to the water, and moss on the big stones that stuck up at the side of the stream. The trees came together like a roof over the old dirt track of the road so it was all shaded, except for light green specks of sunshine. Those were birch trees and some other kind too. And there were some that turned their leaves inside out when the wind blew, so they looked silver. Plenty of pink and yellow and white flowers grew everywhere but nobody had planted them. No one would bother you in a place like this.

Somewhere in those woods there was a sign, with an arrow, marked "Fish Hatchery." He did not know what a fish hatchery looked like, or what anybody did there, but he could learn, considering all he'd been able to learn in Basic. He'd get a job and it didn't matter what it paid because he would need so little. He was going to build his own shack out of logs from the woods and the stones of the stream bed. And later make a vegetable garden. There would be enough money saved up for this from the years in the army. And he would live there, not worrying or thinking about people, or trying to please anybody, for he wanted everything easy and quiet from now on out.

Poppa might kick at first. He'd say he had built up the business for him, it wasn't everybody had a business established since twenty-three years, no debts, all that goodwill, and customers who wouldn't trade with anyone but Mr. Levy. Why couldn't Jacob take over the drugstore like a good son who had his head screwed on straight? Momma would say, leave the boy alone, Poppa; maybe he needs a change, he'll come out of it by himself, just leave him alone now. The guys from Soldan, unless they were killed somewhere in this war, would say what's the idea being a hermit? The girls would say nothing because they would be married. But maybe he wouldn't have to listen to all this gabbling and is-he-right-is-he-wrong. Maybe he'd already be in the place he had chosen, with nothing to hear but the noise of the clear brown water over the stones.

Jacob Levy sat on his heels, tired, a little cold now, unmoving, and thought the same things he always thought. Then he reached inside his overcoat and unbuttoned the breast pocket of his jacket and took out the only personal possession he ever carried with him, which was a calendar. He did not have any ideas about when the war would end and he was not looking forward to a leave. He just crossed out the days on his calendar, and to see each day finished and sure not to come back gave him pleasure.

I wish that sergeant would show up, Jacob Levy thought. His eyes burned and his back was getting chilled from the damp wall. There must be someplace, maybe in the attic or in a barn, where the Headquarters enlisted men slept; or maybe there was a tent he could squeeze in or maybe the guys were out there in the rain, in whatever holes they'd dug. He hoped this new Colonel wasn't the kind that shouted orders at you. They seemed to be pretty nice fellows here in the message center, as if they'd been together a long time and got used to each other and would just as soon be friendly. Maybe he ought to find that sergeant himself; you never could tell how things worked in a new outfit. Jacob Levy slid down so that his legs stretched out on the red tiled floor, his head nodded forward on to the dirty wet overcoat, and he slept.

. . . . ? . . . .

The staff had eaten, making unfavorable remarks about fried spam, Bittelheim, the climate, the Corps M.P.'s who were alleged to have snafued traffic all the way to Paris, this forest from which no good might be expected, and now, still wet, cold, bored, generally disgusted, they had gone to sleep on their various square feet of floor. All except the S-2, Lieutenant Gaylord, and Sergeant Postalozzi, who were taking the first night shift. Major Hardcastle should have stayed up but since he came to supper sneezing and with a feverish look in his eyes, and Doc Weber diagnosed flu, Lieutenant Colonel Smithers was replacing him.

"Why don't you get some sleep, Johnny?" Lieutenant Gaylord asked. "I'll call you if anything comes up."

"I'll stay around." It was no hardship to sit up with Bill; he liked Bill the way you would like someone at home, in peace time. He could act natural but Bill wouldn't take advantage of that. Of course there were a few things they couldn't talk about: the oak leaves and the silver bars pre-

[17]

cluded absolute candor. Lieutenant Colonel Smithers thought, with amusement: look at that guy, would you? As usual, Bill's uniform appeared to have flown together and settled on him. He had folded a blanket on the seat of a kitchen chair, tipped the chair against the wall, stretched his feet out on a box, and now gave the impression of a man gloriously at ease on an overstuffed sofa.

Lieutenant Colonel Smithers was reading a poop sheet that had filtered down from Division. This document discussed the responsibility of unit commanders in the matter of trench feet.

"Why don't they send me some overshoes," Lieutenant Colonel Smithers asked, "instead of this slop?"

Sergeant Postalozzi, brooding over the papers that always accompany replacements, knew that no reply was required from him. And this is Captain Waines' job, Sergeant Postalozzi thought, I'm exploited is what I am. Lieutenant Gaylord did not bother to answer. For two hours that afternoon he had appealed to charity and threatened blackmail, in an effort to find some liquor for Johnny. Johnny needed a drink. Johnny was wound up tighter than a clock. But there wasn't a bottle anywhere or else Regiment was full of lying miserly bastards. He never expected things to be good so he was not upset, the way Johnny was, when things became worse. Besides, he had taken the precaution of borrowing a book called "Murder Makes Merry" from the Regimental S-3; his night was fixed. And meanwhile he had to catch up on L'il Abner.

"Bill," Lieutenant Colonel Smithers said. "You seen my new driver?"

"Just saw him."

"What do you make of him?"

"Oh, I don't know." This was the first Stars and Stripes in four days. Lieutenant Gaylord had saved L'il Abner until last and needed quiet to enjoy it.

"He's a Jew," said Lieutenant Colonel Smithers.

"Fine old Jewish name, Levy."

"He don't seem very bright."

"No?"

"No."

"I can't get over that pan of his," Lieutenant Colonel Smithers went on.

"He ought to go in the movies. He could call himself Jack Lee. He'd have the women squirming from New York to California."

"Yeh."

Lieutenant Gaylord finished L'il Abner, laughed, and said, "It was good today."

"Where's Levy from, Sergeant?" Lieutenant Colonel Smithers asked.

"He didn't say nothing to me, sir." Sergeant Postalozzi was having no part of this business. Could Levy help it if he looked like Victor Mature, only more soulful? The soulful angle came from being in the hospital so long, as anyone could tell except somebody like the Colonel who'd never been hit. Sergeant Postalozzi had been wounded and once was enough. He came from Detroit, worked at the Fisher Body plant, belonged to the C.I.O., and knew about Southerners: anti-union slave-driving KuKluxers, at heart. The Colonel was allright but sometimes he acted like everybody was a dog unless they came from south of the Mason Dixie line. And besides, being anti-semites was one of the reasons for this war, so at least the officers could remember that. And he would like to stuff these papers in the garbage or elsewhere, as the case might be. Levy didn't ask any more questions than he had to, and he knew his job. They could lay off guys just because they weren't southern gentlemen from some hick town in Georgia.

"You never know where you're at with a Jew," Lieutenant Colonel Smithers said.

For God's sake, Lieutenant Gaylord thought, won't he ever stop worrying? He looks for things to worry about. What difference did it make if Levy was a Jew or a Catholic or a Chinaman or an Eskimo, as long as he could drive a jeep? Johnny took this war too personally.

"I never had a Jew in my Battalion."

"Nobody's going to blame you."

"Yeh, I know."

Lieutenant Gaylord was about to observe that Johnny should stop acting like an old woman. But seeing his commanding officer hunched over the mimeographed papers, he thought: it's getting Johnny down. How did he know what it meant or cost, to command a Battalion? He wouldn't want the job at any price; there was no rest for a man. Maybe Johnny worried all the time about everything because he had to, because he couldn't stop; maybe Johnny himself was sick of it.

Out of pity, Lieutenant Gaylord said, "What we need is a trip to Paris." He knew it always cheered Johnny up to think about Paris. There wasn't anything to worry about in Paris.

Paree, Lieutenant Colonel Smithers thought, responding happily and at once as Lieutenant Gaylord had expected. This was the only memory that was anything like what you read about war, or heard or saw in the movies: his forty-eight hours leave in September. Those cute little French girls who walked around on stilt slippers, with their hair in a high wave over their foreheads, and their legs that were perfect but shorter from the knee to the ankle than the girls at home. His ribbons fresh from the PX and his uniform cleaned and pressed and the smell of that French shaving lotion. The night club on the Champs Elysées, all that glass and chromium and pictures painted on the walls and two orchestras and the girls in evening dresses, hanging all over you and chiselling drinks. The carriage in the park, voulez-vous, amour, and a brass bed as big as an LST, darleeng you are so wonderfool, darleeng, more. . . .

"Paree," Lieutenant Colonel Smithers sighed.

Unexpectedly, Lieutenant Gaylord laughed. "You remember that captain from the 12th we saw this morning, Johnny?"

"Yeh."

"Remember he told us how those touring correspondents from home came around and asked his men what they were fighting for and the G.I.'s acted like they had a mouthfull of it?"

Now they were both laughing. They could see those soldiers' faces as if they'd been there: the captain had said he'd nearly choked at the time.

"I wish some correspondents would come around and ask me," Lieutenant Gaylord said. "Gaylord knows, I'd say. Gaylord isn't a dumb slob like most of these soldiers. Gentlemen, I'd say, Gaylord is fighting for one thing and one thing only."

Sergeant Postalozzi listened to the conversation of the officers with bored detachment. He looked at his watch and wondered how he could keep awake for another three hours. The army gave orders about everything except how you should get enough sleep. Suddenly Sergeant Postalozzi was filled with homesickness for the kind of talk he liked: a meeting of his local for instance, where the men would be serious, practical, shrewd and maybe a little angry; angry about something that counted, talking about something that mattered. The stupidity of war depressed Sergeant Postalozzi. Anyhow, Sergeant Postalozzi thought, for Levy's sake it's good the officers are still interested in women. Levy seemed like a pretty nice fellow; he might even belong to a union, where he came from.

> *2* <

THE ROOM smelled of bodies, the thick half-cooked breakfast bacon, damp plaster and stale cigarette smoke. At eight o'clock in the morning there was scarcely enough light for Lieutenant Colonel Smithers to write his weekly V-mail letter to his parents. "Things are pretty quiet up here and we're not doing much but lay around taking it easy," he wrote, paralyzed by boredom. There was nothing he could tell his family, nothing he wanted to tell, and very little he wanted to hear. His parents lived beyond time and measurable space in a world that seemed grotesque to him, a scurrying loud patriotic antheap where everyone babbled his stupid head off about the war as if any of them knew what they were talking about. What next, he asked himself. "I hope you're all getting on fine."

He had been asleep with his eyes open, or simply numb, and was surprised to hear Sergeant Postalozzi say, "Message for you, sir."

He took the yellow message blank and as he read it, he felt what it said, like a gong thudding inside him. There was a cold still second while he listened to this warning. Then he was ready, as he always had been before, and became the certain man, Lieutenant Colonel John Dawson Smithers, commanding the Second Battalion, 277th Infantry, Twentieth Division, U. S. Army.

"Tell Lieutenant Gaylord and Captain Martinelli to follow me over to Regiment right away," he said, and took his raincoat from a nail on the wall, and was gone.

. . . .

The Battalion area seemed to be peopled by men who had all got drunk in the same obsessed way and were now engaged in carrying things idiotically from one place to another. There was a great deal of shouting. "Where's Sergeant Black? Anybody seen Sergeant Black? He better show up. Lieutenant Gaylord wants him." . . . "Where's Lieutenant Grace? Well, for Christ's sake, get him! S-4 wants him." . . . "Where's Captain Weber? How should I know? Regiment wants him." The truck drivers regarded the horses, who were to replace wheeled transport in this mud, with dismay and suspicion. "We're lousy mules is what we are," said a telephone linesman, as he dumped a bundle of blankets on a khaki mound. "Move on, mule," the Supply Sergeant said. The Catholic chaplain came over from Regiment and set up his confessional in a pup tent. The Protestant chaplain wandered around the Companies, saying kindly and encouraging words, and to some he opined that God would look after them. The recipients of this news took it with skepticism, having noticed God's indifference to many of their friends; and besides this was a form of conversation that embarrassed them in broad daylight where other men could hear. At various times they had bargained with God, making many promises and crying silently for help; but that was a man's own private business and nothing you wanted to talk about with a chaplain. PX rations were distributed; old debts of cigarettes and razor blades were repaid. Some men wrote letters home and some did not. They told each other, in the voice of disgust which was also the voice of pride, that whenever the situation was screwed up higher than a kite, their Battalion got called in to straighten out the mess.

. . . .

Pfc Hammer kicked the bedroll lightly and said, "Wake up, Levy."

Jacob Levy did not know where he was and lay on his back on the barn floor, watching dark figures weave before him. Then he remembered. His hands were stiff and fumbling as he laced his boots. He did not taste the breakfast, half eaten, half spilled, under the black dripping trees. Though he could not see the face, he heard the officer's voice saying, "The ditches are full of schu mines. Don't dive for them if the artillery starts. It ought to be pretty quiet now, anyhow."

Jacob Levy carried a metal ammunition box, an angular sack of C rations, his blanket roll, his carbine, and a belt load of grenades. Ahead of him he saw a shadow, swollen and bowed as he was; he could hear the man behind him, grunting sometimes under his load. His mind was empty. You didn't need to think; you looked and listened and put one foot in front of the other; with luck you would eventually get where you were going.

All night men and horses pushed through the mud on this narrow road. The German artillery, harassing other sectors of the forest, camouflaged the noise of the Battalion's movement. There was also something to be said for the rain and the muffled sky. Somehow, as always, despite the darkness, the men who got separated from their units, the men who misunderstood their orders or couldn't see what they were doing, the supplies that got dumped in the wrong places, the horses that went crazy because of the artillery, the radios that were wet and wouldn't work, the Battalion moved up and organized for the attack.

The trees grew clearer and separate, in the before dawn light; they were like no other trees. Hacked and leaning, blown on to each other, burned, the dead trees rose from the endless, sucking mud. Led by guides, the Companies passed communications dugouts, foxholes, aid shelters, half-submerged tank destroyers and anti-tank guns, and finally filtered into the forward outposts of the unit awaiting relief. Now the two-way movement was finished; the sector was theirs; and they alone had the forest and the emptiness of nothing between you and the enemy.

At 0700 hours, which was officially daylight, Easy Company crossed the line of departure on schedule. They progressed three hundred yards to a known minefield, blew holes through the wire, captured the German positions inside this enclosure, took no prisoners, fought off two counter attacks, and were ordered to hold. Captain Politis, two non-coms, and fifty-seven men were killed in the course of this action which lasted one hour and forty minutes. Lieutenant Rodney Blackmer, who took command of the company, felt badly about scooping up Nick Politis and shoveling him into a shell hole. In real life, Nick Politis had owned an undertaking establishment in Trenton, N. J. All the way from Normandy, Lieutenant Blackmer had listened to Captain Politis' conversation about embalmment, caskets, recorded organ music, and suitable floral tokens. It seemed a shame to do such a hurry-up cheap job on Nick.

Fox Company did not move at all, being pinned down by artillery at the edge of a mined road. Without moving, they lost forty-three men, mostly head wounds from tree bursts, and by nightfall the Company commander had a strange look in his eyes. Lieutenant Colonel Smithers, who had listened all day to voices reporting failure, told Lieutenant Gaylord they would get moving at first light tomorrow; there couldn't be two days as lousy as this in a whole war. Meanwhile Easy Company needed ammunition, in its wired-in cemetery.

Thus Jacob Levy became an ammunition bearer. At midnight he joined the snail-like column of men on the mud path, bordered with mine tapes, which led to Easy Company. The bearers were instructed not to stop for wounded; aid men would follow them. "You get the stuff there and get back," Captain Martinelli said, "and be quiet about it." It was obvious that the quieter they were, the longer they would live.

The first man who lost his balance, stumbled and slipped into the minefield beside the path, screamed, but briefly. He was dead before the aid man reached him. The noise attracted machine gun fire but the mortars were more effective. Jacob Levy, swaying from the shock of an explosion, heard a groaning choking sound somewhere in the dark behind him. He walked on, bowed like an old man and dragging his feet. There was no feeling inside him except the hollow coldness of fear.

Lieutenant Colonel Smithers was mistaken about moving; the front did not change for five days. Jacob Levy knew this time had limits, because he crossed off each day on his calendar when he returned from the minefield. He dropped into the hole he shared with Pfc Hammer, shielded for a moment the forbidden beam of his flashlight, and drew a pencil line through the date. Then he fell into a thick buried sleep.

There were days as well as nights, yet they were unreal and dim and only a waiting for darkness. Jacob Levy would wake, in the light that was never daylight, and slowly unbend his body. He slept with his knees drawn against his chest and his head down, and in the morning it seemed that his spine had curved to that position and his legs would not straighten again. With his helmet, he baled water from their hole, then pulled himself over the side and went to cut pine branches for the floor. Towards evening Bert Hammer would do the same; this way they could keep from sitting in a pool of mud as thin as soup. Every morning, Jacob Levy added more dirt and logs to the slanting roof that covered them. Then he crawled back under this shelter and ate C rations without hunger and they tasted like cardboard. He judged the time and the place to empty his bowels, hoping the artillery would not catch him while so engaged.

He listened, always, with his whole body to the shells that seemed to stop in midflight and explode just above the trees.

The German artillery rolled over them in furious cracking waves, and his head felt as big as a balloon, growing high and naked above his shoulders. Then the artillery would stop and the silence was unnatural and threatening. The strange mists of the forest floated in rags through the trees or crept upwards from the ground; the smoke of a phosphorus shell stood fixed in a white plume; branches split and fell; mud-covered figures moved in the shadows; and the silence became as cold as the cold colorless sky. Then the German artillery would start again.

If an officer or a sergeant saw him, he could be sure of getting extra work. Jacob Levy went wherever he was told to go, watching his feet. He was always wet and always cold and he stopped noticing this. There was no other condition of life, and no other world beyond these twilit trees.

Captain Martinelli thought Levy was a good steady man and he meant to tell the Colonel so, when he had time. Pfc Hammer decided that Levy certainly wasn't a sociable fellow but you had to hand it to him, he didn't beef, you never heard a bitching word out of him. Nothing was real to Jacob Levy except the night's journey through the minefield because he believed that it was waiting for him there, the third and last one.

Pfc Hammer was Jacob Levy's newspaper. "We're like those hot beds you read about at home," Bert Hammer said, "the factory workers. One gets in and the other gets out." During these casual meetings, Pfc Hammer would announce: "Marv Busch picked off a sniper last night. . . . Corporal Trask got hit in the head. The wire men are certainly catching it. . . . Some cigarettes came up, I heard from Sergeant Purdy. . . . Captain Waines said there'd be mail in the morning maybe.

. . . Sergeant Postalozzi says they ought to shoot the replacements at the repple depple and save trouble. He says it just wastes time carrying all them bodies back from the road." . . .

Bert Hammer talked a great deal about Lieutenant Colonel Smithers who was the center of his world. "That man can go anywheres and not get hurt," Bert Hammer would state as a fact. "The Colonel's sore because we don't get moving," he said, and Jacob Levy found this amazing, it would not have occurred to him to become angry with doom. "He'll get us out of here allright," Bert Hammer said, and suddenly Jacob Levy wanted to see the Colonel. He wanted to see a man who could get them out of here, not that he believed it was possible.

On the fourth morning, Jacob Levy said, "I think I'll get me some coffee," and followed Pfc Hammer through the lacerated trees. The coffee, if any, would be in the opposite direction; he had come this way only to look at the Colonel. Lieutenant Colonel Smithers was standing at the entrance to his dugout, watching a file of walking wounded pass slowly down a path towards the rear. Then he saw Jacob Levy and thought, that man looks bad. Lieutenant Colonel Smithers smiled. His smile was like shaking hands.

"How you doing, Levy?" He was pleased with Levy; Levy was still alive. Staying alive had become almost a sign of personal loyalty.

"Allright, sir," Jacob Levy said, and smiled back.

The Colonel looks bad, Jacob Levy thought. But it's not getting him down, he's just sore, the way Bert says. He watched Lieutenant Colonel Smithers walk, erect and businesslike, towards the OP and Jacob Levy told himself: he acts like it was no worse than a street at home. If he could look

sore and walk as if he didn't give a fart for this forest, maybe
Bert Hammer had something. Maybe the Colonel will get us
out of here, Jacob Levy thought, handling his new hope with
care.

That night, as every night, Lieutenant Colonel Smithers
studied the casualty list in his dugout CP. Head wounds,
trench feet, pneumonia, the punctured, the dismembered, and
the plain dead: dead getting nowhere, he thought, dead for
nothing. Lieutenant Colonel Smithers' eyes were dull with
fatigue. He signed for the damaged or lifeless bodies and
handed the paper to his executive who was sitting wedged
against his left side. If they didn't move pretty soon there'd
be no one left in the Battalion. Except Levy, Lieutenant
Colonel Smithers thought, and instantly this became a fine
private joke against the Germans. Levy wouldn't get killed;
they'd show those krauts. Kill everybody and not get Levy,
our only Jew, when he's what they got their real grudge on.
It was like spitting in the krauts' faces, for Levy to survive.
Lieutenant Colonel Smithers gave a grunt of laughter and
fell asleep.

Lieutenant Gaylord turned his head and saw that Johnny
was sleeping. Johnny was lucky to dream something funny
anyhow; it was the only way to get a laugh nowadays.

"Our little home smells like those outdoor gents' rooms in
Paris," Lieutenant Gaylord observed to Captain Martinelli.

Captain Martinelli, using his mapboard as a table on which
to write the daily S-3 report, was too tired, busy and depressed to answer.

You wouldn't believe, Lieutenant Gaylord thought, that
people had different smells the way they have different eyes.
How many smells did that make in the world? There were

eight good stinks in here at the minute, and his own was right at the head of the line. Also, in weather cold enough to freeze your balls off, why did your clothes stick to you with a sort of greasy sweat? This place was enough to make you homesick for Harrisburg.

"Can you move your feet, pal?" he said to Captain Waines. "I thank you."

You couldn't even stretch your legs without kicking someone in the crotch.

No one wanted to talk, that was clear, and he had nothing to do until his patrol got back. He could of course sit here and keep busy all night, listening to his stomach rumble over a mess of dog biscuits and pork and apple paste. Only the army would dream up food like that. It made you feel like puking just to think of it. I wish I had a book and a place to read it, Lieutenant Gaylord thought.

He wanted to escape into his favorite paperbound world: dope peddlers, gamblers, blackmail, murder; frightened platinum blondes, draped with rubies, escorted everywhere by ominous hard-faced men; the innocent girl enthralled by a crafty rich old woman who kept Siamese cats, smiled terribly, and drank port; the clues of the bloodstained glove, the trace of perfume in a dark room, a mirror scratched by a diamond; and that infallible man, the private detective, with his mocking smile and cold wit, his chivalry, his magic appeal to women, all women, his Charvet ties, and the client's grateful gift of twenty grand that closed the case. . . . Sergeant Black will call me when the patrol gets in, Lieutenant Gaylord decided; and slept.

● ● ● ● ● ● ● ● ● ● ● ●

On the seventh day, the Battalion had advanced one mile and a quarter, to occupy a hill which looked exactly like any other tree-covered lump in this hopeless forest. They were dug-in and had nothing to fear except artillery and counter-attacks.

Over their heads a pointed, incoming, gnashing, colliding roar repeated itself until it became a ceiling of sound. The overhead metal crashes diminished. There was the shock of silence; and again the screaming wide deep explosions. Jacob Levy sat against the far side of the burrow he had helped to dig.

"I can't wait no more," Pfc Hammer said.

Without answering, Jacob Levy turned his head so that Bert Hammer could be alone. Presently Pfc Hammer was busy with his entrenching tool. He said, to no one, "Like dogs. Just like dogs."

"Can't help it," Jacob Levy said. "I wonder why the Colonel doesn't get hit." He had been thinking about this a great deal.

"What's the matter with you? Why should he?"

"The way he walks around. With anybody else, you'd think he was asking for it."

"Oh that. He's always like that. He's lucky."

"You ever been hit, Bert?"

"No." Pfc Hammer knocked the butt of his Garand three times.

Then maybe the luck is catching, Jacob Levy thought. Maybe whoever worked for the Colonel or was near him got some of it too. He was alive himself, wasn't he, and he'd never have made it in the old days. And the Colonel had taken them out of where they were, anyhow; you could honestly say this hill was an improvement; so in the end maybe he'd get them out of the whole forest. There were lucky and unlucky people, nobody could argue about that, you only had to use your eyes to see it. But maybe some men, who were so lucky that they were different from plain people, could spread their luck around them. You couldn't explain everything that happened. You couldn't say a man was smart, so nothing hit him. Jacob Levy, who had no admiration for bravery, regarding it as an inescapable duty, revered luck. He began to think of Lieutenant Colonel Smithers with respectful gratitude: he would believe in the Colonel's luck and be saved by contamination.

. . . .

No one could tell how many houses had once stood in Wipfel. It seemed a place where, for unknown reasons, truckloads of broken brick, cement, stone and burned pieces of wood had been dumped without plan. Underneath this rubble were some good cellars, and in any case Wipfel was better than the forest. It was human and would not start creeping and crawling on you, after dark. Since something, if not too much, could be said for Wipfel, they were ordered to leave it at once.

At 0655 hours, Fox and George Companies were ready to advance from the edge of the flattened village. It did not look too bad; a long open slope of meadow and field lay ahead, and tanks would spray the forest, preventively, on both flanks of the attack. At least you could see where you were going. At 0658 hours the Division artillery opened up exactly on time. The shells were plentiful and concentrated; they were also short. The men crouched in their scant temporary shelters and the shells landed on them and around them. The whole thing was a regrettable mistake.

The two Companies withdrew to the rubble and the cellars of Wipfel, while Lieutenant Colonel Smithers, with a stony face, discussed the matter with Regiment on the radio. Jacob Levy was pressed into service as a litter bearer: the casualties were heavy, the Germans could not have done better. Doc Weber, working in his dirty sweat-stained undershirt, gave orders that another cellar was to be cleared for the wounded as any fool could see he was falling over bodies in here. The floor of Doc Weber's cellar was slippery with blood, and the smell produced the bitter-tasting saliva of nausea in Jacob Levy's mouth. The patient bewildered look on the faces of the wounded hurt him, as if he were one of them again.

At 1455 hours, the remaining members of Fox and George Companies were again ready to go. The rain had stopped and in the watery afternoon light the open meadow looked, if not attractive, a reasonable piece of ground. The Battalion ought to reach its objective, the Grundheim-Berghof road, in an hour. At 1500 hours exactly, the artillery hit them in the moment when the men were stepping out from cover. This time the shells came from the front and were therefore legitimate. They did an equal amount of damage. The attack was called off for the day.

Doc Weber's two cellars, having been cleared of the morning's wounded, were refilled by three-thirty in the afternoon. Except for Doc Weber, giving orders to the technicians, and the occasional groan or mumble of a man who did not hear the sound he was making, the cellar was silent. Jacob Levy had helped carry in the last of the wounded and stopped near the door to give a cigarette to a soldier who asked for one.

He saw there were others, who looked hopefully at the cigarette. He supposed it was allright to hand them out because no one told him not to. There were times, he remembered, when he'd have been glad for a smoke. He wanted to do what he could to help the poor guys and then get out of this place.

He had given a cigarette to a man who seemed to have no knee, but only a sodden red bandage in the middle of his leg, when he saw the boy with the sad face. The boy was staring at the wall opposite him, and he held himself so still that he appeared not to be breathing.

"Cigarette, Mac?" Jacob Levy said. You felt you ought to whisper down here. This guy must be hurt bad, someplace you couldn't see. Maybe the kid was going to die pretty soon and that was why he had those eyes.

"I'm dirty," the boy said in a queer flat voice, "I'm dirty all over. I can't get clean."

Jacob Levy stood with the lighted cigarette in his hand and began to feel a coldness at the back of his neck.

"Look at my hands," the boy said without moving. "Dirty. I'm dirty like that everywhere. I can't get clean."

His eyes were still focused in the painful stare. "I'm dirty," the boy went on. He did not see Jacob Levy's cigarette.

"Take this, Mac," Jacob Levy whispered. "Or I'll get you some water?"

"I'm dirty," the boy said, and tears rolled down his cheeks though his face stayed numb and expressionless. "I can't get clean."

"Take it easy," Jacob Levy said. His hand, with the cigarette in it, was shaking.

"Dirty," the boy said, and now though the blind eyes and

the unmoving body did not change, the voice became first a cry and then a scream. "Dirty!" the voice screamed. "Can't get clean! Look at me! Dirty!"

Doc Weber who was bowed over the kitchen table at the far side of the cellar, straightened, put his hand on the aching place in his back, massaged it, turned in the direction of the wild insistent voice, said, "Pentathal, Joe," and bent over the table again.

The technician, with the syringe in his hand, said to Jacob Levy, "Move along, bud."

Jacob Levy watched the needle go into a white, clean arm and heard the terrible voice soften until it became a mutter. Then the drug worked and the cellar was quiet again.

Jacob Levy stepped quickly over the bodies of the wounded. Someone plucked at his leg and said, "This guy's dead, I think. You better take him, Mac," but he did not stop, only nodding to show he had heard. He ran up the cellar steps into the air and leaned against the broken housefront.

Low clouds pressed over the shapeless village. Jacob Levy walked down what had once been the main street, listening carefully, for this was a collection of rubble that attracted artillery. He smelled and then saw two dead cows, with flies thick on them despite the cold. There was also the smell of human excrement and the sour smell that hangs around houses which have been opened by high explosive. In a cellar, someone was playing, "Chattanooga Choo Choo" on a mouth organ. A voice droned "Drastic White calling Drastic Six, over." It sounded as if a machine, not a man, was repeating this. "Drastic White calling Drastic Six, over." On the left, the black trees of the forest rose in a jagged wall against the sky.

Jacob Levy found a corner of a barn, intact. It was built of heavy stone and having stood so long it must be a reliable shelter. A capsized farm cart, with bricks and hay blown around it, made a protective mound before the open angle of the building. Jacob Levy slid in and sat far back against the stone wall, hugging his knees. That was worse than being hit; you could heal from a wound. But would a man ever be allright again if once his eyes looked like they were glass and he screamed out crazy things he didn't even hear? Jacob Levy held his knees tighter to keep from trembling. I'm cold is all, he told himself.

· · · · · · · · · · ·

There were three houses left in Glutz. In this way, Glutz could be distinguished from Wipfel. Glutz was located beyond the open meadow and the Grundheim-Berghof road, and Hill 302, only different in number from any other hill. Glutz lay, in fact, seven miles and twenty-five days beyond 0700 hours 4 November, when the Battalion started to fight in this forest. The Battalion's survivors slouched or sprawled in the ruins of Glutz, bearded, filthy, lined with weariness, their eyes dark and brooding, and scratched themselves and shivered in the tireless wind, and looked forward to nothing. Beyond Glutz, the same trees covered the hills to the horizon. The only way out of this forest was on a litter or in a sack.

The battle had curved away from them. To the north other men tried to hammer their way through the pine trees. The soldiers of the Second Battalion did not know this, and waited with an indifference like despair for the next order to attack. Lieutenant Colonel Smithers alone refused to give in to the forest. He walked around the drab wind-beaten mess that was Glutz and gave orders in a harsh voice; he held his shoulders straight and snarled at the discouraged posture of others; he chewed the staff, and drove the soldiers. But at night he could lie sleepless in the dark, cold as they all were, and tired to death, and stop acting. In the night he could mourn his Battalion which he loved. That men had to die in any action was known, and nothing to grieve over. But a man had the right to die for some purpose; the value of death was measured in miles. Whose fault is it, Lieutenant Colonel Smithers asked himself, and hoped it was the fault of the forest.

At night, rejoicing and marvelling, Jacob Levy crossed off another day on his calendar. The Colonel's luck held. The Colonel's a wonderful soldier, Jacob Levy thought, he could command a Regiment if he had to.

• • • • • • • • • • • •

On the twenty-seventh day, the Division was ordered out of the line. They were to move south into Luxembourg and rest and re-equip. Lieutenant Colonel Smithers stood at the roadside in some battered village he did not know, and watched his men get into the trucks. He hated this part. He did not think they blamed him, for they understood he got his orders as they did, and obeyed them. He did not think that the look on their faces was anything permanent, that some part of their brains would always be marked too. He knew they were in bad shape but he had seen them like this before, heavy and silent with fatigue and with the strain of so much effort and fear. They would sleep and eat and wash, get drunk, find a girl. They would close ranks over the dead and wounded, pick up a new buddy, and go on. But right now he hated to look at them. Because, he thought, if these guys had any say they'd have stopped this war long ago. They didn't have any say and he would take them into the next battle and fewer of them would come out. He hated this part because it made him think and he was not paid to think any more than they were.

Lieutenant Colonel Smithers shrugged as if something had caught around him. "Levy!"

"Yes sir."

"Get to the head of the column."

He kept himself sitting up straight and awake until they passed the trucks with his men in them. Then he said, "You know where we're going?"

"Yes sir."

"Wake me if anything happens."

"Everything will be okay, sir," Jacob Levy said, almost choked over the friendliness of the words. Lieutenant Colonel Smithers slept, with his head jolting against his chest. I'll get him there allright, Jacob Levy told himself, and his eyes burned with weariness and his shoulders felt like lead with nails in them. The Colonel didn't need to worry. It was because of the Colonel's luck that he had come from that evil place, without the third and last wound. The Colonel could count on him.

> 3 <

WEILERBURG WAS almost too good to be true; if he had known there was any place like it in the ETO he would have been dreaming about it. These Luxembourg people seemed a lot cleaner than the French, and friendlier, and this was a high class house, whitewashed inside, warm, with white lace curtains and fine furniture. Upstairs his bed had a big feather quilt and sheets with crocheted stuff along the edges and there was a bathroom with hot running water and the toilet flushed. A Regimental commander would be proud to live in a house like this, let alone a Battalion C.O. The men were fixed up good too, they never had it better, and already that look on their faces in the trucks was gone. You couldn't believe it was the same bunch of beat-up dead-eyed soldiers. Everybody happy, thought Lieutenant Colonel Smithers, as he corrected Sergeant Postalozzi's typed copy of the Battalion's after action report.

He was not happy and he felt someone was going to get

chewed for that forest, and yet nobody could have done more than they did. Colonel O'Neal was probably sweating it out, and the General, and there wasn't any way to make it look like a successful operation; it stank just on paper.

"Sixty-five percent casualties for seven miles," he said to Lieutenant Gaylord who was working on his fingernails with a pocket-knife. "I tell you, it keeps up like this and they can send us as replacements to some other Battalion."

He'd have to start training his own replacements right away: bright green, all of them, complete with ten thumbs to each hand. They'd begin on assault craft but since there were no boats he would have the Pioneer platoon mark out the dimensions of boats with mine tape, on the ground, and let the new guys practice finding their places and getting out and maybe the poor dopes would get some notion from that. And borrow a couple of tanks for them to learn close support. And have them throw grenades until their arms fell off. He'd have to move fast if he expected these sad sacks to be soldiers, in time for the next action.

"I hear they got an Officers' Club in Luxembourg City, and Red Cross girls and WACs and Bourbon and everything you want," Lieutenant Gaylord remarked.

"I'm going to see the men get a lot of decorations out of that forest."

That's one thing about Johnny, Lieutenant Gaylord thought, he isn't the heel kind of worrier, always thinking about his own neck. The men knew it too; they knew he did his best for them.

"Not that they'll come through," Lieutenant Colonel Smithers went on, "they don't count how it was, they count what shows in the papers. I'd like to see Levy get something."

"You what?"

"I know I can't put his name in. He didn't do anything outstanding you could mention. But I sure appreciate the way he worked."

"Listen Johnny. When are we going to Luxembourg? I forget what a woman looks like."

Bill was right; the forest was over, there was nothing he could do about it. It didn't pay to think about anything, especially when it was over.

"Allright, sonny, let's go. Tell Major Hardcastle I'm taking off, Sergeant. I'll sign this when I get back."

Lieutenant Colonel Smithers sat beside Jacob Levy in the jeep, with Lieutenant Gaylord in back, and the wind cut at his face though he tried to bury it between his turned-up coat collar and his pulled-down cap. It was cold but it was pretty. They kept their country nice, these Luxembourgers. The land rolled away in soft hills and the clipped brown fields looked as if they were covered in fur. The trees grew on the hills in planted patterns, the smoky purple of birches bordering the blackness of the pines. These are pine trees like Georgia, Lieutenant Colonel Smithers thought, not pine trees like Germany. The hills were like home too, and so was the quiet, and nothing burned at the sides of the roads, and no broken telegraph poles with the white insulators blown into the trees, and no snarled khaki traffic. Inside the sturdy farmhouses people would be sitting down to supper now, the way people should. You had to admire people who could keep their country looking peaceful these days.

The road dipped and crossed a humped brick bridge. A brown stream rushed under the bridge and disappeared into a wood. Jacob Levy greeted this stream with delight; it was not as good as his, and a road interfered with it, but to see clear water running through gentle country was a sort of homecoming. They must be pretty happy around here, Jacob Levy thought.

On the left a hill like a frozen horse's mane flowed dark against the sky; then a black hill rose square like a slag heap. Nearer, a church steeple pointed up above the trees. They passed a grey stone wall with branches drooping over it, and Lieutenant Gaylord turned to see what sort of a house they had in there. It looked like an expensive estate outside Harrisburg; they probably led a gay life in a big stylish house like that.

"Fine place!" Lieutenant Colonel Smithers shouted to Jacob Levy.

"Sure is, sir!" Jacob Levy shouted back. He shared a room with Bert Hammer in a house down the street from Battalion Headquarters. They slept in a double bed; they took off their uniforms at night and slept in their underwear. He could wash anytime he wanted to, in hot water. If war was always like this, you could get a taste for it.

They followed street signs to the Officers' Club, noting with amazement that this city was upright. They were used to shell holes in the streets, a hedge of rubble, and sliced buildings like broken teeth. Luxembourg seemed beautiful simply because it was standing. At the door of the Officers' Club, Lieutenant Colonel Smithers said, "Be back here at ten-thirty, Levy."

"Yes sir." That was a hell of a nice thing to do; most officers would have kept their driver hanging around. Four hours of liberty. He'd leave the jeep in a car park so as not to worry, and find a restaurant if there was one not off-limits, and eat at a table with a white cloth. Boy oh boy, Jacob Levy said to himself, this is the life.

The sky was the beautiful evening color, a dark shining blue with light behind it. If they could have turned on the street lamps you would hardly know there was a war, the city looked so good and felt so good. This was the first place Jacob Levy had seen where people might seriously want to live. There were window panes in the windows. The streets were clean. The houses were big grey stone or cement jobs, mostly, and you could tell the stairs would be swept and there'd be a nice smell of cooking in the halls and not that smell of toilets there always was everywhere in Europe. There were even store windows and things for sale, handbags, cameras, gloves. This really was a city. There was too much rank around though, you couldn't put your arm down for a minute. Now imagine guys who spent the whole war working in a Headquarters city like this. They must be laughing at the suckers who wore the combat infantry badge. Hotels were no good for him; the officers would have taken them for billets. He'd probably find what he wanted on some side street.

There was a flower shop at the corner, then a hardware store, and then this big plate glass window with a sign printed on it in gold letters: Café-Restaurant de l'Etoile. Jacob Levy could not see inside because the black-out curtains were already drawn. The street looked allright, not rich or fancy but respectable. He was shy about opening the door because it might turn out to be a place with headwaiters and a lot of officers, and he'd feel like a fool. Opening the door slightly and peering in, Jacob Levy saw a reassuring room, small, warm, with brownish wall paper and tables and benches around the walls. There was a counter, with a nickel coffee machine and two faucets for beer, and a grey haired woman sitting behind it. Two men were drinking beer in one corner. Jacob Levy decided he was safe here, and shut the door, took off his cap, and saw the white table cloths in the next room. It seemed pretty smart to find what you wanted on the first try in a strange city.

The grey haired woman put down her knitting and smiled encouragingly. She told Jacob Levy, in French, to come in and motioned towards the restaurant. If they didn't wear the same uniforms, she thought, you could never tell they were Americans: some of them looked like Italians, some like Poles, some like Greeks and many of them looked like Germans. She did not know what this one looked like, but not like any others she had seen, like a Spanish prince perhaps. And he was so elegant too, with his trousers pressed and his boots as polished as those heavy boots could be.

"Kathe!" she called.

When Jacob Levy saw the girl come from the kitchen with a menu card, he knew she was what he wanted. Maybe he couldn't get her because there would not be much time. And maybe he couldn't get her anyhow; there were girls who lived with their parents or who were religious or something and wouldn't cooperate under any circumstances. But she was what he wanted and he realized, seeing her, that it had been a long time since the last. In July that was, and then it was no good, in a dirty barn, in a hurry, and the girl scared of everything, of war and soldiers and shells and what was going to become of her. Then there were the months in hospital and afterwards not really wanting anything, except not to be hit again.

Kathe, Jacob Levy said to himself. He pointed to words on the menu. He didn't care what he ate; it would all taste perfect. He understood when Kathe asked if he wanted wine and said, oui oui, and they smiled at each other. While he was waiting he thought about how Kathe looked. She was just right, young and short and not painted and he knew she would smell good, smelling of herself and not of that strong perfume whores always used. Her skin would be just right too. He couldn't stand whores, there was something rubbery and sticky about their skin, and he hated all that phoney sweet talk and the compliments. Kathe had a nice fat little rear and a nice fat little front and good teeth, with a gold filling somewhere when she smiled. And friendly blue eyes and she wore her black hair in a braid around her head. He would like to go where they'd have time, and she could undo the braid and let her hair fall down.

Kathe stood near the table, watching Jacob Levy eat. When she changed the plates, she spoke to him and he shrugged to show he could not understand. But he smiled and hoped she would go on talking anyhow because he liked the sound of the words and the way her mouth puckered up when she said them. He did not move after he finished the apple-cake dessert, and Kathe did not bring him his bill.

There were other people in the restaurant now. Three men with owl-like horn-rimmed spectacles sat at one table. A white haired man sat with two thin middle aged women, who had the pinched red-nosed look of poor circulation, and wore identical brown felt pots as hats, with identical brown cabbages of ribbon bobbing on the front. By the door, a gnarled old couple whispered for the salt or bread or the wine bottle and were otherwise silent. They all wore dark baggy clothes

[47]

and had the kind of faces that cannot be remembered. They spoke in French but they looked more like Germans, Jacob Levy thought, not mean the way he imagined Germans in Germany looked but as if they were the sort of Germans who lived on the south side in St. Louis; only sadder. They seemed to know Kathe and they spoke to her, jokingly, but he could see there was nothing tough or on the make about it. She talked back too, in her funny voice, and it was like a nice girl waiting on her family's friends in her own house. He enjoyed watching Kathe bring in the trays, with her little bottom moving under the thin black wool of her dress.

Then it was nine-thirty and the other customers were leaving the restaurant. Jacob Levy had been afraid the people would stay too late and he would have to go before he could see Kathe alone. He kept looking at his wrist watch and lighting one cigarette from another. When the last customer had left, the woman behind the coffee urn asked Jacob Levy a question in French: she had to close up and be home before the civilian curfew and she could not miss the only streetcar that went to her part of town. Kathe brought the bill. Jacob Levy was relieved to see how cheap this place was because he planned to eat here every night he could get off.

When he had counted out the money, Jacob Levy said, "Take a walk with me?" Kathe smiled at him, not understanding. He pointed to her, "you"; pointed to himself, "me"; pointed to the door and then he made his middle and index fingers walk crookedly across the table. Kathe laughed and nodded and then she was back, buttoned into a black coat that was tight across her hips and her breast. She pulled on a pair of green knitted mittens, embroidered with yellow daisies. Jacob Levy looked at the mittens and he wanted to pick this girl up and fondle her like a puppy. He had forgotten there were such things as mittens.

Kathe led him to the park alongside the river. It was not far to walk but Jacob Levy worried about the time. Four hours had seemed plenty and now he was left with not enough minutes of it. They were standing in the cold deserted park, with the narrow river shining in a ravine below them. He pulled Kathe towards him, not hard or fast because he did not want to frighten her. He had to stoop far down to reach her mouth. Kathe put her arms around his neck, like a child he thought, and he was touched and scandalized by the trustfulness of the gesture. She oughtn't to act like this with soldiers. Her mouth was soft and trusting too, and she did not kiss the way girls did when they'd had a lot of practise. Jacob Levy held her and was afraid to do all the things he wanted to do. He held her and thought of her little body tight and warm and full inside the healthy skin, inside the modest black clothes. He thought her petticoat and underpants would be made of starched white cotton. He felt dizzy with the effort of holding her like that against him, and keeping his hands still, and not kissing her as he wanted to.

Then he remembered the time and pointed to his watch and took Kathe's arm to make her hurry. He left her in front of the restaurant because he could not ask where she lived and he had no time now to go wandering around the city.

"I come back tomorrow," Jacob Levy said slowly. Again he acted it out, pointing to himself and the restaurant, and making a circle with his finger on the crystal of his wrist watch. Kathe understood, and smiled, and standing on tiptoe, she put her arms around his neck and kissed him.

Now I really have to make time, Jacob Levy thought. If there was a password for after dark, he didn't know it; and if he kept the Colonel waiting this first night, that would be his last chance, he'd have to sit in the jeep like other drivers. Why didn't he get started sooner? He hoped the Colonel had a fine time at the Officers' Club and would want to come in every night.

Jacob Levy was waiting in front of the modern chromium-trimmed restaurant, which had a cocktail bar and deep leather chairs and a juke box and murals of never-never-land peasants, when Lieutenant Colonel Smithers and Lieutenant Gaylord came out. A crowd of officers and two Red Cross girls came out with them. Jacob Levy saw Lieutenant Colonel Smithers talking to one of the girls, bending over her, and he thought the Colonel was holding her arm high-up where he could feel her breast against his hand. Nice work, Jacob Levy said to himself. That was what he needed, a good hot Red Cross girl for his Colonel.

In the jeep, driving without lights through the blacked-out town, Lieutenant Colonel Smithers turned to Lieutenant Gaylord and said, "I liked that Dotty!"

"I like that cute little blonde WAC."

"Hell of a nice club."

"You bet."

"I wonder where those fellows get all that Bourbon?" Lieutenant Colonel Smithers asked.

"I guess they don't go without, in a Headquarters like this."

"Rugged!" said Lieutenant Colonel Smithers.

"Yeh, hard life those boys got here. No women, no liquor. You see that major I was talking to?"

"Yeh."

"He lives in a six-room apartment with two other majors."

"They break my heart."

"He told me we could borrow a room anytime."

"Maybe he's not too bad a guy."

Jacob Levy rejoiced. It would have been the end of all hope if the Colonel had come out of that Officers' Club, sober, bad-tempered, saying the place was a sewer and the girls were a bunch of cows.

"Dotty's got her night off day after tomorrow," Lieutenant Colonel Smithers remarked in the direction of the back seat. But Lieutenant Gaylord was sunk into his coat collar, and the wind made a cold whistling noise, and he was figuring out how soon he could get Lucille, his WAC, to give him a date at that Major's apartment. 72 rue Philippe, Lieutenant Gaylord repeated to himself, second floor; as if there was any chance he'd forget.

．　．　．　．　．　．　．　．　．　．　．

Sergeant Postalozzi, who thought of everything, owned an English-French dictionary. Jacob Levy was sitting on the edge of his bed, with his fountain pen and a block of airmail paper beside him, looking up words. "Where is your house?" Slowly, this became, "Ou être votre maison?" He printed this on a half sheet of paper. There was another sentence he ought to fix, just in case, so as to avoid confusion. "I'll be back later." This was harder and he decided to use "come" instead of "be back" and as he did not see any word for "later," he thought "late" would do. He printed, "Je venir tard," on another half sheet of paper. Then he folded them both and buttoned them into his breast pocket and returned Sergeant Postalozzi's dictionary.

"What's the matter?" Sergeant Postalozzi asked. "Can't she read it in your eyes?"

"It's a place I saw where I want to buy me a Christmas present for my mother," Jacob Levy answered.

The whole Battalion was busy, secretly, noisily, in groups, in pairs; the Battalion was busy returning to life. There were the ones who loved food or drink, there were those who pursued women, there were shoppers, souvenir hunters, camera specialists, sightseers, gamblers. There were even athletes and letter writers and one or two who read books. Every man was furiously occupied; searching, moving, scrounging, borrowing money, lending money, giving addresses, picking up addresses, laughing, being shrewd, helping a pal, looking after himself; all making time reward them, greedy, grateful and alive.

This was what they would remember if they were around to do any remembering. This was what they would have to remember of their youth in foreign lands.

> *4* <

JACOB LEVY gave Kathe the first piece of paper when they left
the restaurant at ten. Now he was memorizing the turnings
and when he stood at the door he noted, number 14, and the
street was called rue de la Boucherie. He kissed Kathe in
the dark before the big door, before the high old building
with many windows. He could not keep his hands still, he
wanted her too much, there was too little time. But her out-
grown coat was buttoned up to her chin and he could only
pass his hand, steadily and softly, across the rough wool over
her breast. She seemed puzzled but not afraid, with her head
bowed watching. She stayed close to him and then she turned
her face up and smiled. He had to go; it was a long way
back to the car park. He'd have to run and you never liked
to run in a dark city with a lot of trigger-happy rearguard
sentries and M.P.'s around. Kathe looked disappointed. If
he could only talk this stupid French and explain to her.

Tomorrow was Dotty's night off, tomorrow there would be time. "Honey," Jacob Levy said, "Kathe," and he kissed her once, harder than he had dared before, and turned and ran. He remembered on the way that he had forgotten to tell Kathe he would come back tomorrow night but he couldn't stop and she'd have gone inside and it was almost ten-thirty this minute. What if tomorrow was her night off, too? She might go out visiting friends; she might do anything. He'd find her if he had to knock on every door in Luxembourg. It all depended on Dotty now; if only she wasn't going steady with some jerk of an officer, if only she wasn't the hard-to-get kind. He needed time; he needed time just once.

. . . .

Jacob Levy had been thinking about this all day, planning, foreseeing, and making alternate plans. He borrowed Sergeant Postalozzi's dictionary again and the Sergeant was funny about Christmas presents but Jacob Levy was too concentrated to joke back. "What floor? What number?" That was a big house, there must be ten apartments in it anyhow. How could he have been so dumb as to overlook a thing like that? He flicked at the dictionary, urgent and bungling. There were three choices for "What": why couldn't those French make up their minds? Jacob Levy printed under "Je venir tard," the second line, "Quoi etage? Quoi numero?" Then he felt safe and returned the dictionary to Sergeant Postalozzi.

There was plenty of work to do but the good thing about it was, it stopped. They operated on the eight hour day, you might say, like normal people. The old hands weren't knocking their brains out. To date, he had had it soft, driving the Colonel to the Companies and to Regiment and keeping the jeep clean: no work at all. He observed with sympathy the poor godforsaken soldiers who had to crawl through these little peaceful woods, practicing all the things they'd done wrong in that hell forest; and the other godforsaken soldiers standing around on the range; and the poor dumb replacements sweating out everything anyone could dream up for them. It was his considered opinion that a jeep driver had the best life of anybody because he saw the world and had nothing except his jeep to worry about.

But now, when every minute was a waiting for the end of the day and the Colonel saying: "Okay Levy, let's go," that Motor Sergeant had to get a notion the cylinder block on the jeep was cracked. This was the sort of craziness a Motor Sergeant invented when he didn't have enough to do. The jeep was perfect. The Motor Sergeant did not wish to listen to reason. "Get over to Regiment and see if you can find what you need there; if the Colonel wants transport before you get back I'll send him a jeep from the pool."

Jacob Levy stood outside the barn that was Service Company's repair shop, in the village of Ettelroth, and pleaded with the mechanic to hurry. "Take it easy," the mechanic said, from under the jeep's hood. "Your Colonel isn't gonna shoot you if we don't finish in time." Anxiety wore Jacob Levy out, and left him bemused, waiting in resignation of spirit for the worst to happen: he would return and find that the Colonel had gone to Luxembourg with another driver.

I was never like this before, Jacob Levy told himself. He could not remember when he had made any plans in this war.

He didn't care what he did; he went along with anybody; it never mattered. There was only time to live through, and though the present was interminable and tomorrow was more of today, and all of it endless, his only real occupation was waiting. He waited for the calendar to get crossed out. I was never like this, he thought. You exposed yourself, as soon as you started to hope.

• • • • • • • • • • • •

The evening began to happen on schedule, according to plan. At the door of the Officers' Club, Lieutenant Colonel Smithers said, "You know where the Transient Mess is, Levy?"

"Yes sir." You always said "Yes sir," to questions like that.

"Pick up some chow and get right back. No more than an hour."

"Yes sir."

Jacob Levy had imagined that was how it would be. The Colonel would feed Dotty at the club, give her something to drink first of course, and then he would want to leave as soon as he could persuade her. He would need his transport ready and waiting.

Jacob Levy drove the jeep to the Café-Restaurant de l'Etoile. He locked it with a chain through the steering wheel, and a padlock. He wasn't going to let some joker pinch his jeep tonight. The restaurant was empty. Jacob Levy smiled at the coffee urn lady and she called Kathe. He sat near the front window where he could hear if anyone tried to monkey with his jeep.

When Kathe stood by his table, they stared at each other, serious-faced and silent. Jacob Levy felt he had been away a long time and was just getting back now, from a great distance. He wanted to put his arms around her, he didn't want to eat or remember the Colonel, he wanted to go to a warm room of their own and stay with her. He wanted to talk to her too, but he knew he couldn't. It was bad to have so much to say to a girl and no way to say it except Sergeant Postalozzi's crummy little dictionary. Jacob Levy shook his head; all this was in his way, there was important business to settle.

"I only got a half hour to eat." He showed Kathe thirty minutes on his watch and made gestures of eating. She nodded and looked sad, somehow tired and sad, as if she saw ahead the terrible disappointments: the life of the war always coming before their life, the fearful relentless lack of time. Jacob Levy pulled the printed slip of paper from his pocket and spread it on the table and beckoned Kathe to come close and read. The coffee machine lady can see, he thought, but what's the difference, she can't see the words.

Kathe bent forward to read. She smelled better than he had dreamed, a sweet warm smell, something only women had, that you couldn't name exactly. Jacob Levy watched her. Kathe read slowly; then, without anything showing on her face, she folded the paper and put it in her apron pocket. She doesn't understand, Jacob Levy thought, there's something wrong with the dictionary. What could he do now; how could he show her by signs?

Kathe offered him the menu card and Jacob Levy said, "Anything," shrugged, pointed to his watch and pushed the card away. She went through the door to the kitchen but he was not looking at her. He was thinking, fast, maybe there's some Luxembourg boy in the Officers' Club kitchen that can speak English and I could send him to explain to her. No, it would never work; it was too complicated; it would get too late; he couldn't send her a stranger with a message like that. He wanted to break something; he wanted to beat somebody up. Why couldn't they all speak the same language? Why couldn't the lousy dictionary get the words right?

Kathe stood in the kitchen waiting for Monsieur Steller, the proprietor and cook, to finish with the plate. There were two fried eggs, two fat wienerwurst sausages, some mustard pickles and a big dollop of fried potatoes. Now Monsieur Steller was going to fix some lettuce, with sweet dressing, as a side dish. Kathe held the tray and felt her heart beating with fear.

It was only going in and coming out that there was danger. The long tunnel of the hall led down the apartment, past the parlor and the dining room, the Hefferichs' bedroom, the bathroom and the kitchen, to her little room at the end. Once inside her room they would be safe for it was far away and they would keep quiet. Unless the Hefferichs heard something strange, they would not come out into the hall. She was only a boarder and they did not visit together in the evenings. She could wait downstairs just inside the big front door, and lead him upstairs when he came.

But if the Hefferichs saw him they would put her out, naturally. And maybe they would tell Madame Steller, and she would lose her job. And maybe Madame Steller would tell her mother, who lived in Müllerhof with her brother's wife. And then, and then.

It was the most dangerous and important decision she had

ever had to make and she had no one to consult, but even if there was time to think she could not ask anybody. This was not a matter a girl could talk about to anyone. If he took off his shoes, surely the Hefferichs would not hear him. But perhaps they would hear the front door closing when he left?

Kathe picked up the tray and carried it to where Jacob Levy sat, listening for the safety of his jeep, waiting, trying to think and having no thoughts that followed each other or made sense. He looked up at Kathe and his wide black eyes were pleading and stricken. Kathe needed a pencil but she could not borrow one from Madame Steller.

Jacob Levy stared at the full plate of food. I can't even touch it, he thought; he had not known he could feel so awful. There had been no place in his plans for this fatal misunderstanding.

Kathe was making signs, writing signs, and she had opened his printed note, shielding the table from Madame Steller with her back. Jacob Levy gave her his pen quickly and she wrote: 14 rue de la Boucherie, chez Hefferich, 3 ième étage. He picked up the paper, took the pen, just brushing her hand, and the beautiful mouth that she wanted to stroke with her fingers, smiled.

The food tasted marvelous, now. He was swallowing as fast as he could; above all, he must not be late for the Colonel. Jacob Levy left the tip with his bill, paying at the beer and coffee counter, because he was ashamed to give Kathe those crumpled dirty notes. Then he smiled at everything, the tables, the advertisement for beer, the water color of the Cathedral, the photograph of the Grand Duchess, Madame Steller, Kathe, and saluted as if he were sweeping off a plumed hat, and was gone. Kathe thought it was scarcely possible that any human being could be so handsome and so graceful and she had to lean against Madame Steller's chromium counter for a moment before her legs became steady.

She could sit down now in the back of the restaurant, and think. Madame Steller would not talk to her; they were not loquacious people here, though they were kind and good natured. They did the work between them, in friendliness, and no one talked much.

Kathe knew she had done what she ought to do. If there was trouble afterwards it would be dreadful trouble, for her people would not forgive her. She did not worry about her soldier; he was not wicked and he would know that she was not wicked. In real life, where everyone was safe, this could not happen to either of them. He would be home on his farm and she would be home on her farm. It did not matter that she could not talk this over with him, or explain, he was certain to understand it as she did.

And Kathe knew too that this had always been going to happen; she truly had no choice. She had been waiting for it these last four years. In the beginning, when the Germans came, she was like everybody else; she shrank inside of herself, she seemed to go blind and deaf at once, she felt herself shrivelling to a little place within her, and even this secret part of her was quiet. That was during the first two years when they were still on the farm. You could not believe it was the same farm or that people had been happy there, or ever had a birthday party or her brother's wedding or a Christmas tree or gone sledding in the winter or laughed and kissed Henri Laroche, in a haystack in the summer. That was the two years before her father died, when they all worked like animals and had nothing to say to each other or to look forward to. Her father probably died from over-work, after her brother and the hired man ran away so they wouldn't have to go in the German army or go for the labor service, in Germany. Her father wanted them to run away. He said he had seen the Germans walk into his country twice, as easily as opening a door. He didn't even seem to love his family, after the Germans came, he seemed too dis-gusted with life to care about anything. It was like being dead to live on that farm, dead from tiredness and hopelessness, and with the Germans around them like a hateful silence.

Then after the funeral her mother went to Müllerhof to stay with Charlotte, her brother's wife, in the house of Char-lotte's father. But Kathe would not go. She was seventeen and she dreaded sitting at night, in the kitchen in Charlotte's father's house, nothing but women and old men, night after night, just waiting. Her mother did not try to make her come. Her mother went to Müllerhof because Charlotte took her, but she did not seem to mind what she did, with her son disappeared and her husband dead.

The cousin who worked in the bakery near the fishmarket found the room at the Hefferichs'. Mrs. Hefferich bought her bread at the bakery so the cousin knew that Mr. Hefferich, who was a bank clerk, couldn't afford a maid any more be-cause everything was so expensive and they would just as soon rent the back room to a quiet decent girl. Kathe got her job in the restaurant by herself; the only things she knew how to do were work on a farm or in a kitchen. Monsieur and Madame Steller told the Germans Kathe was their niece, their only near relative, and that they could not run their restaurant alone because they were growing old and if their niece could not stay and help them they would have to close it. That way she avoided the Labor Service and Germany but Kathe thought she would have killed herself rather than go to that country which was only a few miles away across the river and looked entirely different, and dark and cruel.

At the start it was exciting to be grown-up and independent and earning wages every week and seeing new people. It was a good respectable restaurant too. The same people came there to eat year after year. The German soldiers or officers could come if they wanted, but when a German sat at a table the regular customers ate very fast, not speaking at all, and left; and this lawful hostility and the modesty of the restaurant chilled the Germans, so that for the last year none of them patronized the Stellers. The Etoile customers were all nice old people, nice the way everybody used to be before the Germans came, and Kathe liked them and the work was easy. Still, she only worked and went home; that was all she had of her life. It was waiting again, and the waiting began to hurt her, the time passing hurt her. She could almost feel it going by, the way you could feel every step if you had a nail in your shoe.

There were no young men that she could go out with, to walk or skate or have a beer in a café. The good ones were gone like her brother, or the Germans had taken them; those who stayed were poor things who got on with the Germans or else they were too sickly to be worth taking. Kathe did not notice the hardships the war brought because she was used to very little, and now there was only a little less. She did not care about that anyhow; she only cared about the four years, her four years that were going by without joy in them, winter or summer.

The Hefferichs did not own a radio and Kathe never read

the newspapers and she did not follow or understand the war. She would hear things in the restaurant, the old customers talking together prudently, but she did not understand. She knew, from school, how Luxembourg looked on the map: it was so little you could barely see it and the map of Europe was enormous, with all the great far off countries in different colors. The Germans were everywhere; it was hard to believe that anybody would ever come to Luxembourg and drive them away.

Kathe had begun to think it would be like this forever, for her whole life, with those grey uniformed men in the streets and the city silent and sad and the little country forgotten and rotting. Then she heard the Americans were coming. The French would have been everyday, though heaven-sent as anyone not German would be. She had no ideas about the English. But she had seen a moving picture before the war, before she was fifteen even, and it was American. That was when her father brought her to Luxembourg City, perhaps because he had to have a tooth pulled or maybe it was a question of taxes, and gave her money and she went to the theatre. Kathe had this one vision of Americans who lived in a land made of splendid beaches, long fields of sand with the crested sea coming in, and they were a golden brown race, like the finest bread, tall, slender, and almost naked. They laughed together, the girls and the young men, and ran and played on the beach. Kathe imagined that when the Americans came, they would come across the fields of Luxembourg like a great wave, tall, glorious, sunburned, and singing.

The Americans did not come as quickly as expected and they were preceded by panic rumors which everybody in the city heard and repeated. It was said that the Germans would shoot one out of ten of the people of Luxembourg, if they saw they were losing the city; and that they would poison the water; and destroy the castle and the cathedral. But above all, they would dynamite the Adolphe bridge, so that the Americans could not cross into the heart of the town.

It was this rumor which started Kathe's great daydream.

She was going to save her city and the beautiful Americans. She would be on the Adolphe bridge, and she would find the package of dynamite the Germans had left; she would throw it back on them, and it would explode and they would not be able to come across the bridge to fight the Americans. The Americans would be marching down the Avenue de la Liberté, forty abreast, you could not even see the street they would be so thick on it, a wide river of them, all tall and young and singing. They would sweep on to the bridge and the most beautiful one would be leading, and he would come to her and give her a rose. Kathe knew this was a silly story, she told herself it was silly and selfish too; why should she be the main one, in the saving of her city, and besides it was stupid, really stupid, even in her thoughts to pretend that anything about Kathe Limpert mattered when the whole world was so unhappy. But she could not renounce her dream: she needed one fine and memorable event in her life, after all the years of nothing.

Then the Americans did come and Kathe did not see them, being in the kitchen with the Stellers at the restaurant, with the iron shutters down and the lights off, hushed and listening and terrified like everyone else. Later she saw the jumble of tanks and jeeps and guns and trucks and ambulances, everything looking used and dirty as it had to in war. No one seemed to be marching. The Americans were young and cheerful and noisy and they were fine brave boys, the saviors of her country, but they did not look like the ones she remembered from the moving picture. They were not really very good looking or very tall and they wore hideous metal pots on their heads. When the city was entirely cleared of Germans the young Americans stood around together, near all their strange automobiles, and whistled at every girl who passed which was clearly a custom of their country and allright since that was their manner but it was not what she had dreamed; not the beautiful respectful one, coming forward with such grace to give her a rose. Kathe could not speak to the American soldiers and besides she had her work to do and the war was not over and presently she was waiting again. Though she thanked God they had come to free her country, and she prayed for them in church on Sunday and she was grateful with her whole heart and she knew that it was shameful to think of herself and be disappointed.

When the soldier came into the restaurant Kathe felt it was no accident; he came because she was waiting. He had come alone, with no one to show him, directly to her, and he looked at her with love. He brought no flower but in every other way he was the one she had dreamed of meeting on the Adolphe bridge.

It doesn't matter, Kathe said to herself, I will find another room and another job and I will tell my mother that I am sorry but she would understand if she was nineteen and had waited her whole life without even anyone to think of or remember or write a letter to, and he came all this way for me as I knew he would, and I am not ashamed, not ashamed.

Her soldier had come suddenly and he would go suddenly,

she was sure of that. Kathe could tell he was of those who fought, not of those who worked in the big office buildings across the river. The ones who fought were a different kind of man. He had only a little time too. She saw this in his eyes. God will not punish us, Kathe thought, let them say what they want, I don't care. I know it is not wicked. We have no time.

"Kathe," said Madame Steller, peering over the coffee machine, "what is the matter with you, child?"

Kathe did not realize that she was beating the table softly with her fist and snuffling to keep the tears back.

"I think I'm getting a cold."

"Take an aspirin," Madame Steller said.

"Yes, I will. Thank you."

Kathe turned her head away so that Madame Steller could not see her. She would wait for him inside the big street door and they would go up the stairs hand in hand and not make a sound.

> 5 <

JACOB LEVY began to sorrow for his Colonel. The poor bastard,
he thought, Dotty's stringing him along. She's making him
buy her drinks and she won't say yes or no. I'd like to go in
there and tell her a thing or two. I'd like to tell her all the
time she's been sitting in a fine warm house, he's been up
there in that death-hole forest. About the least a nogood,
spoiled, rich bitch of a Red Cross girl could do would be to
make the Colonel happy for a while.

Here it was eight thirty and still they didn't show. Jacob
Levy sat bowed over the steering wheel and ached with cold.
Slowly he realized what this meant to him. The night would
not go on forever. And what he wanted was sweet and willing and put her arms around your neck like a child.

But if Dotty said no, they would drive straight back to
Weilerburg and he couldn't even tell Kathe not to wait. He
imagined Kathe sitting on a chair in her room, waiting all
night. He'd like to choke that Dotty.

This would teach him to let himself get happy, as if there
was anything good in war. This would teach him to make

[67]

plans. Cold and despairing, Jacob Levy said to himself, stick to your calendar. All you can expect is for a day to finish.

Then suddenly the Colonel and his girl were there. They must have sneaked out of the door so no one would see them or hear them. Lieutenant Colonel Smithers helped the girl in the back and jumped in beside her. He had his arm around her already; Jacob Levy could feel this, without seeing it. It was all going to work out for the best.

"72 rue Philippe, Levy," Lieutenant Colonel Smithers said. "You know where that is?"

"Yes sir." Jacob Levy had heard Lieutenant Gaylord giving the address to the Colonel last night, and he had located it on a street map. No time would be lost in transit, if he could help it.

It didn't look much different from Kathe's house and it wasn't even too far from the rue de la Boucherie. Perhaps he could find a car park up here somewhere and save time. He was cold all through. That was bad. That would feel bad for Kathe.

"When shall I tell him to come back?" Lieutenant Colonel Smithers asked the girl. She had walked ahead towards the door of the apartment house, and was a shadow in the bare lightless street.

"Oh, about one, I think." Her voice upset Jacob Levy. She sounded as if she didn't care whether she stayed or went.

"Two will be allright," Lieutenant Colonel Smithers said softly, and crossed the pavement.

Jacob Levy grinned and saluted the Colonel's back. That was a man who couldn't be discouraged, that Colonel, and why should he? He'd sweated out worse things than one Red Cross girl.

Lieutenant Colonel Smithers followed Miss Dorothy Brock of Des Moines and Miss Leighton's Finishing School and the Junior League, into the hall of 72 rue Philippe and up the stairs. She has nice ankles, he thought. Not even those flat-heeled black oxfords could spoil her ankles.

"I don't know what this place is like," he said.

"All the houses here are very comfortable." Ugly, heavy, overstuffed, color of mustard, Dorothy Brock thought, with scratchy cloth on the chairs, glaring chandeliers and oil paintings in gold frames. She had been in a good many of these apartments with various officers. The Germans pinched the apartments in the beginning; then we took them from the Germans. Thus everyone is cosy except the natives, Dorothy Brock thought.

"He said it was good and warm."

"Fine."

He, being Major Havemeyer, had also told Lieutenant Gaylord who relayed the information, that the beds were big and soft and to use the room down at the end of the hall. If there was anybody home now, Lieutenant Colonel Smithers would introduce himself and they'd hang around and have a drink and act casual, until the other guys got the pitch and went to their own rooms. Much, much better if no one was home. He was not sure of Dotty, though she ought to have a rough idea of what this was all in favor of.

Lieutenant Colonel Smithers rang the doorbell and a maid opened it. She asked no questions. Strangers barging in must be S.O.P. here, Lieutenant Colonel Smithers thought. The maid showed them the living room and disappeared into a long greyish hall.

"Nice place," said Lieutenant Colonel Smithers.

"Lovely," she agreed. It was exactly as she had imagined it. Suddenly she thought, these are the bordels for ladies.

"What're you smiling about?" Lieutenant Colonel Smithers asked. He didn't know if he liked this girl.

"Nothing," Dorothy Brock said. "Are there drinks?"

Major Havemeyer had also said to help themselves. Lieutenant Colonel Smithers saw bottles in the dining room that led from this parlor. What a soft life. As far as he was concerned, they could drink all the liquor and tear the place down. Lieutenant Colonel Smithers felt these rooms belonged to him; he had earned them, not the two Intelligence Majors and the other one from the Public Relations office. It was nice of Havemeyer to loan his apartment, but Lieutenant Colonel Smithers understood the self-imposed guilt that forced the offer, and that released him also from gratitude or responsibility. You're damn right they're generous, he thought.

"Pick up a nice comfortable chair," he said. Dorothy Brock had taken off her cap and was combing her hair. She's got pretty hair, I like that color brown, Lieutenant Colonel Smithers thought, pretty ankles, a good build, the kind that went all to the chest and nothing to the hips. She's not too hot in the face, he went on, weighing what he'd got; sort of sallow, and there was something disturbing about her face too, or her eyes, as if she thought different from what she was saying. Lieutenant Colonel Smithers poured a big drink for Miss Brock, as he was in a hurry.

"Here's to you, sir." She smiled at him over the rim of the glass. What we use nowadays instead of a fan, Dorothy Brock told herself, and furthermore flirting is done with a hammer in the ETO. Not that he had to be warmed up, this handsome hunk of bravery. It was only politeness that made her shine her eyes that way.

"Here's to you, sweetness," Lieutenant Colonel Smithers said.

Mother of God, she thought, I really can *not* take "sweetness".

"Tell me some more about Georgia," Dorothy Brock said, and stopped listening immediately. Lieutenant Colonel Smithers talked of Georgia, but without enthusiasm. Georgia would not lead them down the hall to the last bedroom and the advertised soft bed.

It was very easy to smile, to nod, to widen the eyes, to say "Oh, My!" to say "Honestly?" and hear nothing. It was so easy that if there was anything worth hearing, she would probably miss it. Dorothy Brock had stopped listening almost two years ago, and men found her perfect to talk to. Dotty seemed to know what you meant, even when you couldn't say it right.

Two years ago, when Dorothy Brock came to England, she had listened earnestly and tried to give each one what he wanted, sympathy, jokes, advice. She had been convinced that without the Red Cross girls, standing behind the men, their everpresent tireless friends (mothers, sisters), the war would fail. They needed her and her only desire was to help them.

Two years was a long time, or else you learned the technique and it required no further attention. Like working in a button factory, she thought, you could punch button holes all day long but you wouldn't have to think about buttons. And how boring they were, how endlessly and drearily they repeated themselves. Dorothy Brock did not blame them. She had lived in the camps in England and, since coming to

France, in the bleak villages where Divisions rested or trained. If their lives were so limited, you could hardly expect these men to make scintillating conversation. They seemed to Dorothy Brock to be trapped animals, trying to make the best of it; and when they left the security of her coffee, doughnuts, magazines, games, and went away in trucks, they exchanged the boredom for something, to her, unimaginable. She had worked in hospitals too, and where the men went in trucks was the place that gored and gouged and chopped them up, ready for the hospitals. Dorothy Brock was always sorry for the soldiers but that did not make it necessary to listen. They liked her just as well when she never heard a word.

She took a professional pride in her clubroom, all the same, and in making the men as contented and comfortable as she could. This war wasn't a scream of laughter from anybody's point of view, and she would not tolerate complaints from herself. She no longer believed that her job had much effect on the outcome of the war, and she did not care. They were all in an endurance contest; she meant to perform as well as the next person.

The officers were another matter. Some unwritten law restrained Red Cross girls from going to bed with enlisted men. With the officers, however, it was a permanent open season. Dorothy Brock had a private taboo on the rearguard; if they were lonely, sex-starved, homesick or overworked, that was their business. It seemed to her they took a lot of unjustifiable liberty, making passes to right and left, as if they did anything more hazardous than travel between their offices and their billets. The fighting types had their own excuse. A man was not automatically attractive because he flew a Thunderbolt, rode in a Sherman, or commanded infantry in battle, but he was explained; he had all the necessary reasons. It was then up to her to decide whether she was going to be eager, compassionate or a good friend. They did not repel her with their insincerity and their haste; she would have been the same in their place. They very often bored her. Dorothy Brock thought perhaps everyone in armies was always boring. They were certainly predictable. But what they had, finally, was their bodies. They had them at least for however long they could keep them. And since, really, there was nothing else they wanted of her, she would settle for that too. It might make them both happy for a while, or take their minds off their problems, and anyhow it passed the time.

Only I wish, Dorothy Brock thought, that I could tell him to stow Georgia and let's get to bed. That's what we came here for, and this room isn't a place I'm just thrilled about sitting in.

Lieutenant Colonel Smithers was mixing a second drink. If we don't start soon, he thought, those Majors will come home from the Club. He handed Dorothy Brock the drink and as he did so, he bent down and kissed her hair.

"You've got pretty hair," he said.

"I'm glad you think so," Dorothy Brock said, mocking him and mocking herself.

With his glass in his hand, Lieutenant Colonel Smithers kissed her on the mouth. She had turned her face up, obligingly.

"Honey!"

"Let's take our drinks with us," Dorothy Brock said. She hoped it sounded breathless and overcome with passion, and not simply practical. She thought she could not stand any more talk, she really hated it, it made her sick. This Lieutenant Colonel was a big handsome man, and he had come from a bad place, and she would be very nice to him if only he'd keep his mouth shut.

Lieutenant Colonel Smithers was now sitting on the edge of the bed, unlacing his boots. Dorothy Brock had walked in, put her glass on the bureau, and unbuttoned her coat. Methodically, she hung it over the back of a chair and started to pull down the zipper of her skirt. She said nothing. He turned his back then and went to the bed. Light blazed from a chandelier that looked like a piece of knotted glass intestines.

Lieutenant Colonel Smithers was shocked and hurt. Whores acted like this, only at least they'd say something agreeable while they were about it. And he knew she wasn't a whore, she was a nice girl, she had come from a good family. They checked up on all these Red Cross girls before they let them join. It was awful to think American girls got like this, just wanting it the way a man would.

No respectable girl, where he lived, would behave like Dotty. They'd let you neck them as much as you liked, but you'd have a tough time getting them to bed and then only if they were so crazy for you they couldn't help themselves. With Dotty, you had the idea that the line formed on the right. He wouldn't mind with a French girl; you expected it. But Dotty made him feel cheated and disgusted, and ashamed for American girls, the good ones at home. Here I go worrying, Lieutenant Colonel Smithers told himself, what do I care how she acts? Okay! she wants it, I want it; she'll get it. But he stood up, abruptly, and went to the door where the switch was, and turned off the light. Somebody had to have some decency around here.

Dorothy Brock did not speak and she understood the rebuke and the anger. What a delicate fellow, she thought, he wants everything complete with lies. My God, I'm tired; it would be nice just to sleep. Well, sleep was not exactly what she had to look forward to. Why did I bother; I don't need him and he'd have found somebody else. I could be home in my snug little cot, with a hot water bottle and nourishing cream on my face and nine lovely hours until morning.

I'd just as soon give her a hundred francs and get the hell out of here right now, Lieutenant Colonel Smithers thought.

In this state of mind, silently, and in the dark, they climbed into bed from opposite sides.

She was naked. (What did I expect? Did I think she'd have on her chiffon negligée? I forgot to bring my pyjamas myself, that are in a foot locker in Durham England.) Lieutenant Colonel Smithers put his hand on her, pulling her closer. She was warm and her skin felt soft, unbelievably soft. The smoothness of that skin acted on him as nothing else did, for it was like nothing else. Ah, he said to himself, you may be a hard little bitch, but you feel like heaven to me.

Lieutenant Colonel Smithers stopped thinking. Dorothy Brock had stopped thinking when his hands rested on her waist and he lifted her towards him.

She was sleeping on her side, with her face against his chest. His arm stretched above her head, like a frame. Lieutenant Colonel Smithers lay on his back, plunged into a black drowning of sleep. He woke, sickened by the suddenness of it, and sweating. He sat up in bed, and said in a low furious voice, "Get them over that road! I don't care what's hitting you!"

At once, he was aware of a girl's body by his side, of a bed, of four walls and the quiet of a sleeping house in a sleeping city. He held his breath. Then he knew where he was. He had been saying something; he hoped it wasn't some dumb whiney stuff; he hoped Dotty hadn't heard him. He lay back, moving gradually and in silence.

Dorothy Brock had heard. She did not understand what the words meant and she was confused by sleep, but she felt they were words from a nightmare. This man would have had many chances to pick up nightmares. She stirred, pretending to be asleep, and laid her arm across his chest. She did this without plan, in pity, so that he would not be alone. It was her first gesture of tenderness.

This thin girl's arm seemed to Lieutenant Colonel Smithers like safety itself. He did not remember what he had been dreaming, but her arm was against those dreams. It was what life was meant to be, and would be, when he got home again. He let out his breath carefully. She was soft and gentle and he did not know how to thank her.

"Dotty," he whispered, "I love you, darling."

When they said that before, it meant they were trying to buy you with easy words. But when they said it afterwards, they were trying to be nice, or squaring their consciences, or something. Anyhow, it was sweet and sort of pathetic. "Of course you do," Dorothy Brock murmured.

Why didn't she just give me a good hard slap on the puss, Lieutenant Colonel Smithers thought. Dotty was breathing regularly; she had gone back to sleep. Allright, he thought, that's how you want to play it. Allright: I don't love you, and you don't love me, but there's still something we can do together. Come on and do what you're good at.

Oh my, she thought, feeling the strong demanding hands, he certainly doesn't want to miss a single opportunity.

> *6* <

THERE WAS still time to catch Kathe at the restaurant. Jacob Levy drove fast in the dark and saw her walking down the street with quick small steps. When he pulled up at the curb she walked faster and he could tell she was scared. Maybe guys bothered her in the night when she was going home alone. She ought to have somebody to take her home every night. She didn't know anything; she was too young; she couldn't look after herself. He called to her and Kathe ran towards him with her face surprised and joyous. Jacob Levy lifted her in his arms and put her on the front seat, though it was against orders to drive civilians. Kathe seemed delighted with the jeep; not shrinking from the cold wind but jolting with the car and laughing, as if to bounce were a special treat. Jacob Levy made her get out and wait at the corner while he drove the jeep past the sentry into the wired enclosure of the car park. If he came back and found any soldier bothering her, he'd kill him.

When Kathe opened the big front door she put her finger on her lips. Jacob Levy wanted to laugh. If he could only talk to her, he would tell her that he knew how to move without making noise if he didn't know anything else. He had learned when it was a lot more important than now.

Kathe turned once on the stairs, because she thought he had not followed her as she could hear nothing. How foolish I am, she told herself, why did I ever fear this? The Hefferichs would not hear him; no one would hear him. He was also different from all others in that he was silent as a cloud.

Jacob Levy had locked the door of her room so cautiously that she did not hear the key turn. Kathe drew the black-out curtains and switched on the little lamp by the bed. It had a mottled pale blue glass shade and a chromium base, and she thought it was beautiful. She hoped he would not think her room a poor place. No doubt in America all the rooms were very big with carved mahogany furniture and satin hangings at the windows.

They sure don't spoil the civilians with coal, Jacob Levy was thinking. When you compared this little icebox with his room and his stove at Weilerburg, you saw how good the army had it. Maybe he could scrounge some coal for her; the cook might let him have it if he said it was for old people that were sick. Kathe kept her room just the way he knew she would. The white iron cot had a clean white cotton bedspread and there was a starched curtain hanging flat like a table cloth over the window, and her washstand with the flowered china pitcher and bowl was so neat you'd think nobody used it. The marble top of the washstand was cracked and the legs were scratched but that wasn't Kathe's fault. Now that bureau or chiffonier, or whatever it was, was a good practical idea; built with a place to hang your clothes on one side and drawers on the other. Kathe could do with a new piece of mirror though and that straight chair would stand a new seat on it. And she was a Catholic allright because there was the picture of the Sacred Heart and another of the Virgin, the way everyone seemed to have in Europe. Well, he had guessed Kathe would be a Catholic and what difference did it make? She'd be warmer if she had a carpet on her floor.

They were both standing. Kathe had not moved to take off her coat. She knew now that he was disappointed; he was used to better rooms. She had nothing better to offer, she could get nothing better. She always thought it was nice here until he stared at it this way.

Jacob Levy noticed Kathe watching him with a funny look in her eyes; not being able to talk made things awkward. He smiled and crossed the room to kiss her. Kathe let him kiss her but she did not seem to be happy. What's gone wrong now, he wondered. He started to unbutton her coat. They'd freeze if they didn't get into bed quick. I'm pretty big for that bed, Jacob Levy thought, it's going to be a tight fit.

Now that she had brought him here, and whatever it was would start, would happen, Kathe felt wretched and dazed with uncertainty. There were too many thoughts churning in her head, and even if he understood her she would not know where to begin; her hands were cold and she wanted to hide. They had to talk first; she needed to hear him say something, she needed to tell him something, but she did not know what this must be. She must explain to him who she was, so he would realize about the war and the Adolphe bridge and all her life.

"Je m'appelle Kathe Limpert," she said. She had taken hold of both his hands and stopped him from unbuttoning her coat. If only he could understand, she would tell him everything. Jacob Levy looked down at Kathe's hands, and his face was puzzled. Didn't he know that she was telling him her name? Not that her name explained her, but perhaps he would see that there was her father and mother and brother and the farm, in her name. Or maybe it was because the name sounded German? Oh dear Lord, he must not think that! Almost all the people have German-sounding names, Kathe said to him in her mind. Our own language is much like German. We know German too. But after the Germans came we tried only to speak French even if it isn't the best correct French the way people in France speak. No, he couldn't think anything so terrible. He would hate her, and go away.

"Kathe," she said again. "Tu comprends? C'est mon nom. Kathe Limpert. C'est un nom Luxembourgeois."

Jacob Levy did not understand what this was about, but she looked worried. "I get it, honey," he said. "Kathe." He sat down on the bed and took her on his knees. She was scared maybe. He knew she didn't have much experience of men. Well then they wouldn't hurry, was all. He didn't want to scare her.

"Toi," Kathe said. "Comment t'appelles-tu?" He did understand her name and now she would learn his name, and that would make it closer and better between them.

Jacob Levy shrugged and shook his head. Too much French, he thought, her hands are cold. I could keep her warm in bed.

Kathe frowned a little, because it was necessary for him to understand. She had fixed on this; if they knew each other's names, they would know each other, and there would be no danger of a mistake or any ugliness. It would not be as if they were strangers.

"Moi," she said again, pointing to herself. "Kathe Limpert.

Toi?" and she pointed to him and waited. Jacob Levy knew what she wanted. He looked at her, his eyes narrowed and veiled, and said very fast without really knowing what he said, "John Dawson Smithers."

Then he was horrified at what he had done. What if Kathe ever came asking for him and the Colonel found out? The Colonel would think he'd been playing some cheap joke on him. He must be crazy; why had he said such a thing? The trouble he was fixing for himself. What made him tell a stupid lie like that; he must be nuts.

But he knew why and he was ashamed. He said "John Dawson Smithers" because of the Sacred Heart and the Virgin and the fear that Kathe would not want a man named Jacob Levy.

"Jawn," Kathe said happily. Everything was allright now, for they knew each other. Jawn and Kathe.

Jacob Levy realized at once that John was as much as she remembered; so there would be no trouble later with the Colonel. There would only be that bad feeling of having used another man's name because your own wasn't good enough. He shivered, and Kathe—remembering that her room was unheated—pointed gravely and shyly to the bed.

Well, Jacob Levy thought, that's what I did it for so I may as well get some use of it. He lifted Kathe from his knees and began to undress. She turned out the small blue-shaded lamp; it was easier to be brave in the dark. But she stood still and was too frightened to move; everything she knew about animals came back to her and it seemed revolting and she would not be able to.

Jacob Levy stopped undressing. "Kathe," he whispered. "What's the matter?" He was barefooted on the cold floor boards. Oh God, he thought, this is too much complications for me.

No, Jawn would not hurt her; not that gentle voice and those kind hands. And if she let him go now, she would have only herself to blame for the lost years behind and the uncertain years ahead. She loved him and there had to be a beginning for every woman.

Jacob Levy waited and heard the bed springs creak and said to himself, I guess it's okay now. He took off his underclothes, and the cold of the room was solid around his nakedness, and then he slipped into the narrow bed.

The need and the nervousness left him at once. He had never imagined this would be possible, that you'd go to bed with a girl you were crazy for and the only thing you'd want to do was laugh. He couldn't help it; maybe he ought to see a doctor about his brain.

Sex-mad Levy, he thought, and this only made him want to laugh more. Me and my fine plans: Charles Boyer Levy. How he'd worked it all out, what a sweat of a hurry he'd been in, couldn't live until he got his hands on her. The big moment arrives, he told himself, and our hero lies on his back and laughs his stupid head off.

Kathe was certainly the most comical kid in the whole world. And he was right about that petticoat; it felt like a straitjacket with ruffles on it. If he could turn on the light, and look at her, she'd be just like those dolls you saw in the store windows, the Christmas presents for little girls: made of pink and white plaster, stiff, with open doll's eyes and wearing a white doll's dress starched like a board. And this comical bed too; he hardly had room for his shoulders. He couldn't help it, it was the funniest damn thing he ever saw. I'm in a kindergarten bed with a Christmas present doll, Jacob Levy thought, and laughed softly but aloud. Then he gathered Kathe in his arms and said, "You funny little kid," and patted her as if he had been presented with a baby to hold, soothe and put to sleep.

"Jawn," she whispered.

"There, there," he said and went on laughing to himself. Honest to God, who'd ever believe it? Experience of men, hell. She didn't have to say anything; you'd know it if you were blind, deaf and dumb. I bet she's the only virgin in the ETO, he thought. The petticoat was the funniest thing of all. The poor ignorant kid, she was probably scared out of her wits right now. He was sorry he'd taken off all his clothes because that would scare her worse if she noticed. Don't know the first thing, Jacob Levy thought. I'm sure glad it's me she stumbled on. Yeh, well, it wasn't so funny after all. What if it had been some guy that didn't give a damn and would have thought, "too bad, baby," and gone ahead anyhow. They oughtn't to let young girls around loose, Jacob Levy told himself indignantly, they don't know what can happen to them.

Sure, allright, it had to happen someday but then it ought to be with a fellow that would look after them. You could see how it would scare them, not knowing anything, and maybe hurt them, too, how did he know? He couldn't even remember how it was for him in the beginning, it was so long ago; some floozy of a Wop girl and he was sixteen, that was six years ago. For a long time the girls knew a lot more than he did and they could always take care of themselves. It wasn't the same.

Kathe lay in his arms and he could scarcely believe that

he had desired this helpless pitiful little creature. It was as if you'd get all steamed up about a lost kitten. I sure know how to pick them, Jacob Levy thought, and had a pleasant feeling that there was more nonsense in life than he had guessed and you did not have to be so serious about it. Kathe was trembling: no, what was she doing? Crying? Yes she was, and trying not to show it.

"Kathe," Jacob Levy said, "Don't you worry, honey. Nothing's going to happen to you. I know how it is, see? Nothing's going to happen."

But girls were goofy when you thought about it. How could Kathe tell he'd leave her alone, as soon as he guessed? What a hell of a chance to take. He wished he could talk to her and explain she oughtn't to take such chances. He wouldn't touch her for anything: it didn't work him up to think a girl was a virgin. But there were plenty of guys who'd think it was a picnic.

"Go to sleep now, honey. You're allright with Uncle Jacob."

"Jawn." She did not understand what he said; she did not understand anything. She clung to his name, for safety.

John, hell, Jacob Levy thought, lousy business. Never mind. Oh you, he thought, and shifted her so that they would be more comfortable in this box of a bed. Oh you sweet little dopey kid. He did not feel excited at all; he felt relaxed and peaceful. Maybe just lying here was the nicest thing he'd ever done with a girl. He felt good about it anyhow.

Jacob Levy kissed her hair and tightened his arms around her. She fitted him as if she had been specially constructed to his measurements. "Goodnight, Kathe," he said. I'll wake up at one o'clock, he promised himself, and she won't even hear me go.

> 7 <

The Colonel didn't look right. He had bags under his eyes and he seemed sort of sour, as if his stomach had gone bad or he was having trouble at Regiment. He acted slow, too, like he was pooped-out and didn't give a damn for anything. Jacob Levy stood inside the parlor door and waited for orders. What happened with him last night, Jacob Levy wondered.

"You want to go to town, Bill?" Lieutenant Colonel Smithers asked.

Lieutenant Gaylord was sprawled on a purple plush chair near the stove, reading. The chaplain had come around in the morning with a box of paper-bounds to give out to the men: morale department. Lieutenant Gaylord kept all the detective stories he wanted and sent the rest on to the Companies. Now he was half through the Saint's adventures in Hongkong. He was comfortable.

"Not specially. Lucille's got a date. I'd just as soon take it easy tonight."

"Me too. I could do with a good night's sleep."

This is really bad, Jacob Levy thought.

"Got any more books?"

"On the table," Lieutenant Gaylord said. "By the window."

If Lucille didn't loosen up by tomorrow night, Lieutenant Gaylord decided, he'd find a nurse. Nurses were the fastest operators of all; after the way they handled men in the hospitals, they didn't have any girlish coyness. You couldn't blame them. It made them sort of rugged, but what the hell. He didn't have all year to hang around after Lucille.

What am I sore about, Lieutenant Colonel Smithers thought. Why've I been going around all day like I wanted to kick myself? What did I expect her to say when I took her home? Dotty had patted his shoulder after she opened her front door, and said, "Goodnight darling. Be seeing you." Friendly enough, but as if she didn't care one way or the other. Did she think she was too good for him or what?

Lieutenant Colonel Smithers remembered his driver. "Nothing more tonight, Levy. I have to be at Regiment at eight. Come around at seven-thirty."

Jacob Levy had walked up the street to his billet, scuffing over the cobbles and thinking. Now he sat on the edge of his bed, thinking some more. Maybe the Colonel would never go to Luxembourg again. He could get a pass someday, but it wouldn't be overnight and Kathe had to work. She would worry herself sick; he felt sure of that. How come he knew so much about what Kathe would think; he wasn't a woman specialist. He never knew what girls thought; that was their business. But he knew about Kathe; she'd get her head full of foolish notions because he didn't show up tonight. She'd sit in her room, worrying and thinking she'd done wrong.

I might as well turn in, Jacob Levy thought. He wished

he had a particular buddy in the Battalion, so he could talk this over. Sometimes two guys had better ideas than one. Or if you couldn't get off, the other one would be free and could get around and fix things up. He was friendly with everybody but there was no one he felt really close to, no one he'd like to ask for help or advice. I might never see her again if things keep up this way, Jacob Levy said to himself. He stood, holding his jacket in his hand, and wished he hadn't thought anything as awful as that.

Pfc Hammer put his head in the door and said, "Come on down to the kitchen, Jake. The Sarge is giving away cigars and licker."

Bert Hammer looked flushed and happy. His eyes shone and his shirt was marked with sweat under the arms.

"Why?" Jacob Levy asked. It wasn't Christmas or anything, yet.

"He's got *four* bottles of cognac. He's having a baby," Bert Hammer said and clumped down the stairs.

Jacob Levy put on his jacket. By God, he thought, that Sarge is a fast worker. He was delighted for the Sergeant. Old Postalozzi, you'd never think of him having a baby. He knew the Sergeant was married to a WAC who worked at the Seine Base Section in Paris. He got married on his last leave in September. The WAC came from Detroit too. You had to hand it to the Sergeant, he was a fast worker allright.

The kitchen was brightly lighted by a hundred-watt bulb hanging from the ceiling. It was steaming hot and smelled of sweat, cigar smoke, cognac and an unappetising general smell of food. Sergeant Postalozzi stood at the kitchen table, pouring cognac into water glasses. In the center of the table, spread on a clean khaki handkerchief, was a small pile of PX ration cigars.

"Come on in, Jake!" Sergeant Postalozzi said. "Have a drink."

"Thanks, Sarge. Well, congratulations!"

Sergeant Postalozzi's small grey eyes gleamed in his large grey face. His thin colorless hair had come unstuck and was hanging in wisps, glued with sweat to his forehead. He was smiling so much that his cheeks seemed to push against his ears. Now he laid his finger alongside his nose, though he had intended to place his finger across his lips, and said, "Ssh! Agnes said not to tell anybody. If they hear, they'll ship her home. She wants to stay in Paris long's she can so we can see each other."

"I sure hope you get a great big baby, Sarge," Bert Hammer said.

"Here's to the Sarge's baby," said Royal Lommax, the cook.

"We ought to break the glasses," Dan Thompson remarked. He was a code clerk who had come over from his billet to visit the cook, and been invited to join the celebration.

"You sure as hell won't break them glasses," the cook said. "These're damn good glasses."

"Here's to Agnes," Jacob Levy said.

"Who's Agnes?" asked Marvin Busch, a truck driver from Headquarters Company, and a friend of Bert Hammer.

"His wife, you dope, the mother of the baby," Bert Hammer said.

"Here's to my Agnes," Sergeant Postalozzi said, smiling and smiling. "Fill them up, you guys."

"That Sarge," the cook said. "He's always got stuff stored away for when you need it."

"I wish we had some music," Sergeant Postalozzi said. "You need some music at a party."

"You want me to eat some glass for you, Sarge?" Marvin Busch asked.

"I what?" said Sergeant Postalozzi.

"Eat glass," Marvin Busch explained. "You know, instead of music."

"Well, damn *me,*" said Sergeant Postalozzi.

"He can, too," Bert Hammer said. "I seen him."

"What kind of glass?" the cook asked. "What is this, for Christ's sake?"

"You show them, Marv," Bert Hammer said, encouraging his friend. "Here's to Sergeant Postalozzi's son, Mr. Postalozzi Junior."

"I need a light bulb," said Marvin Busch.

"What the hell is this man talking about?" the cook asked. Dan Thompson stood on a chair and tried to reach the electric light bulb in the ceiling.

"Leave that alone," Sergeant Postalozzi said. "If he eats that, we got to sit in the dark. Have a cigar, Jake?"

"Well, thanks Sarge. Couldn't we get Marv the light bulb from the can?"

"Now you're talking," Bert Hammer said. Dan Thompson, who seemed the one for decisive action, left the kitchen.

"I hope it's a girl," Sergeant Postalozzi said. "Then she can cook for us when we're old and she won't have to join no bitched-up army. Agnes is a corporal," he added. "Did I ever show you a picture of Agnes, Jake?"

"No, Sarge," Jacob Levy lied. He was staring, in apparent admiration, at a colored photograph of a girl with yellow cement-like curls under her overseas cap, and rimless glasses, when Dan Thompson came back. The Sarge is sure going to have an ugly baby, Jacob Levy thought. He liked the Sarge; he wished the Sarge could have a baby that would look like Shirley Temple when she was a kid, ten years ago maybe.

"Will this one do, Marv?" Dan Thompson asked.

"Listen," Bert Hammer said, "he can eat beer bottles if he feels in the mood."

"You hear that?" Sergeant Postalozzi asked generally.

"Now I need a towel," Marvin Busch said. They watched him wrap the electric light bulb in a towel, which the cook supplied, and then break it like an egg against the kitchen table. Marvin Busch spread the towel on the table, and they gathered around him in silence as he picked up the first morsel of glass, with his little finger crooked, and put it in his mouth. They listened to the glass crunching against his teeth and saw his adam's apple rise and fall, as he swallowed. Marvin Busch, smiling politely, chose another piece of glass, chewed it, and swallowed again.

"See what I mean?" Bert Hammer cried.

"Well, I'm goddamned is what I am!" said Sergeant Postalozzi.

"Didn't you ought to have a drink to wash that glass down, Marv?" Dan Thompson asked.

Marvin Busch shook his head.

"He can't talk when he's eating glass," Bert Hammer explained.

"Is he going to eat it *all*?" the cook said.

"Sure is," Bert Hammer answered. "One night in Puntrimmy, he ate four."

"For Christ's sake," said the cook. "You'd think he'd get

little holes all around his stomach. You'd expect him to bleed somewheres."

Marvin Busch, calm but concentrated, delicate-handed and elegant, went on chewing glass.

"Is he going to eat the metal part too?" Jacob Levy said.

"Naw," said Bert Hammer. "He don't fool with nothing but glass."

Then the towel was clean, except for the metal screw fixture and the fine interior wires of the bulb, and they were all beating Marvin Busch on the back and saying that was the goddamndest thing they ever saw in their whole lives. Sergeant Postalozzi filled a glass full of cognac and said to Bert Hammer, as if Marvin Busch could no longer understand English, "Is it okay for him to have a drink now?"

"Sure," Bert Hammer said. "Do him good."

Marvin Busch looked very pink and a bit rigid, with pride and with the effort of eating the light bulb thoroughly and correctly. "Here's to you, Sarge," he said.

"Say! Here's to you!" Sergeant Postalozzi answered. "Have another cigar, everybody."

They felt exhausted from seeing a man eat so much glass, so they sat on the kitchen chairs and on the floor and drank in comfortable silence. This is a swell party for the Sarge's baby, Jacob Levy thought. He only wished he could do a good trick, with cards maybe, or juggling. He would like to contribute to the Sarge's fine celebration. If he remembered any jokes, he wouldn't tell them so they'd turn out funny. It was a shame not to be able to do something nice for his friends.

"Cognac?" Sergeant Postalozzi asked. They could drink it all. You didn't get your first baby every day.

Royal Lommax, who was sitting against the wall by the stove, stirred from deep contemplation, and said, "Ever seen any knife tricks?"

"Can you do knife tricks, Roy?" Dan Thompson answered. "Why didn't you tell me before?"

"Yeh," said Royal Lommax, "I can do a certain number."

"Well come on, pal," Sergeant Postalozzi said. "Drink up, you guys. We got plenty."

Royal Lommax began to unlace his boots. Languid and affable, they watched him and it seemed as if he were taking his shoes off under water or in a slow motion dream. Then they looked at Royal Lommax's bare feet, which were somehow unusual; it made you wonder, thinking every man had these curious objects hidden inside his shoes. You almost never saw a man's feet, when you thought about it.

Royal Lommax, too, appeared to be surprised by these large pale appendages. There was black around the nails and the cuticle, and a tuft of black wiry hair on each toe below the joint, and a hard corn on both little toes. Royal Lommax stood up, took a bone clasp knife from his pocket, and placed himself carefully, spreading his toes as if they were fingers. The men made a circle around him.

"Give him room," Dan Thompson said.

Royal Lommax caught the tip of the knife blade between his teeth, jerked his head back, and there was the knife, quivering in the floor boards between the big toe and the second toe of his right foot.

"God Almighty!" Sergeant Postalozzi cried. "It's worse than eating glass!"

"You'll kill yourself! You'll amputate yourself, Roy!" Bert Hammer said.

The others were too impressed to speak. Roy hadn't even looked where that knife was going. It had a blade like an ax and it went spinning down like a jet-propelled top.

Royal Lommax grinned and put the knife in his teeth again. It would be awful, Jacob Levy thought, if the next thing they saw was a handful of cut-off toes and the floor covered with blood. Roy couldn't even walk without toes; that would be a hell of a note for poor old Roy if he couldn't walk.

The knife hurtled down and landed between the second and third toes of Royal Lommax's right foot.

"I can't look," Sergeant Postalozzi said. "Is he allright?"

"He sure is," Marvin Busch said, with generous admiration. "I wouldn't try that trick for anything."

"I need a drink," Dan Thompson said. "You're going to cut the hell out of yourself some day, Roy."

"Been doing it for twenty years. Never had an accident yet."

Jacob Levy and Bert Hammer and Dan Thompson knocked wood, quickly.

"Look at them feet," Sergeant Postalozzi said. "Look at them just standing there."

The knife was now trembling in the tight space between the fourth and little toe.

"Take a drink, Roy," Jacob Levy urged.

"Don't push your luck, boy," Sergeant Postalozzi said, handing Royal Lommax a glass. "A fellow's got only so much luck is what I always say."

Royal Lommax took the glass, bowed to them all, and drank it in long swallows.

"Here's your shoes, Roy," Dan Thompson said. He wasn't

going to let his friend play with knives after a straight glass of cognac.

"Thank you," Royal Lommax said. When they saw that he could not lace his boots, being unable to find the holes, they realized he had been drunk all the time. A man who could throw a sonofabitching sharp knife at his own feet, when drunk, and not cut his leg off, was a man who could really hold liquor. They spoke to him about his performance, with respect.

"Been practising for twenty years," Royal Lommax murmured.

"Well, what I mean is, thank God you still got your feet," Sergeant Postalozzi said. He sat down at the kitchen table. They were all exhausted again.

Presently Dan Thompson asked if they knew the story about the G.I. from Texas in the Paris whorehouse. They knew a hundred stories about G.I.s and whorehouses but it wouldn't have been friendly to say so. They laughed when Dan told his story because nobody wanted to hurt his feelings; but it wasn't a very good story and anyhow it didn't seem right to talk smut when the party was for the Sergeant's baby. Bert Hammer started to whistle "Lili Marlene." He was a famous whistler and he ornamented the melody, and they hummed with him or tapped the time. Everyone felt contented and warm and a little sentimental. Suddenly Marvin Busch said, " 'Scuse me," and ran for the back door.

"I guess it was all that glass he ate," Bert Hammer said. He stopped whistling. Marvin Busch returned, with tears still in his eyes, looking yellow to green. He drank a glass of water at the sink and said in a subdued voice, "Sure has been a fine party, Sarge. Thanks a lot. I better get going."

He waved vaguely to the others and walked out the back door.

Sergeant Postalozzi was nodding at the kitchen table. "Gotta finsh ma work," he announced and rose and moved like a sleep walker on a window ledge, towards the hall.

The party was over.

Royal Lommax took the half empty bottle of cognac and put it on the top shelf of the cupboard where the Sergeant would find it tomorrow. There were no cigars left on the khaki handkerchief. He collected the glasses in an unsteady hand and laid them in the sink.

"Bed," he said. "Bed, now, everybody."

Jacob Levy followed Bert Hammer up the stairs. Bert slept next to the wall so he had to wait for him. Jacob Levy took off his shoes and socks and his shirt, but his trousers proved unmanageable. I just don't feel like jumping up and down or balancing till they fall off, he told himself.

"We sure gave the Sarge's baby a swell send-off," Jacob Levy said.

"Sure did," Bert Hammer answered and took a deep breath that was almost a snore.

Jacob Levy burrowed his face into his pillow. Pretty, soft, little pillow, he thought, pretty, soft, little Kathe. When me and Kathe get a baby we'll invite Marv Busch to eat some glass for it.

> *8* <

I GOT TOO much on my mind, Jacob Levy thought. He was
leaning against the side of a farmhouse, out of the wind, let-
ting the sun warm his face. The farmhouse was made of
knubbly white concrete, covering the old stones. It had a red
tile roof and was built according to no design, but had
grown as the farmer's fortunes allowed. This was G Company
Headquarters, a mile down the road from Weilerburg. A
window opened and someone threw out an empty khaki tin
can. Cheese from the C ration, Jacob Levy noted: it made
the place messy, they oughtn't to throw cans around a nice
farm. He had heard Lieutenant Colonel Smithers' voice,
briefly, through the window. "You got to put a stop to that,
Paul." Lieutenant Colonel Smithers sounded angry; he would
be chewing Captain Paul Willcox of G Company.

That's my trouble, Jacob Levy decided, I got too much to

[97]

think about. They were working hard now and he did not like it. They could have transport, weapons, and personnel inspection every day of the week if it made them feel good. He would drive the Colonel back and forth from the Companies to Regimental Headquarters and all over this pint-sized country, fourteen hours every day, and not mind it. But Jacob Levy watched this faster and faster movement of the Battalion, watched the new men being trained until they were expert, the weapons repaired or replaced, the supplies piling up, the whole machine tightened and readied, and he knew what it meant. The army wasn't running any free winter vacations: the outfit got in shape and then they used you.

Time, Jacob Levy thought, time, time. It would be a matter of days. Allright, how many days? It was better to know than to worry. Those poor bastardly replacements, he said to himself, and observed eight wooden-faced soldiers and two contemptuous sergeants working with light machine guns. Nothing the soldiers did pleased the sergeants, and they looked half frozen.

The replacements acted like they wanted to beg your pardon but at the same time they tried to seem tough. They were young was what, twenty or so, or maybe younger, and fresh from home. And they were all thinking the same thing: *what's it like?* And they were all scared they'd be scared, when it started. And they all wished they were back in camp in the U.S.A., where they'd spent their whole time wishing they'd get going.

Ah stuff the replacements, Jacob Levy thought. If he could only dope out the Colonel now, that would make things easier. It was the uncertainty of it. He couldn't figure where the Colonel stood with Dotty. Why didn't they get themselves fixed up so you could say for sure they'd be dating every night? This way he couldn't make his own plans, with the Colonel maybe liking Dotty, maybe not liking Dotty.

And there was no use kidding himself it was life's young dream with Kathe; it had been rough last night. He couldn't take it this way much longer. Last night he felt as if his body was full of hot wires, jumpy and hurting. There she was and there he was and nothing happened; a guy wasn't made of stone. If he could talk to Kathe, maybe they could straighten it out. But what if he did look up some words in Sergeant Postalozzi's dictionary, then what? Ask her, "what do you want to do?" How did Kathe know what she wanted? And he was afraid to start; he didn't have any idea how virgins were. Kathe could get disgusted, or scared off, and she wouldn't want any more to do with him.

His mother wrote him a letter today, when he had all this on his mind besides, and said: I keep hoping you'll be home for Christmas. She couldn't be so foolish as to think he, or anyone else, had a prayer of being home for Christmas. But he could imagine her, his good pretty little mother who didn't look old at all, and who didn't understand anything, and just baked some more cookies and boiled some more fudge and sent her son another package, because she didn't know what else to do. It must be kind of tough on them too, sitting there in the house by themselves.

When did it start that he got so much to think about all of a sudden? Jacob Levy kicked at the thin crust of frost on the grass and thought: snow next. That'll be fine to fight in, fine and dandy. Snow was the only thing he'd missed; rain mud heat dust and the Italian flies, but no snow. His heart began to beat heavily. No, Jacob Levy warned himself, skip it, cut it out, leave it alone. *No.* That Colonel's got luck for two.

"Ah, to hell with it," Jacob Levy said, under his breath.

• • • • • • • • • • • •

Lieutenant Colonel Smithers came out of the farmhouse, pulled up his coat collar and said, "So long, Paul." He climbed into the jeep and muttered, "H Company now." He sat hunched into his coat and all Jacob Levy could see of him was a thick brown eyebrow which looked as if it had been dented, and a chill blue eye.

Allright, Lieutenant Colonel Smithers said to himself, they've got it easy and they want to live. Who doesn't? That's what's eating them. Rod Blackmer, commanding E Company since old Nick got knocked off, was not up to the job. He wasn't using his head or else he didn't have enough experience. It was half-witted to put the replacements through weapons drill, as if they were still at home, instead of sending them out on tactical problems so they could learn what to do with their weapons, aside from fire them in the general direction of the enemy. The platoon leaders felt Rod's lack of confidence and pretty soon the men would too. And the paper work beat Rod entirely; here he was four days late in sending up the court martial papers on those two corporals of his who had to stand trial. Knowing he wasn't doing things right made Rod sullen; he took it out by beefing. That beef about snow suits, for instance; sure, there was going to be snow and plenty of it, sure the men would show up like big black targets against a white background; sure, he himself requested snow suits from Regiment who had already requested them from Division. No doubt Division spoke to Corps, Corps spoke to Army, Army spoke to Ike and Ike spoke to the President. Result: there were no snow suits. It wasn't Rod's business anyhow.

Joe Huebsch, commanding F Company, was tired. He was so tired he couldn't relax. He was just the opposite of Rod and was driving his men crazy, running after them like a cop the whole time, raising trouble about the kitchen not being clean enough and the latrines not deep enough and the vehicles not shiny enough, and the men were getting sore, and had reason to. They were old hands and they did their work allright; Joe had the fewest replacements of any Company and could have worked them into the outfit easily enough. Instead it almost smelled like mutiny down there and that was no good either. Joe was going nuts on chastity, maybe, being faithful to that blonde basketball player in Belleville Illinois. He'd have to get Joe over to his CP and fill him full of drinks and try to make him loosen up. But he wished Joe would shake himself out of it; there was enough to do around here without worrying over mental problems.

As for Paul Willcox, at G Company, that cluck seemed to think this was the Christmas vacation or something. Half his transport had the radiators frozen and ten of his men were in hospital with clap and the whole Company was having a high old time, enjoying the pants off themselves. He had had to chew Paul and now Paul would feel like a heel and he felt like a heel himself; you couldn't want a better man in combat than Paul and this Battalion hadn't been out of the line enough to train a Company commander in rear area discipline. It wasn't Paul's fault but if he didn't hurry up and change, he'd lose his command.

And now we will see what kind of trouble there is at H Company, Lieutenant Colonel Smithers said to himself. Then he had to go back and finish writing those letters to the families of the dead. The General encouraged unit commanders to write personal letters and it probably was a decent idea but he hated this more than any other single feature of his job. How do I know what to say to a mother, Lieutenant Colonel Smithers thought. And half the time he didn't even know who the guy was that got killed, or how he got killed. If he could write the truth he'd just say: Dear Madam, when you've seen as many deads as I have you stop noticing; they aren't people once they're dead; and the best thing you can do is forget them because you know there will always be more anyhow and what can we do about it?

The only pleasure he had was watching Bill Gaylord train his Intelligence section. Bill was making a bunch of murderers out of those boys. They were goofy the way Bill was, but getting a kick out of it. Bill was full of new tricks and ideas and he'd have a time holding Bill once they got back in the line. Probably Bill picked up all these fancy angles from those mystery stories he was always reading. The army got in Bill's way a lot: what he would have liked was to operate with his section as a private task force, committing heroic deeds behind the enemy lines.

I guess Bill will want to go to town tonight, Lieutenant Colonel Smithers thought. He wasn't sure he ever wanted to go to Luxembourg again and he couldn't figure himself out. Dotty was giving it away, as generous as you could ask for, but how did he know she didn't lay some other guy the night before and the night after him? She had plenty of opportunities and there was nothing to stop her. She didn't make any bones about being his girl: easy come, easy go was her motto. He wasn't in love with her, so what law said she had to be in love with him? She was straight about it anyway. But he didn't have any satisfaction for himself; he couldn't fool himself it was Johnny Smithers she wanted. If she'd just say something once, he thought, I don't even care if it's a lie.

And Dad writing about the chicken farm; okay, they were too old to handle it if they couldn't get help. But he'd bought the chicken farm from the money he saved for five years, by selling cars in La Harpe to people who couldn't afford them and then collecting the installment payments like pulling teeth. It was mean work and that money was supposed to keep his folks so he wouldn't have to worry. Now he had to worry all over again. The old man was bound to be robbed when he sold the place; Dad knew no more about business than a poor dumb flea.

"Ah, to hell with it," Lieutenant Colonel Smithers said, under his breath.

> *9* <

Jacob Levy sat with his hands inside his sleeves, hugging himself. He was bent over as with cramp. A drizzle, that was almost ice, fell on the sagging canvas top of the jeep. At ten o'clock the last soldiers came out of the Red Cross Club and walked fast, in the rain, towards their billets.

They looked cold and bored. You couldn't help thinking about Christmas and naturally that made everyone feel sick. The rain didn't help; the cold didn't help. Ten o'clock and this dead foreign city closed down. Everybody has something except me, they thought, walking inside their loneliness. Might write a letter home. What can you say? I love you, for you are heaven and earth, you are everything I have lost, you are more beautiful than the morning because you are mine. Hell, what could a fellow say in a letter? Maybe there'd be mail from the U.S. in the morning. Write to me: write to me on pink paper, on blue paper, on a ruled pad from the dime store. Write to me with a pen, with a pencil, put a stamp on the envelope and address it with my name. So that I may know I am someone, came from somewhere, am waited for, loved, and exist. But Christ, you sweated out the mail and when you finally got it, you read it over and over, and you didn't know, you couldn't tell, everybody seemed different. What can anybody say in a letter? When you're so pissed-off you don't know what to do with yourself, when you're so pissed-off you don't even want anything; when you're so pissed-off you wouldn't move if a truck was going to run over you, you can always climb between the khaki blankets and sleep. The street lay oily and empty, under the rain.

Jacob Levy shivered and hugged himself tighter. The Colonel would be out soon. The Colonel probably stayed in the office until the men left. It wouldn't look good for him to hang around where the men could see him, though they must know he was there. Dotty wasn't too smart, but maybe she didn't give a damn anyhow. It looked as if she was saying to the guys: I'm paid to work for you but I date the officers.

What Dotty did was her business but it would be very nice if she would hurry before he became a corpse. Kathe was waiting in this rain, too. He was tired of this street, and the night that settled on your skin like leeches, and he was tired of thinking about Kathe and the unfinishedness of Kathe, so Jacob Levy went to his stream in the Smokies. It was spring and there were small pale flowers between the trunks of the birch trees. From his shack, he could see the fast water making mirror flashes in the sun. He was building a field stone fireplace now and it was a big handsome job that took up the whole east wall of his shack. He was going to make the sides of the fireplace like steps, so he could put stuff on them, a clock, or a cigarette box, or some magazines. The question was, how to finish off the top? Would it look better with a sort of board for a mantelpiece, or should he leave the plain stone?

The voices, loud and confident, banged against the invisible housefronts and echoed in the street. Jacob Levy came back from the Smokies, slowly. You could get arrested for making so much noise. They were talking under the glass and iron porte cochere of the Red Cross Club, and could not see him where he was parked on the street at the end of the curved private driveway.

"But I can't walk, Sammy!" She don't have to scream like that, Jacob Levy thought. That would be the other Red Cross girl, the blonde one with the baby-talk face.

"Where in the hell is that beautiful dumb driver of yours, Johnny?" A man's voice, must be a friend of the Colonel's, the baby-talk's date.

"What?" the blonde said. "Have you been holding out on me, Johnny? What's this about a beautiful driver?"

"Haven't you seen him? He's Johnny's pet. Name of Jacob Levy," the man's voice answered.

"Oh *no!*" the girl said, laughing.

Jacob Levy tried not to listen. He would act as if he were asleep and pretty soon the Colonel would come looking for him. He could not drive up now, and know they'd know he had heard them. Why did they have to talk about him; he wasn't anything to them; he'd never gotten in their way.

"He's very nice," that was Dotty; Jacob Levy knew that cool precise voice. "And he's always on time."

"Look how Dotty sticks up for him!"

"I've *got* to see him," the girl squealed. "But *why* do you call him Jacob Levy? Or did you make that up?"

[107]

"Because it's his name," Lieutenant Colonel Smithers answered. "Why are you Ruthie Maxton, as far as that goes?"

"Say, what're you sore about?" the man's voice interrupted. "Who did anything to you? Lay off Ruthie."

"Lay off Levy," Lieutenant Colonel Smithers said.

"Well, for Christ's sake, what is this? Come on, Ruthie, let's go. We can walk."

"I don't mind." She would have had to toss her head, as she said it. They started down the driveway towards the Officers' Club. Ruthie's voice drifted back, "I can't *stand* people who pick fights."

"Levy's probably asleep," Lieutenant Colonel Smithers said. "I'll go and see."

"I'll come with you," Dorothy Brock said.

Jacob Levy kept his eyes shut until he felt Lieutenant Colonel Smithers' hand on his shoulder. "Wake up, Levy! We've been waiting for you."

"Yes sir," Jacob Levy mumbled, pretending to wake. "I must of fallen asleep."

"That's allright. Rue Philippe, now."

Miss Dorothy Brock sat silent in the jeep, hating the cold and thinking that her partner Miss Maxton was at once too stupid and vulgar to live, and that Miss Maxton's beau, Major Ricks, was too stupid and vulgar to live, and that Johnny was really a nice man, though not an interesting one, and that she needed a vacation because everyone was beginning to get on her nerves.

"Usual time, Levy," Lieutenant Colonel Smithers said, as he jumped out of the jeep.

Lieutenant Colonel Smithers followed Miss Brock into the

ugly parlor, and walked past her to the table of bottles in the dining room.

"What're you thinking about, Johnny?" she asked. Now why chandeliers? Of all the hideous, cheerless, unbecoming light in the world.

"Nothing."

"Yes you are. Not too strong for me."

Lieutenant Colonel Smithers brought her glass.

"Don't these guys ever use their apartment?" he said.

"That's not what you were thinking."

"I was thinking I was glad Levy was asleep so he didn't hear those jerks."

"Yes."

"That fat-assed Ricks was never anywhere he could get hit."

"True."

"Oh well, the hell with it. Here's to you."

They drank in silence. The room, though heated, was not a place you felt like taking your coat off in.

"Why didn't you ever get married, Dotty?" Lieutenant Colonel Smithers asked.

"I don't know."

"Why don't you go home and find yourself a good man and have kids and settle down?"

"There aren't any men at home now. Remember?"

"This is no life for a girl," Lieutenant Colonel Smithers observed. "It's just no good. There's nothing good about it."

"It's allright."

"No, it isn't. You meet a lot of men but they——" He had started to say, "take what they can get," and it did not seem a tactful remark, considering that he was one of them.

"Aren't serious?" Dorothy Brock asked. "Is that what you mean, Johnny? Maybe I'm not serious, myself."

"That's what's wrong about it. A girl gets mixed-up about things and then the war will be over——"

"It'll never be over," Miss Brock interrupted, lightly.

"It sure as hell will. I'm going back to Georgia, I am."

"And find a good girl?"

"You bet. And have kids. And live the way people ought."

"I'm not arguing."

Lieutenant Colonel Smithers tried to find a comfortable position on the sofa. It was covered in grey velours, dented with upholstery buttons as if strewn with navels, and it was unyielding. It had muscles of its own and if you moved, they flexed and hardened against you. He sighed and said, "Want another drink?"

Dorothy Brock handed him her glass. She was staring at the empty grate under the marble mantelpiece. The mantelpiece would look lovely in a mausoleum. How had anyone ever lived in this loathsome apartment?

"You see," Lieutenant Colonel Smithers began, holding the two glasses, "a man gets to thinking after he's seen some action."

He could find no place for his shoulders on this lousy sofa. Better drink and forget it. "He certainly doesn't want this sort of life."

"I know. Georgia. A good girl. A white picket fence. The little toddlers."

"What's wrong with that?"

"Nothing," Dorothy Brock said. "Nothing."

What was she sneering about then? Did she imagine this was what a man was fighting for; to sit around strangers' houses that were so miserable you had to get drunk to be comfortable, with a girl who didn't mean a thing to you.

"I have a friend," Dorothy Brock said, "awfully sweet girl, from Charleston. We were together in England. She fell in love with a paratrooper. She never thought of anything except how to get to Leicester or how to meet him in London. She'd sit up all night in a train, and go to a pub and hold hands with him for two hours, and come back. She wrote him twice a day and if she didn't get a letter she couldn't eat. Then his Division parachuted in, on D-Day. She read about that in the papers but she didn't hear from him. She walked as if she had rheumatism and I wouldn't have been surprised if her hair had turned white. She got frightfully thin, and she wouldn't talk about him. We shared a room and I'd hear her thrashing around and crying all night. I kept saying, I know Dick's allright, and she'd look at me as if it wasn't a thing you could speak about.

"This went on for ten days, and then she got a letter from Dick. He was perfectly okay, not even wounded. First she cried like a baby, just lay on her bed and sobbed. She couldn't stop. Then she slept for about twenty-four hours. We were in a big camp then and the other girls and I agreed to say she had a light case of flu, because there was a sort of field supervisor woman poking around.

"Then Grace, that's her name, came out of it. She drove us mad by singing all the time and she joked with the men and looked as pretty as a picture. She was a lovely girl, with long ash-blonde hair. She wrote four letters a day to Dick and had it all planned how she was going to get to France.

"So everything was divine for two weeks and then she got a letter from a friend of Dick's, who knew about her, saying that Dick had been killed. Sniper, I think it was. Anyhow, I gather it just happened on an average day when there wasn't anything extra going on."

Lieutenant Colonel Smithers finished his drink. "What became of her?"

"They shipped her home. Nervous breakdown from overwork, I think it's called. I haven't heard from her since she left."

"Poor kid."

"Yes."

"Still, she had something."

"Had what?" Dorothy Brock said. "What sort of life is that? You call that having something? I call it hell and insanity. Listen: my father's too old; I haven't got a brother, nor a husband, nor a fiancé, nor a man I'm in love with. Have something! All I want is not to have anything."

Her voice sounded very strange to her; why did she let him get under her skin with that stuff about true love and babies. Who wanted to talk about the war? Why couldn't they drink and stick to gossip or stories about the places they'd been?

"But Dotty, after the war——"

"After the war!" This voice did not belong to her; it couldn't. "After the war!" Suddenly Dorothy Brock hid her face with her hands. "I think Ricks and Ruthie are horrible, too! I hate mean people! I hate killing! I hate doughnuts!"

Lieutenant Colonel Smithers was too shocked to move. Did I do this? he thought. She doesn't even know what she's saying. She's gone all to pieces, crumpled up, gone to pieces. This was the hard girl who didn't show anything.

"Dotty, honey, I didn't mean to," he touched her hair awkwardly, and Dorothy Brock moved her head to get rid of his hand.

She's all alone here, Lieutenant Colonel Smithers thought, and she works like a dog at that club, she's up at six-thirty every morning and she's tired and she sees how things are. It's got her down. She can't keep it up all the time, being so tough and independent. She's just a girl, after all. He felt that he was the one who was sure, he was the strong one, he was necessary. Dotty had broken up, the way girls had a right to, and now he would take over.

"Honey," Lieutenant Colonel Smithers said, "I'm going to put you to bed. You need some sleep."

Dorothy Brock was quiet now, but still hidden behind her hands. She shook her head.

"Oh yes you are," he said. "You're going to bed. And to sleep. Nothing else, hear? And if you feel like crying you go ahead. I could cry myself, plenty of times."

Dorothy Brock looked smaller, hunched in the bulging armchair, and younger, and at last she was behaving the way Lieutenant Colonel Smithers expected a girl to behave.

"Come on," he said, "up you get."

She could not look at him and she wanted to run from the room and disappear before she died of shame. How could she have let herself go like that? And she still felt stunned by the emotion she could not stop, and lost in the loneliness that had made her cry. What has happened to me, Dorothy Brock thought, am I cracking up? Her eyelashes were stuck together in points, and her nose needed powder and her smooth brown hair was rumpled around her face.

Lieutenant Colonel Smithers took her hand and led her down the hall as if she were a child on a dangerous street crossing. "People aren't getting enough sleep around here," he said.

Dorothy Brock stood inside the doorway of the bedroom and looked at it as if she had never been there before. Lieutenant Colonel Smithers turned on the small table lamp and said, "Sit down, honey, while I take your shoes off." She obeyed in silence. This was not the Dotty he knew; she had cried herself into another girl. You could really fall for this girl because you'd know you mattered to her. He was happy undoing her coat and taking off her blouse; happier than he had been when the other Dotty, willing and indifferent, undressed herself. And she still wouldn't meet his eyes, she was shy now, and this made her more desirable than ever before but Lieutenant Colonel Smithers repressed himself. He was going to leave her strictly alone. She'd had enough wolves making passes at her. That was why she put on the tough act. She was a sweet kid at heart, and if she'd acted like a hard little bitch that was because there were too many guys who'd take advantage of her if she let them. He was sorry for her, here all alone, and worn-out, and she could relax and trust him. He was in charge now.

He turned his back while Dotty pulled her slip over her head, and then he put out the light.

"You comfortable, honey?" Lieutenant Colonel Smithers asked. Dorothy Brock murmured something he could not hear. It was fine having his arm around her, and her head resting just below his chin, as if she knew it was a safe place and she belonged there. Lieutenant Colonel Smithers lay on his back, and felt his body loosen in contentment. He did not know exactly what it was that he wanted, but he knew he had found it.

▷ *10* ◁

Usually Kathe told him the events of the day. Jacob Levy was always amused by the way she bounced at his side and chattered in her funny voice with every sentence rising to a question. It was unimportant to Kathe that Jawn could not understand. Perhaps he could understand for often she paused, in between telling him how expensive eggs had become and that Madame Verney came to the restaurant wearing a new blouse of figured crêpe de chine, and asked, "Tu comprends, Jawn?" Then Jacob Levy would smile down at the eager little face, somewhere near his elbow, and say, "oui, oui." Sometimes Jawn stopped and hugged her in the middle of a sentence. And then they walked on, with Kathe's conversation like a breeze around them.

But tonight she was silent. She felt the cold through her thin old coat and the cold was part of the darkness and sorrow of the city and part of the war which went on and on. The trees looked starved and bony against the night sky; the squat stone apartment houses that lined the street seemed empty. No one was happy; no one was even alive. Kathe felt this terrible weary waiting of the world, of the people and the houses and the abandoned land, and she was lost in it. She had wanted her own happiness, however brief, and now she was losing it; she could feel Jawn going away from her.

They walked down the cobbled street and Kathe listened to the noise of their feet, and shivered with cold, and thought that soon she would have nothing at all, not even this sad and lonely walk home through the night.

Jawn was sitting on the straight chair now, at the end of her bed, and his legs stretched out nearly across the room. He kept his cap on, which showed how he felt. He would not keep his cap on unless he were unhappy, for he was the most courteous man she had ever seen: he always held doors open and took her arm crossing the street.

"Dis-moi," Kathe said, "Dis-moi ce que je dois faire. Je veux te plaire, Jawn, je veux que tu sois heureux."

Jacob Levy looked at her and smiled.

Kathe sat at the foot of the bed and reached around the white iron bedpost to take his hand. "Jawn, pleeze," she said.

"It's not your fault, honey." Jacob Levy patted her hand and put it away from him.

Kathe was trying not to cry. Jawn had not kissed her; he had not unbuttoned her coat. He came to her with love and she had failed him, and he would go away for he could have whatever he wanted and why should he waste himself sitting on a chair in Kathe Limpert's bedroom. He would go away and that would be the end, and she could only blame herself.

"Tu viens te coucher, Jawn?" Kathe pointed to the bed timidly.

Jacob Levy shook his head. "I can't take it, kid." His mouth seemed to want to smile and his voice sounded as if he were saying something to smile at. "Not being made of iron," he went on, "it gets a fellow down. And then, you see, I guess I'm pretty hungry too and it wouldn't do you much good to be raped, now would it? We better leave it be, honey, though I'll regret it."

He looked at his watch. A long long time to sit on a chair, Jacob Levy thought. Might as well go out soon and chew the fat with that sentry at the car park. Or find some woman, just to stop thinking about women. And lose Kathe because he was a dope and didn't know how to act. Maybe she'd thank him for it someday but it made him feel pretty sick right now.

The light went out. He could hear Kathe undressing. She'll be warmer in bed, Jacob Levy thought. He'd give her a brotherly goodnight kiss and beat it. This was a fine life and he was enjoying every minute of it. If the car park sentry had been stationed here a while, he'd probably know some cat house addresses. No, not tonight anyhow. Maybe not tomorrow night either. Maybe he just thought he needed a woman.

"Jawn," Kathe whispered.

Allright, one brotherly kiss and beat it.

Kathe did not want to be kissed; he could not understand what she wanted. She was trying to find his hands in the dark. Now she had his left hand, by the wrist, and was pulling him towards her. Jacob Levy sat on the edge of the bed, mystified. Kathe whispered something, and guided his hand.

What was all this? Then he felt a warm round naked breast, and recoiled as if the skin conducted electricity. Kathe had stopped whispering; she was holding her breath. She's taken off her petticoat, Jacob Levy thought, she hasn't got a stitch on.

"Kathe! Kathe, you mean you want to?"

"Viens vite, Jawn!" I am only shivering from cold, she informed herself.

Jacob Levy took off his clothes and threw them on the floor. If she wants to, it's different; it's not like putting something over on her. He remembered to slide slowly into the cot; he remembered the rusty springs. Then he had Kathe in his arms; cold feet against his legs, cold hands at the back of his neck, and all the rest warm, silk soft against him, all his, all given to him gladly. He had never felt this way, only holding a girl, and his blood pounded in his throat and his temples.

I feared this, Kathe thought, I feared it. No wonder people would die for love, no wonder there were all the poems and songs about it. She wanted to laugh with joy. She was breathless and tingling as if she had rolled in snow. She could not hold Jawn close enough; and she had all the lost time to make up for, the nights she had thrown away because of her ugly imaginings.

Jawn moved. Come back, Kathe thought, do not let me go. Now he was moving her. What did he want her to do? This would be some new delight which he understood in his wisdom. Yes, she thought, anything; Jawn knows; he will show me what I must do.

"Ah non!" Kathe whispered. Jawn would stop and they could be as they had been before.

[118]

"Non, Jawn, non!" Kathe gasped.

"Relax, Kathe," Jacob Levy mumbled, "loosen up, Kathe."

Her muscles had contracted; she lay like a stone. Jacob Levy could feel the sweat on his forehead and his lip. Millions of people got married all the time; girls mostly didn't know anything when they got married. It couldn't be so bad or they wouldn't get married, millions of them. There had to be a first time. Take it easy, go slow, it'll be allright if you take it easy.

In the dark, Kathe's eyes were open and staring at Jawn's blurred face. What had happened to the floating joy; this was like the animals. The animals could not be blamed, they knew no better; but it was shameful horrible wicked for a man to do this. She was crushed and in pain and Jawn panted as if he had been running. He was hurting her with his hands, with his shoulders, with his hips, with all of him.

"Arrête! Arrête!" Kathe commanded, and tried to free her hands and push him away.

Can't stop, Jacob Levy thought, can't stop, mustn't stop, has to be one first time, can't, can't, can't.

"Don't worry, Kathe. I won't make you a baby. Don't worry, honey."

Jawn sounded as if he were crying, and suddenly he groaned. Kathe caught her lip in her teeth and put her hand, that was useless to protect her, over her mouth. At least she must not cry out and wake the Hefferichs. Her face was smeary and hot with tears and Jawn didn't care if he killed her. Then Jawn said something, and wrenched himself from her, and rolled over on his back.

Kathe turned her face to the wall and lay in a tight ball of misery, crying into the pillow and feeling the pain blunt

itself and spread in a dull ache through her body. She listened
to Jawn, gulping in air, and she thought he had tricked her
and destroyed her and how could he be so cruel to a girl
who had never harmed him.

"Kathe," Jacob Levy whispered, "are you allright?"

She would not answer him. She would never speak to him
again.

"Kathe. Say something."

He thought he could kill her and she would still speak
to him. If she didn't hurt so much, she would turn over and
beat at his face. I'll never walk again, Kathe thought, I'll
never speak to him and I'll never walk.

Jacob Levy reached out to stroke Kathe's shoulder and she
shook his hand away.

Oh God, Jacob Levy thought, I guess I must of hurt her,
I guess she's sore. But she'd have to find out someday. I did
the best I could. I took it as easy as I could. I didn't want to
hurt her.

"Kathe, I'm sorry if I hurt you, honey. It's bound to be
rough the first time."

I hate you, I hate you, Kathe said in her mind. How dare
you talk to me after what you've done?

"Va-t-en," she said, forgetting that she had meant never to
speak to Jawn again. "Va-t-en. Je ne veux plus jamais te
voir." She had to bury her face in the pillow to keep from
sobbing aloud.

I guess she's sore, Jacob Levy thought. This took all the
pleasure away. There had been a rugged stretch when he
thought he'd give it up but it would be just right now if he
could hold her in his arms, with the hunger satisfied, and
only the quiet and goodness left. As it was, Kathe spoiled

everything; he felt like a heel because she was sore. But she did take off her petticoat; she certainly seemed to invite him. How could you ever get things straight with a girl?

Might as well go, Jacob Levy thought, no sense staying here being unfriendly.

He got out of bed carefully. Those springs must have sounded like a command car on a mud road. Thank God nobody came, anyhow. He felt heavy and hollow and stupid; it was no good if it ended like this. I didn't want to hurt her; she might understand that.

Dressed, Jacob Levy stood by the bed and looked down at Kathe, shrunken into a lump against the wall.

"I'm sorry, Kathe."

There was no answer.

"Je venir demain," he offered.

The lump shook, disagreeing. From the pillow, in the muffled voice of a bad cold, Kathe said, "Non."

"Okay, if that's how you want it. But it seems pretty stupid to me. You had to find out sometime. And you're not going to get a baby or anything."

"Non," Kathe said again.

"Goodnight, then."

There was silence. Kathe sat up in bed and called, "Jawn!" She wanted him to put his arms around her and comfort her; she wanted him to tell her everything was allright, that this was the way life happened and that it was only difficult and painful until you understood it. She wanted to cry in his arms and be petted and loved and made safe. And then too, she had taken a unique decision and suffered all its consequences, and she deserved to be thanked a little, and admired. "Jawn," Kathe whispered. But he was gone.

> *11* <

AFTER HE left Lieutenant Colonel Smithers at the rue Philippe, Jacob Levy took counsel of the car park sentry. He wanted a drink, he said, he wasn't after anything more. The place the sentry recommended seemed to be a speakeasy, a small storeroom lined with bare shelves, behind a shoe store. There were five wooden tables and the clientele was all soldiers. The civilian who served cognac and beer, the only drinks, looked nervous. The soldiers talked quietly too; nobody wanted the M.P.'s on their necks.

He listened to four soldiers talking football; then he listened to three soldiers talking automobiles. He attended, with indifference, an argument on the relative merits of life in Texas and Arizona. He was invited to join a muted poker game, with matches for chips. It seemed to Jacob Levy that the night lasted a week.

The next night Jacob Levy decided to wait for half an hour and drive back to the rue Philippe. It would be warmer inside that downstairs hall and he had a blanket which he used as a seat cushion in the jeep. He could wrap himself up and sleep on the floor.

Miss Brock and Lieutenant Colonel Smithers found Jacob Levy, curled in an architecturally useless niche that had been built into the lobby wall.

"He's something to look at, isn't he?" Dorothy Brock whispered.

"He looks sick to me. I've been keeping him out a lot, lately."

Lieutenant Colonel Smithers woke Jacob Levy and asked, "Do you feel okay, Levy?"

"Yes sir. It was warm in here." He was embarrassed that the Colonel and Dotty had seen him sleeping and he managed to appear more awake than he felt. On the way back to Weilerburg, in the cold dark, Jacob Levy said to himself: I couldn't feel lousier if I was dead.

.   .   .   .

Lieutenant Colonel Smithers stretched and stacked the papers he had been signing. He looked around this comfortable room and wondered, briefly, what had happened to Mr. Haas, the notary, who once owned it. Probably came to a bad end, poor fellow, and it would be harder on a man who had such a good place to live. Lieutenant Colonel Smithers admired once more a fringed lamp shade, the figured rug on the floor, an oil painting of two cows and an oil painting of a sailing ship. This was what everyone wanted:

a fine home of your own, settling down, knowing today what you would be doing tomorrow.

The letters to the families of the dead were written; the recommendations for citations and promotions were signed; the after action report was in; the poop about heroes, for use by Division P.R.O. who would try to peddle the stuff to home town papers, was collected and handed over. All the sweeping-up was finished. And the Battalion was fat again. The men were rested, fed, re-fitted; the new ones were getting some idea of the score; and in fact, he had a ready Battalion. This time now, with all pressures off, was pure gravy: too good to last for that reason. But for this little time, he could feel easy in his mind and stretch and be grateful.

"Women are funny," Lieutenant Colonel Smithers said.

"Sure are," Lieutenant Gaylord agreed. He was reading the sports' page of the Stars and Stripes. He did not mind talking as long as he was doing something else too. What he did not like was just to talk.

"They change around."

"Sure do." Now who would have believed that Northwestern could lick Purdue? He'd have taken a bet.

"One time they're one way. Then you figure it out: okay, the girl is a simple straightforward bitch. Then they're another way. You say to yourself, I got this babe all wrong, she's really a good kid. Then they're something in between. Nothing you can put your finger on."

"Yep," said Lieutenant Gaylord.

"How's Lucille?"

"Oh Lucille. You know something, Johnny? They ought to take action against those WACs. I've heard more damn gossip about this headquarters. What her Colonel said to

Mabel's Colonel. What Mabel's Colonel said to Gladys' Colonel. If I was a spy, I'd know every last thing that goes on in this place."

"There's too many women hanging around this war."

"You ought to hear those girls talk, Johnny. They talk about operations like it was something that happened at a ladies' bridge club."

"Bill, I got a hunch we'll be moving soon."

"I wish you'd get a hunch we were going to Cannes."

"Cannes, France?"

"That's the one."

"Why not New York, New York while you're about it?" Lieutenant Gaylord picked up "The Poisoned Orchid Case."

"Do you know anything, Johnny?"

"No."

"Just got a hunch?"

"Yeh."

"I wish this war would get over. I need to make some money. Seems my wife's starving to death."

"The minute you turn your back, they make a balls of everything. My old man's fixing to sell our chicken farm."

"I saw Paul Willcox today. He seems kind of upset."

"I know. I'd hate to see him lose his company."

"Johnny, I'd like to use bazookas on combat patrols."

"Bulky."

"I think they'd be worth it. And there ought to be more B.A.R.'s; the proportion's wrong. You get in a little fight, coming back, and you'd have a big advantage."

"Could be."

"Sergeant Black picked me a new man from the replacements, name of Wedemeyer. He talks kraut better than they do. I've got ideas for that boy."

"Pretty good job Luke Hermann's done scrounging us warm clothing, isn't it, Bill? He's one of the best S-4's in the business."

"He's a good man. You know that kid in F Company, Lieutenant Heller?"

"What about him?"

"Nothing. But he's smart. He's somebody to keep your eye on. Do you think we'll be going up to the Roer, Johnny?"

"Maybe. That's mean country. I wish we could have got boats for the men to practice on."

"Fixing those mock-ups for them helped some."

They were back in their work, their only work, that wiped out and made unreal the past, that limited all plans and endangered hope and changed the present from life into waiting; the final urgent work of managing nine hundred men whose function was to avoid death or damage as much as possible, while inflicting both on others.

· · · · · · · · · · · · ·

Jacob Levy worried in silence until he could no longer bear this wordless discussion with himself. He had to talk to someone. The conversation began in the middle, assuming that whatever needed to be taken on faith and forgiven between him and Kathe was already accepted and even forgotten. You could not talk to a person unless you were friends. Nothing interrupted Jacob Levy's monologue with Kathe, and in the simplicity and beauty of dreams she now understood English as well as he did. Driving on the roads that were covered with a thin mustard slush, waiting for the Colonel in the hall of their Headquarters, or in the message center at Regiment, cleaning his jeep, oiling his gun, sweeping his room, eating, lying in bed at night, Jacob Levy spoke to Kathe. He had never done so much talking in his life. It amazed him that he had all this to say.

I love my old man and my mother, Jacob Levy explained to Kathe, they've always been wonderful to me. They gave me everything they could. We never wanted for anything at home. My old man would of sent me to college only the war came. He said I could go anywhere I liked; he said if I wanted to go to one of the big colleges in the East, he had plenty of money saved up. I never did care about college much; I'm not too smart with books. It was hard work in highschool getting good enough grades so I could play football. Then the highschool was in our neighborhood and I had a lot of friends. Fellows, you know; we had our own crowd since I was a kid. We'd fool around, all the stuff you do, after school and Saturdays and Sundays. A bunch of us dated girls together; I never went with one special girl like some of them. I liked the girls allright but I couldn't see getting stuck with any one. I didn't have to worry about parties and going out and who'd be my friends and everything; you live in a place a long time and you don't have to think about those things. But I'd go away to one of these big eastern colleges and the first thing there'd be fraternities. A fraternity is a sort of club, Kathe, which the boys run themselves and they ask new boys in every year. It's just a social club where the fellows have fun together and eat and maybe live in the same house and give dances. You don't have to belong to a fraternity to go to college, you understand, but that's where they have their fun and get to know each other. So you wouldn't be all alone in one of those big schools, with nobody to talk to at meals and things. Well, you see, I wouldn't get asked for one of those fraternities from what I hear because of being a Jew and it isn't that I mind so much only you get the idea you're different from other people. See what I mean, Kathe, it's as if you were born in Luxembourg and you didn't know any other place but they told you you were French maybe or Italian. You'd feel funny and out of things and as if people were watching for you to make a wrong move.

I never did talk to my old man about this, because I figure he's the same as I am. It don't make no difference to him being a Jew; there's nothing to do about it and there's no sense getting sore if people are snotty, and I guess my old man said to himself when he was a kid, like I did, the best thing is to get along and not have any trouble. . . .

"Here's your plate, Jake," Royal Lommax said.

Jacob Levy was bewildered to find that he was in the kitchen at the Weilerburg CP. In his mind, he had been sitting in Kathe's restaurant, talking to her alone, with the black-out curtains pulled and the other customers gone for the night.

"Thanks, Roy."

They could hear the staff eating in the dining room; the officers were talking and laughing as if this was a party or they'd just met each other at a reunion or something. This is as classy as a hotel, Royal Lommax thought. A lady in the village gave him a bunch of flowers for the Colonel and though it seemed pretty funny giving flowers to a man, he stuck them in a jar and put them on the dining room table and suddenly he felt very pleased. It was high living, with flowers on the table. And even in the kitchen the men got washed before they came in and didn't slop around the way they usually did, and he had it all clean and good in here. Maybe I'll run a nice classy restaurant when I get home, Royal Lommax thought.

Jacob Levy poured catsup over the stew and the floury hunks of potato, spread marmalade on a slab of army white bread, and ate. He might have been eating straw.

Bert Hammer and Royal Lommax were now talking about how much money movie stars earned. Jacob Levy, who had only paused to chew and swallow, returned to Kathe.

．　．　．　．　．　．　．　．　．　．　．　．

"Damn cold," Lieutenant Colonel Smithers said, and swung into the jeep as on to a saddle. "Go to Regiment, Levy."

"Yes sir."

They sat, side by side, hunched into their coats, their faces scraped by the painful wind, and Lieutenant Colonel Smithers wondered what dirty job his Battalion would have to do next, and Jacob Levy said to Kathe:

I wish you could see my father, Kathe, he's really a handsome man. He's about forty-four and he's got a little grey hair at the sides but the rest of his hair is black with a nice wave in it. He's shorter than I am but he's got a fine build and he's a sharp dresser but not the flashy kind. He wears mostly dark blue suits and ties with a little stripe in them and I swear he looks like a million dollars. He's smart too. I guess I must of taken after my mother more, because

Momma's the sweetest woman you ever saw and as pretty as a girl but she's not smart like my old man.

My old man could of built up his business and bought some other drug stores and maybe had a chain of stores in the west end. But he didn't want to. He told me once our store was a good family property, and it didn't kill a man to run it, and he knew he could always make a steady eight or nine grand a year, and we didn't need more for the three of us. He said he could take two weeks off in the summer, and we own our house and we've got the car, and Momma can buy all the little things she wants, and the best thing is to have a good plain life with no worries.

They got their own friends in the neighborhood, the Grulichs and the Johnsons and Mr. and Mrs. Kraus and the Weinbergs and the Isaacs. They play cards with them or go to a show or have a little supper party sometimes. My old man don't belong to organizations or clubs and he don't see any other Jews but the Weinbergs and the Isaacs because he says if you get in with a lot of Jews the first thing you know everybody's got trouble, and their families have trouble all over the world, and you can't help anyway and there you are, choked up with problems. He thinks if Jews would stay quiet and not get together and make a squawk and mind their own business and pay their taxes, pretty soon people would stop picking on them. Like he says, he's had his store for twenty-four years and no arguments with anybody.

Anyhow I think he and Momma are the happiest when they're together. They been married twenty-three years, Kathe, that's a lot of time. And they're just as crazy about each other as they ever were. He takes Momma out driving in our car, we got a maroon Pontiac four door sedan, a 1940 model, and they look like a young couple that's just met and making a big play for each other. I guess they feel comfortable together, Kathe; everybody else, even friends, is always a stranger. You really only got your wife and your kids that you can count on. . . .

"Levy! What's the matter with you, man? You've been over this way fifty times," Lieutenant Colonel Smithers said.

Jacob Levy looked at a perfectly strange road. He had been on another road, in another country, with Kathe, whose face was flushed by the wind, listening. My God, Jacob Levy thought, I'm sure getting things jammed-up here. He'd have to cut Kathe out, before he got in a worse fix. Where was he now, anyhow? Where was the brown barn that marked the turn to Regiment? He'd never seen that church steeple sticking up by the next hill; it might be Germany for all he knew. It wasn't even safe to get lost in this two by four country, you'd run over the edge without knowing it. Where was that barn; it couldn't walk off by itself.

"I must of missed the side road, sir."

"Well, go back and make it snappy. I have to be there in fifteen minutes."

"Yes sir." Now that's serious, Jacob Levy thought, I must be talking too much. He'd have to watch himself. Better think about something practical now, and keep his mind on his work. Besides Kathe, there was only one other subject which interested him.

"Sir," Jacob Levy said, because he wanted to know and also to distract the Colonel's attention from his mistake, "are we going anywheres soon?"

"What do you think?" Lieutenant Colonel Smithers did not mean to jump on Levy, but Levy was acting too dumb these days. He ought to know better than to ask questions like that; and miss the turn for the Regimental CP. Maybe Levy had bad news from home; men went haywire if their letters upset them. Why couldn't those silly civilians at home keep their bellyacheing to themselves?

"I'm sorry I asked you, sir," Jacob Levy mumbled.

"Forget it."

Forget it, Jacob Levy thought, forget it. We've got days is all, nothing more than days. And then what's to happen to Kathe and me?

It was a pleasure to be rid of the Colonel and to know that he had at least an hour, when no one would ask him anything or tell him anything. The afternoon was cold, with a pointed wind, and the sun looked like a lemon hanging in the pale sky. Still, if he went indoors to the kitchen or the message center, he would have to talk to the other fellows and keep a lookout for the Colonel to be ready when the Colonel wanted to leave. It was better to stay out here, where he could be alone with Kathe. Jacob Levy slumped down on the seat and pulled his helmet forward to shield his eyes, so that it would appear he was sleeping.

So anyhow, Kathe, as I was saying, I enlisted right after Pearl Harbor and that was that about college. Momma cried like she was going to die and my old man lectured her and said all the young men in America had to fight for their country and she shouldn't cry as if her son was the only one going away. I wouldn't tell anybody but you this, Kathe, but that first night after I enlisted I came home and when I went up to my room I cried too. I don't know why either. I guess I was excited. I thought the Japs were going to land in California next week and I was scared for America and for everybody and I thought I had to hurry out there and fight so they wouldn't get to St. Louis. I don't know what I didn't think. Then of course nothing happened and about six months later I began to kick myself for enlisting like a dumb cluck because anybody could see St. Louis wasn't in danger of any kind, or America either for that matter. But once you get in, you're in.

Then I was crazy to come overseas, which just goes to show how crazy a guy can be. I don't know why either except that camp in Louisiana was so godawful and I was so sick of the army and I guess I thought it would be interesting to see foreign countries. That's really funny.

You know, Kathe, I never could see what we're in this war for. I understand Hitler's got to be kicked out but I should think the people he was causing trouble to ought to kick him out. He couldn't ever get to America; he couldn't even get across that little English Channel. I know it was rough on everybody in Europe having the krauts in their countries; but they live here and if they don't like these wars why don't they move someplace where they don't have wars or else cut out fighting among themselves all the time. Well, anyhow, I can't figure that out but I certainly don't see what Americans have to do with it. Naturally after you've seen some action, you hate the sons of bitches. Your friends get killed or guys you know and believe me I been hit twice and I hate those krauts like nothing on earth. That's only natural but I still don't see what we came here for in the first place.

Of course I've heard what they been doing to Jews, putting them in ghettos and killing them and so maybe I ought to take more interest in this war than the other fellows. But Kathe, it don't stand to reason that the American government and the whole army and navy and airforce would go to war with Hitler because of the Jews. I mean, take a nice fellow like my Colonel, and a fine soldier too, now that guy's not going through the crap we have to go through because Hitler wants to rub out the Jews. I *know* that isn't why we're here. I'm sympathetic to these poor Jews over here and if I wasn't American I'd probably be exterminated myself by now, but honestly Kathe, why didn't the Jews get out of Europe a long time ago? What did they want to hang around here for, if there's nothing but trouble and misery for them? My grandfather had the sense to move and he was a poor man.

You read a lot of stories about what the krauts do to people, not only Jews you understand, in the Stars and Stripes, and we even heard some lectures at camp in Louisiana, and there was stuff in the papers in St. Louis too. I don't read the papers much but there were a lot of horrible stories. And I don't doubt it's probably true but two things I don't see: what are Americans doing here, and why didn't the Jews clear out of this stinking Europe long ago?

.   .   .   .

"You want some coffee, Levy?" Joe Henckel asked. He was cook at Third Battalion H.Q. Lieutenant Colonel Smithers had gone to pay a combined professional and social call on his friend, Lieutenant Colonel Gallagher. Lieutenant Colonel Smithers had said, "You better wait in the kitchen, Levy. It's pretty wet out here." So he had to thank the Colonel and go in whether he wanted to or not. This Joe Henckel seemed a nice fellow and the kitchen was empty because probably everybody else was sleeping now, or maybe on a pass to Luxembourg, or maybe they had something to do. But it

[135]

looked to Jacob Levy as if most of the work was already done, and that was the worst sign of all.

"If you got some, Joe, I could use a cup."

The coffee, hot, oversweetened with condensed milk, tasted like water. Jacob Levy did not feel it as he drank it.

"I got the gloomy notion we'll be moving soon," Joe Henckel said.

"Yeh, I guess we had about all the rest that's coming to us."

"I wish we'd move home," Joe Henckel sighed.

"For Christmas," Jacob Levy suggested.

"For any old time," Joe Henckel said. Then he went wherever he went, in his mind, and Jacob Levy said to Kathe:

I had to talk to you about Jews and being a Jew, Kathe, because of that lie I told you and I hope you'll forgive me. I never would of lied to you if I could talk to you and explain things. But not being able to, I was afraid you'd get wrong ideas. You see, Kathe, it's different about being Jews and Catholics. I was born a Jew but I'm not religious. I've never even been inside a synagogue. My folks aren't religious either. I don't know if I believe in God, as far as that goes. There seems to be a big choice in what God you want to believe in anyhow, and I'm in no hurry. Men get religion over here that could take it or leave it before, but I don't kid myself that God is going to show any interest in what happens to Jacob Levy or the Second Battalion. I sometimes see guys praying and I think they've got a nerve expecting all that special attention.

But if you're born a Catholic, you're religious too. You can't help it, that's the way it is with Catholics. I don't care if you're a Catholic; I mean it's fine for you to be a Catholic and I'd never get in your way. I'll be a Catholic myself if the Catholics haven't got any rules against it, and if you'd like that. Religion don't make any difference to me one way or the other, I just don't want you to worry. So you see that's why I told you the lie about my name but you could ask a priest if they had any rules against Jews and if not, we'd fix it up in a church somewhere and I'd be a Catholic and then everything would be okay. You don't need to think you couldn't see any Catholics in America because it's not like that. Maybe Jews can't get into fraternities but you could see all the Catholics you wanted to. At highschool, a boy that was one of my best friends was a boy named Mike Murphy and he was a Catholic. There's nothing against it at all, honestly there isn't. . . .

A sergeant came into the kitchen. "Colonel Smithers' driver?" he said.

Jacob Levy did not hear. Kathe was telling him she would arrange it about her religion and not to worry.

"Wake up, Levy," Joe Henckel said.

"What?"

"Are you Colonel Smithers' driver?" the sergeant asked. He thought it was a good thing they didn't have mush-brains like this guy in the Third Battalion.

"Yeh."

"Well get a move on, pal. He's waiting for you."

"Okay. Thanks for the coffee, Joe."

Jacob Levy walked slowly around the farmhouse in the rain. He was wondering if Sergeant Postalozzi might be a Catholic so he could ask the Sarge if just anybody could apply for transfer to their church.

• • • • • • • • • • •

"You sure keep a nice fire in here," Jacob Levy said.

"Make yourself at home," Sergeant Follingsby said.

Jacob Levy tipped his chair back against the wall and closed his eyes. This room became Kathe's bedroom, only warmer than it was in life, and there was a big sofa and they were sitting on it, and he had his arm around her. They understood each other now, and were at peace together. He had been wanting for a long time to tell her about their shack, but he had to get the rest cleared up first.

We'd be living in our shack, Kathe, and we wouldn't see many people. We'd be more like my old man and Momma, Kathe, just the two of us. I know you'll like our shack, not that I've exactly got it yet, but I'm sure to have. And you'll love that little stream. It's the cleanest prettiest water you ever saw and it makes a noise like wind, even when there isn't any wind. The trees are beautiful too. I can't describe it, you'd have to see it for yourself. It's better than anything I've seen in Europe and I've been to Italy and England and France and Belgium. When you had to buy things or you wanted to go to the movies or eat in a restaurant maybe, we could get to one of those little towns they got down there. We may not have a car but there's bus service everywhere in America, and those little towns are very up to date, they've got just about everything you'd want in them.

The shack's got two rooms, a big room for a parlor and dining room combined, and a bedroom. We'll have a dinette to eat off of, and there'll be everything you need in the kitchen. I don't know about electricity but I'm going to look into that. It would be nice for you to have an electric washing machine and an electric stove and maybe a dish washer, wouldn't it? I got to figure all that out, and the bathroom too; because, before, I was going to live there alone and of course a man don't need so much. I planned to burn wood in the stove and rig up some kind of old bucket contraption for a shower but I guess that wouldn't be convenient for a girl. I'll fix it up good, Kathe, you can depend on that. I wouldn't expect you to come all the way to America and not have everything nice for you.

And then we'll just live there, see, Kathe. You won't get sick of it. There's plenty to do in the woods, and we ought to make a vegetable garden. And we won't have anybody to bother us, or look at us, or get in our way. We'll have our life. . . .

"Jake, are you feeling allright?" Sergeant Postalozzi asked.

Jacob Levy tipped his chair forward from the wall and said, "Sure Sarge." He was puzzled for a moment as to who the sergeant was, or what this room was. He had been very far away from the Battalion message center, and Sergeant Follingsby and two runners and a code clerk playing poker, and Bert Hammer whittling a boat for his sister's kid, and the Supply Sergeant practising on a new mouth organ.

"You look kind of worried. Had some bad news from home?"

"No, Sarge, same as usual. You know: hope you'll be home for Christmas. How's Agnes?"

"Agnes is fine. Only she's scared about showing the baby." Sergeant Postalozzi counted on his fingers. "I don't know— three months maybe. Got any idea when a woman starts to show, Jake?"

"No I haven't, Sarge."

Sergeant Postalozzi was obeying orders. A few moments before, in the front room, Lieutenant Colonel Smithers had said to him, "What's eating Levy, Sergeant? You noticed him lately? Did he get some bad news from home?"

"I don't know, sir."

"Well, see if you can straighten him out. I want everybody in the Battalion in good shape, when we get ready to move."

"I'll see what I can do, sir."

When Sergeant Postalozzi had gone, Lieutenant Colonel Smithers said, "I'm lucky to have a steady man like Postalozzi."

"He's allright," said Lieutenant Gaylord who was reading a magnificent book about nymphomaniacs, dope peddlers and gunmen in Key West.

The staff had separated after supper, as was their custom. The two Captains had found girls in the village and spent their evenings visiting in parlors much like this one and waiting for the parents of the girls to go to bed. The other officers were going to lust over Betty Grable in a movie at Regiment. Major Hardcastle, always diligent, was upstairs studying a book on business management. It was a waste not to be in Luxembourg, but if Colonel O'Neal would call meetings of Battalion commanders for 2030 hours, that settled it. Bill was duty officer; he said he needed a rest; it was a good thing he had to stay home some nights.

"You know something, Bill? You know Dotty?"

"Naturally I know Dotty."

"I don't get it. I'm not crazy about her and she's not crazy about me, but I *like* her."

"Sounds okay to me."

"No, but I mean you're either crazy about them or you're out to get what you can, but you don't expect to *like* them."

"You're lucky you don't have to listen to that awful office

gossip. I'm so sick of Lucille's Colonel and all the rest, I don't get any enjoyment out of it."

"What you need is a little combat to warm you up."

"It's not that bad," Lieutenant Gaylord said. "Nothing's that bad. Ever been to Key West, Johnny?"

"No."

"It must be a hell of a rough place. Boy, the way the people carry on there scares me."

Lieutenant Colonel Smithers returned to the letter he was writing. Painfully, carefully, he explained to his father the intricacies of selling a chicken farm. But he felt it was too late. The old man would be well and truly robbed by now.

> 12 <

LIEUTENANT COLONEL SMITHERS was singing. Since they had just left G Company Headquarters, from which he usually emerged in a frowning temper, this was a remarkable change. Lieutenant Colonel Smithers did not know all the words of the song. He knew, "Oh what a beautiful morning, oh what a beautiful day," and after that he hummed. Jacob Levy wanted to open his mouth and shout the song too, but drivers did not sing with colonels. The sun burned in a moonstone sky; frost covered the fields with spiky glass; the farmhouse roofs were red as holly berries; the pine trees were green as pine trees; the road was an old companion whose failings could be overlooked; and somehow all must go well in this weather.

"Captain Willcox is a fine officer," Lieutenant Colonel Smithers remarked.

"Yes sir. The men think a lot of him."

"Couldn't find better." Paul had lost that half peevish, half hang-dog look, and gone back to work. I've got the best Battalion in the whole damn army, Lieutenant Colonel Smithers thought.

"Oh what a beautiful morning, oh what a beautiful day!"

Such pleasure was catching. Jacob Levy forgot time. The hours were not counted as they passed, lived with regret, and bitterly lost. We're not going anywhere, he said to himself. It was against nature to fight in perfect weather and, by some accurate dispensation, nobody ever did. You only had to start to fight for the weather to go to hell in a basket, in his experience.

"I'll be leaving early tonight, Levy. I want to get to the Officers' Club in time for supper."

"Yes sir." And I want to get to Kathe's restaurant. I am going back as if nothing had happened; that is what I am going to do and I was a dope not to start sooner.

"By God, what a day!" Lieutenant Colonel Smithers said.

Without making a sound, Jacob Levy sang, "I love you, I love you, I love you: You are the girl of my dreams."

.   .   .   .

Jacob Levy walked back and forth on the pavement across from the Café-Restaurant de l'Etoile. There was, after all, great risk in entering that door. For perhaps Kathe would look at him with anger, even hate; perhaps she would look at him as though she had never seen him before. And then he would be truly alone and the long silent conversation, which had kept him company, must end.

St. Louis was so far away that Jacob Levy could no longer

believe in it; maybe it was there, as he remembered, but it had nothing to do with his life. His parents were faultless and beloved and dim, remembered as the dead are. The only personal connection Jacob Levy had with himself was carrying trays behind that plate glass window. Kathe had replaced his calendar, his despair and his resignation, and he could not imagine himself without a reason for getting up in the morning, and a hope that was clothed in a body and called by a name. I need her, Jacob Levy thought, I don't care about the bed part, I'll do what she wants. He had talked to Kathe more than to anyone else in his life, at last he had explained himself and everything he thought, and he was safe with her. We're close now, he told himself, we couldn't get on by ourselves anymore.

Jacob Levy opened the restaurant door. He did not know that his face looked pale and stern. Kathe, who had watched that door every day and turned grieving from the unwanted faces, stared at Jacob Levy across the heads of the usual evening diners. She held a full tray in her hands and she did not move while tears swelled in her eyes, gathered at the corners and rolled down her cheeks alongside her nose. She turned and pushed through the swing door to the kitchen. Jacob Levy found her in the passage leading to the pantry. He took her in his arms and Kathe leaned against him, still crying. Neither of them spoke.

Look at the time we've wasted, Jacob Levy thought. Three whole days and two whole nights. You might never have so much time, twice. It's a crime; it's a shame. Years from now, by their stream, they would remember how crazy they had been in 1944 in December; but it would not happen again.

Kathe's head, which was burrowing somewhere near Jacob

Levy's breast pocket, moved and she pushed him away and stood back. Her nose was pink, she was sniffling, the tears had smudged against his not too clean overcoat, she was everything he loved in the world, and he felt like eating a whopper of a big dinner with a bottle of wine. Jacob Levy lifted Kathe until her face was level with his, and kissed the tip of her nose. He put her down, slapped her bottom lovingly, and went into the restaurant.

"Oh Kathe!" he said, seeing the plate Kathe brought him. It towered with food; he would have to eat his way through to the wiener-schnitzel underneath. What a wife he'd found himself; you wouldn't believe anyone could have luck like that in this war. Kathe was something like Momma who knew how to look after men and steadfastly, optimistically, fed them as a solution to all problems.

At the door of 14 rue de la Boucherie, Jacob Levy stopped and said, "I'll leave you here, honey." Kathe waited as she always did when he spoke to her in English. Jawn would now explain in signs what he meant. Jacob Levy stooped down and kissed her. It was a tender but careful kiss. Then he waved and started to walk towards the car park by the river. Kathe ran after him.

"Non, Jawn, non. Viens avec moi. Je veux que tu montes. Je suis sûre que tout sera bien maintenant."

The words meant nothing. Kathe held his hand and began to pull him towards the house. She looked very little and determined. It's up to her, Jacob Levy thought, and took satisfaction in what now seemed an old habit, a family custom, which was to walk like a ghost down the Hefferichs' hall.

Kathe could not invent two different acts of daring and

welcome, so she repeated what she had done on their last night. Jacob Levy was uncertain. It would be terrible to begin another misunderstanding and lose her again. Kathe insisted, with her arms around his neck.

Later Jacob Levy whispered, "Kathe, as far as I'm concerned, you're the best wife in the world."

"Mon amour," Kathe sighed, in contentment. All you need in life is courage, she told herself. The first part had been as she remembered it; that was when their bodies touched, like cream. The second part had not been painful, only uncomfortable, and it did not matter. The second part pleased Jawn. Kathe felt that she was finally a woman; she had experienced the great sorrows and the great joys that belonged to women, and having triumphed through all trials there was nothing further to do but settle down to happiness. As she could not reach Jawn's mouth without wriggling her way up the bed, and as she was warm and well installed and sleepy, she kissed his shoulder.

> *13* <

By NOW HE knew this road as if he had been born here, and
he loved it. He knew the curved bridge and the grey stone
wall and the roadside shrine and the square hill behind Bet-
tembourg and the house called Belvedere with the colored
glass porch roof and the water tower and the farm of the
Nelles-Spaatz family with the chickens scratching and flut-
tering around it. He passed them all with a sense of possession and permanence, and this belonging somewhere was part
of his happiness. Jacob Levy waved, with friendly pleasure,
at a jeep going in the opposite direction. He overtook two
red-cheeked girls, whose bright wool kerchiefs blew like
flags in the December wind, and he thought how nice they
looked, pulling their cart of firewood, and he was glad to
have them on his road. He waved and smiled at them too.
Down here a ways that kid would probably show up, driving

his cows home to the barn back of the second clump of pine trees. He was going to give that kid all his chewing gum before they left. It was a fine thing to live someplace. He'd lived here for nine and a half days now. You could really establish yourself in nine and a half days.

My Colonel is a prince, Jacob Levy decided. Lieutenant Colonel Smithers had said, "I fixed up a little deal with Major Havemeyer, Levy. He's getting some bottles for me. I want you to pick them up at his apartment. I won't need you here before six."

I'm going to see my Kathe in the daytime, Jacob Levy thought. He did not know what Kathe looked like, by day. And there were fifty things they could do in the afternoon. Well, anyhow, they could walk around and look at the store windows. Look at the windows? Go *in* the stores and buy her presents.

For the first time, Jacob Levy realized that Kathe was poor. He had not considered this before. Those trays must be heavy for her, and she was on her feet all day and what she had to go home to was that icebox of a room and no running water. Kathe always wore the same black dress and coat, the same shoes; because she didn't have any others, of course, because she couldn't go out and buy herself little things she might want or need.

That's no good, Jacob Levy thought. Momma would open the newspapers and see something advertised (that was why she read the papers) and she'd say to his father, "Jacob, do you think I'd look nice in this?" and his father would say, "Now Elsie, you know you're going to buy it anyhow." She was always coming home with hats or blouses or house dresses or shoes or electric egg beaters or lamp shades or sofa cushions or dresser sets or bath salts or soap made to look like flowers. That was women's fun, going to Famous-Barr or the Grand Leader and walking around in the afternoon and picking up some knick knack they liked and talking to each other about it on the telephone and showing it to their husbands.

In his life Jacob Levy had never worked for money. You couldn't count helping out around your own father's store as working for money. And you certainly couldn't count the army. A person wouldn't go into the army to earn his living; there wasn't enough money in the world to pay them for combat. No one would sweat through twenty-seven days in that forest for a salary. The army gave you spending money, was what it amounted to. But Kathe had to live; she couldn't throw her wages away on foolishness.

I'm going to get her a bathrobe and a blouse and a silk slip and some stockings and a handbag, Jacob Levy planned. But how much money did he have himself, when you got right down to it? He stopped the jeep and took out his wallet: the wad of francs added up to thirty-eight dollars. That wasn't too much when you wanted to buy everything for a girl. Usually thirty-eight dollars would seem a good-sized roll.

Kathe was sitting at a table in the back of the restaurant, darning table cloths. The café and the restaurant were empty, except for Madame Steller behind the coffee urn, adding up figures in a ledger. Kathe's just a young kid, Jacob Levy thought, only a kid could look so serious about doing a little job. His tenderness surprised him; it was new; he had never expected to feel this way nor known such a way of feeling existed; and it was sad too, something like being sad anyhow; you could feel like this if you heard a certain kind of soft music or if you were visiting someone you liked who was sick. Then too, because of what the sight of Kathe did to him, he had become the old one, the sure one, the man. He had to be, for he stood between her and a hard world which she did not even know about and from which he was bound to protect her.

I want to give her everything, Jacob Levy thought, I don't want her to go short of anything. She's been looking after herself long enough.

Kathe raised her head and was amazed to see Jawn here, in the middle of the afternoon. She bunched the table cloth and could not move for joy. Sun, slanting in through the clean plate glass windows, made the brownness of his skin golden, and lit up his dark eyes. He looked even more beautiful in the daylight, happier, easier. What sort of life would it be, Kathe thought, when you could see the one you loved all the time, any time, for as many hours as you could keep your eyes open.

"Promenade?" Jacob Levy asked. This was a word from Sergeant Postalozzi's dictionary.

Madame Steller managed the situation, because Kathe seemed content to sit where she was and stare and smile. Madame Steller told Kathe to take the afternoon off, she need not return until six-thirty, hurry child, it's a lovely day. Madame Steller was glad that she and her husband were old and childless: war could only ruin their lives, it could not break their hearts. Kathe's young man would leave, one day soon; war seemed a rush and a disappearing for the young men. Let Kathe be happy.

"Come on, Kathe," Jacob Levy said, "we got a lot to do."

He had noticed a shop, near the car park, with women's clothes in the window. They did not look like the goods at Famous-Barr or any first class American store but probably the girls here hadn't much to compare with so they'd be satisfied. Kathe was puzzled when Jacob Levy opened the door of the Jardin des Femmes. He led her in because she did not seem to want to pass that etched glass panel.

"Do you speak English?" Jacob Levy asked a solid bosomed saleslady.

"Un moment, Monsieur."

The lady with the steely marcelle and the competent smile spoke English as if she were cracking a whip. The solid bosomed saleslady was nicer, but language-bound.

"I want to buy a bathrobe for my fiancée," Jacob Levy told the marcelled interpreter.

"Perfectly. What color, sir?"

"Light blue."

There was a quick earnest conversation between the interpreter and the saleslady.

"Follow please," the interpreter said.

Across the shop a glass case held raincoats, overcoats, suits and bathrobes.

"This will look very beautiful," the interpreter stated, as an order.

"Do you like it, Kathe?"

"Monsieur demande si ce peignoir vous plaît, Mademoiselle," the interpreter explained. She was holding a blue quilted rayon dressing gown, whose collar and cuffs were trimmed with pink rosebuds.

"Non, merci," Kathe said. She would not allow this woman to tell her what Jawn said; she and Jawn had always understood each other without the help of a meddling stranger.

Another dressing gown was taken from the glass case. It was practical and modest, made of thick blue flannel and tied at the waist with a silk cord sash.

"Et ceci, Mademoiselle?" the interpreter asked. "Do you appreciate this one, sir?"

"Whatever you want, Kathe."

"Monsieur dit qu c'est à Mademoiselle de décider," the interpreter said.

Kathe flushed with anger. She could not enjoy this excitement of going into a shop with Jawn, and him buying her a lovely present; she could not talk it over and take her time because of this hateful woman who pretended to understand English.

"Try it on, honey," Jacob Levy urged. He took the bathrobe from the saleslady and Kathe started to put it on over her coat, was corrected by the interpreter, blushed, and finally was tied into it. She looked like a fuzzy blue cocoon and Jacob Levy laughed at her.

"You take it, Kathe. It'll be warm for you at night. You look pretty in it."

"Tu l'aimes, Jawn?" Kathe turned in front of the mirror. It would be very expensive. Perhaps Jawn did not know how expensive everything was in Luxembourg. And she could not understand why he was giving her a present. Was it a day when people gave each other presents in America, like Christmas or Easter? It was kind and sweet of him but she did not want him to spend all his money on her. What would the salesladies think, seeing her accept a bathrobe from a man?

"How much is it?" Jacob Levy asked.

There were more consultations and Jacob Levy did division and multiplication in his head. That would come to $15. It was cheap to dress a girl. Kathe, seeing the bills he held out, looked troubled; but she could not discuss their personal business before the overhearing woman.

"Now we'd like to see a blouse, a silk petticoat, some stockings and a handbag," Jacob Levy said. He wanted to say something more about his fiancée. He had never used this word but it was a fine one. When they were back in St. Louis, he would go with Kathe to Famous-Barr when she did her shopping. It made him feel like a big shot to give the saleslady orders and see everybody running around to bring Kathe what she wanted.

"My fiancée would like to see a blue blouse," Jacob Levy remarked suddenly. When it was time for the stockings, he could say, "my fiancée has very small feet."

At a glass counter the saleslady displayed blouses. They seemed hideous to Jacob Levy but Kathe touched them with admiration. She could not believe there were so many different styles. She thought a pink one, with buttons like real pearls, was the loveliest thing she had ever seen. But I have no skirt to wear with a blouse, she remembered. Perhaps I could buy one later. It would take three months or more to save enough, and I must have it now to wear for Jawn. She did accounts: 100 francs for her rent every week and 2 francs fifty for morning coffee and 35 francs to Maman in Müllerhof. That only left 17 francs fifty for the extras such as soap and money in the church box on Sundays and savings. She kept her tips but they did not amount to much. A skirt would cost at least 300 francs and probably 400.

"Merci, je n'ai pas besoin d'une blouse," Kathe said.

"Mademoiselle does not desire the blouse," the interpreter announced.

"Je ne porte pas de tailleurs," Kathe added. "Seulement des robes. Les tailleurs ne me vont pas."

"Mademoiselle says she does not wear suits. Only dresses. She says suits do not become her."

It didn't seem right of Kathe not to want his presents. And he wouldn't have enough money for a dress. Instead of feeling like a big shot, he felt like a tightwad; but he couldn't ask to look at dresses and then have Kathe choose one and not be able to pay for it.

Since Jacob Levy knew nothing about his face, he also did not know how it changed. He felt, at the moment, worried and somehow cheated and his face took on an expression of grave and noble sorrow.

Kathe always watched this face and misjudged it and responded to the emotions Jacob Levy showed but did not feel. She was, she decided, a heartless fool; it was Jawn's joy to buy her presents; she should take what he offered gladly; and she had caused Jawn pain. But how could she now declare that after all she wanted a blouse more than anything in life? It was the fault of that conceited shop woman, and somehow they must leave this place.

"Quelle heure est-il, s'il vous plaît?" Kathe asked the interpreter.

"Ah, trois heures un quart," Kathe repeated with mock anxiety. "Il faut absolument que je rentre. Veuillez faire un paquet du peignoir, je vous en prie."

"Mademoiselle says," the interpreter began.

"Monsieur est au courant," Kathe interrupted.

The interpreter went to get the package of the bathrobe.

That little provincial slut was angry about something; impossible to understand the minds of such people. Now she would take the soldier to another shop until he had spent all his money. It was infuriating to lose the business. That girl—his "fiancée," these soldiers were fantastic—probably had arranged with some other shop to receive a percentage on the customers she brought in.

"Kathe, what's the matter?"

"Ssh, Jawn!"

Kathe took the package and pulled Jacob Levy from the shop. She went on pulling him until they reached the corner where he planted his feet and looked forbidding. He was not going to be dragged through the streets like a dumb animal. This had started out to be his party; why did Kathe have to bust it up this way?

"Je connais des magasins bien meilleur marché, Jawn."

"I want to buy you some more clothes." He showed Kathe his grimy roll of banknotes.

"Oui, mon amour. Viens un peu. Je te montrerai un magasin merveilleux."

There was nothing to do but follow Kathe, and when Jacob Levy saw the other shop, La Femme Elégante, he understood that Kathe had her own preferences. His mother always said she wouldn't trade at Nugent's for anything.

It wasn't so much fun for him because he couldn't give any orders, as there was no interpreter; but it seemed to be more fun for Kathe. Jacob Levy removed himself from the clatter of women's voices discussing color, quality and prices and thought about being a man who took care of a woman. He understood why his father didn't go shopping with his mother; you could see that the kick would wear off pretty fast, and you felt in the way too. But it was a good feeling to pay; it made you own something; it was much more important than buying a girl drinks and dinner and taking her to a show or dancing.

Already Jacob Levy foresaw a lifetime of Kathe coming home with her purchases. He recognized his future self being indulgent, happy to know that he provided. Kathe, buying clothes with his money for the first time, became a familiar Kathe who had been spending his money during the long contented connubial years.

He had a daytime life now, as well as the life after dark. He had the security of being depended on, the protection of being needed. He had responsibilities for he was the head of a family, the man who paid. He had been happily married for as long as he could look ahead. This war delayed his plans but if you were living safely in the future the war couldn't upset you. You didn't have to worry, you only had to wait.

Kathe hoped she was doing the right thing in accepting all these luxuries which she had never coveted. She hoped Jawn was happy. But they had spent more money than she earned in a month and to let Jawn ruin himself further would surely be wicked. They divided the packages and Jacob Levy carried the bathrobe and the box with the imitation black leather handbag. There is some natural law which makes it impossible for men to carry women's parcels without a sense of disgraceful encumberment. Soldiers, lounging by, their hands in their pockets, looked at Jacob Levy with good-natured contempt. Jacob Levy envied the other men with their arms free. He felt stupid now; Kathe should have told those store people to deliver the things. He was relieved when they got on the side streets and definitely eased when he could get rid of his burden at Kathe's front door.

It was five o'clock and time to think of Weilerburg and the Colonel.

"Goodbye, honey." Kathe was just visible above the layers of packages.

"Je te remercie des beaux cadeaux, Jawn. Tu es vraiment gentil pour moi."

He could not hug a lot of boxes so he kissed her on the forehead.

"Take care of yourself, Kathe."

"Je t'aime, Jawn."

"Oui, oui," he said gaily and crossed the street. He was in a hurry so he did not look back though Kathe waited.

That was a nice afternoon, Jacob Levy thought, a nice homey afternoon. And he had $4.00 left which was enough for cigarettes and shaving cream and candy bars until next payday.

Kathe spread her gifts on the white iron bed: the blue bathrobe, a pink artificial satin slip trimmed with machine lace, two pairs of mustard colored rayon stockings, a red coat sweater, a shiny oilcloth-leather bag with a gilt fastener. They were all handsome and stylish and Jawn was generosity itself. But the first afternoon they had ever shared lay wasted in the shops, the very first afternoon, and she had nothing of Jawn to remember.

> *14* <

LIEUTENANT GAYLORD said, "That was certainly lousy chow tonight. I don't know what's the matter with Lommax. He oughtn't to dish us up garbage like that."

"I didn't think it was so bad," Lieutenant Colonel Smithers said.

Lieutenant Gaylord walked to the window and opened a chink in the black-out curtain.

Across the cobbled street were the same little square concrete houses, with their dull faces and their long badly proportioned windows. Behind them were the same flat, frozen fields. The sky was simply black. You could not even take an interest in the sky.

"Don't you ever get sick of this place, Johnny?"

"This is a hell of a nice place. We got a fine house, we can go to town, the Battalion's shaping up good. What do you want?"

"Nothing, I guess." Lieutenant Gaylord took his usual chair by the stove and picked up a book that was lying face down on the arm. This was a story about a rich old mad-woman in Carmel and her neurotic daughters and a murder they were involved in, though guiltlessly, due to gambling debts. The detective was very tough and epigrammatic and had a yen for one or both of the daughters.

Lieutenant Colonel Smithers said, from behind the Stars and Stripes, "Why doesn't this Division ever get any pub-licity? You always read about the gallant First or the heroic Eighty Second or God knows what. Now here's a lot about the Third Armored. What's the matter with us? Haven't we got glamor?"

"The old man's got no time for the correspondents."

"They can by-pass the old man. I'd like to see some of my men get a write-up once in a while."

"Don't you ever think about anything except the Bat-talion?"

"What's wrong, Bill?"

"I'm disgusted," Lieutenant Gaylord said. He started to rip the flashy cardboard cover from his book and stopped and looked sheepish. "I'm sick of sitting still. We sit on our asses and the goddam war will last forever."

"Take it easy, Bill."

"I haven't got all this time to waste!"

"Hey!" Lieutenant Colonel Smithers said. "Take a drink."

So now Bill was getting the meemies. He could feel it him-self; it was a beating of the heart for no reason, brief point-less angers, a quick knot in the stomach, a short headache over one eye. This was the way it was. There was combat and the first doped pleasure of rest; then some fun, anything you could get and as much of it as possible; then a kind of stale tiredness that you didn't understand and couldn't explain;

and then this restlessness, this fretful waiting for something
you hated and hated to wait for.

"Have a drink and remember to tell me what a dump
Weilerburg was, the next time we're in the line," Lieutenant
Colonel Smithers said.

"You're a sensible guy, aren't you, Johnny?"

"I'm a good sensible old man."

"Shall I fix you a drink?"

"Sure. Let's polish off the bottle and go to bed."

At two in the morning Lieutenant Colonel Smithers was
wakened by a dispatch rider from Regiment. At seven o'clock
in the morning dark, the men of the Second Battalion lined
up along the junction of the Weilerburg-Frisange road, waiting for the trucks. They were cold and depressed. At noon,
the trucks arrived. The soldiers climbed into them and the
trucks headed north.

.   .   .   .

One thing about the army, Jacob Levy thought, you can't
ever count on it. You get all set for something but no! that's
not what they have in mind. This last deal beat everything.

The replacements had heard about the forest; the veterans
could not forget it; the trucks had seemed like hearses rolling
slowly through the pleasant country. Everyone was prepared
to huddle in the cold and freeze their way north. Everyone
was set for a ride that would shake your guts out and freeze
your face off, and after that some more forest. The old hands
tried to keep their minds empty and make their bodies as
easy as possible. They had started to take the long breath
that must last them until this next misery was over.

[163]

And after all that, they drove not more than twenty miles to the northeast of Luxembourg City. The men offloaded; the sun shone brightly down; they dispersed in the fields and small woods that lined the road, lit fires, ate C rations, swapped rumors and slept. The guns, working over the front two miles away, sounded like lazy range practice. At dusk, the 20th Division proceeded to relieve the 108th Division which looked uncommonly cheerful for an outfit coming out of the line.

By 2030 hours, Lieutenant Colonel Smithers was standing in a small dirty room, like countless rooms before it, listening to Captain Huebsch announce over the field telephone that F Company was in position: the Battalion transfer had been completed.

"You've got the sector," said Lieutenant Colonel Warren of the departing Battalion. "Have a nice time."

In a state of grateful disbelief, the Battalion settled down to a quiet night. They seemed to be holding a lot of land but that meant more farmhouse cellars for shelter. The previous occupants had done a thorough job of digging in, leaving behind them deep machine gun emplacements and foxholes and communications dugouts. Though it was as cold as you could wish, charred remains of small fires in all these showed that it was safe enough here to make yourself comfortable.

This was not, of course, the hotel life of Weilerburg but for a front it was the best thing yet seen. The krauts were beginning to get some sense. Maybe they were running out of men and ammunition, at last, the way you always read in the papers. Maybe the fighting in the north kept them busy. Maybe they were fixing to surrender. Whatever it was, since you had to be at the front, this was the one to pick. Aside from occasional artillery on the roads and occasional mortar fire on the forward positions, and useless machine gun racket at night, and the alleged minefields on the river bank, this was as safe as any Army Headquarters.

At night, lying in his bedroll on the floor of the disheveled little farmhouse that was Lieutenant Colonel Smithers' CP, Jacob Levy said to himself: it keeps up like this and maybe I'll get a chance to go back to the city and tell Kathe why we had to leave so she won't worry. The Colonel might want more liquor, and send him for it. And then he would think: nothing can be this easy, and he would have a sick feeling that there was a catch somewhere. But in the morning the front was the same. The replacements acquired a smug expression: if this was all there was to combat, the old hands were the biggest lineshooters out of jail. The replacements volunteered readily for night patrols. The veterans did not dispute the honor with them.

Bert Hammer said, "I got nothing serious against this place, Jake. For war, it's solid. The only thing is we ought to get some good latrines. Closed-in, like real outhouses. So you wouldn't freeze every time."

Royal Lommax said it was foolish to come over here for nothing; they could hold this front as well from Weilerburg. The krauts weren't up to anything. The krauts were all played out.

Lieutenant Gaylord said he guessed he'd go out tonight and look around the river. "Okay, Bill," Lieutenant Colonel Smithers said. Bill never did know how to wait; but it wouldn't do him any harm to wear off his energy playing Indian. Lieutenant Colonel Smithers thought the Division must be even more chewed up than he knew, if they were only fit for sentry duty. You couldn't call this a front. It was fine by him. He had ceased to thirst for glory long ago. He wanted his Battalion to do whatever was expected of it; if nothing was expected, so much the better.

He told Captain Willcox to get a few prisoners and to find out about the mines on the river bank. But no one was to pick a fight. They were supposed to stay nice and calm while the real business went on up north, along the Roer. There were seventy-five miles of front here, with four Divisions holding it, and with nothing behind them. The last thing anybody wanted was to excite the Germans.

"Just bother them a little," Lieutenant Colonel Smithers said to Captain Willcox. "So they won't get fat and happy."

You couldn't ask for a better place to break in the new men. Any soldier who kicked about this ought to get shot. It was so quiet he might even send Levy to Luxembourg and bring Dotty back for supper. She'd be as safe as in town, the way it was here. She would be used to guys disappearing without any excuse but he hated to break a date and not have time to explain. And he certainly wouldn't be cheating on his work if he took a few hours off to eat with her. There was really nothing to do but sit back and watch the bombers, high, neatly wedged and silver, flying over to Germany. They made vapor trails in the clear sky, like giant chalk marks. It was pleasant to think of the krauts being blown to hell while you drank a cup of coffee and smoked a cigarette and the Battalion operated like a little angel. The only casualties in two days had been a couple of men whose jeep skidded and turned over in a ditch and one dumb bastard who killed himself experimenting with a hand grenade.

> *15* <

THEN WITH a suddenness the High Command could never quite explain, the Germans attacked this tissue paper front. The weather went over to their side and a thick dripping cloud settled low above the trees. It was iron cold and snow began to fall, as if to order. The Germans attacked through the snow, the pine forests, across the rivers and over the dumpy hills. Nothing like this had been seen; it was no counter-attack. They seemed driven by a final and furious hope. The front broke.

At the southern extremity of the Germans' drive, on what was officially called "the shoulder of the penetration", the 20th Division attempted to hold. It had a better chance than the inexperienced outfits to the immediate north but three Companies in the flank Battalion of the 256th Regiment were overrun; in effect, it was as if the snow had swallowed them. German tanks plowed through this gap all night moving to the west. German infantry, in tight mobile clumps, had infiltrated behind the rest of the Division's front. German artillery worked over the roads to a depth of ten miles, and

---

Regiments were out of communication with each other and with Division.

At 2400 hours on the night this break-through started, Lieutenant Gaylord, purple with cold, came into Lieutenant Colonel Smithers' farmhouse CP in the village of Hackenthal. He announced, with surprise, that a routine patrol had been badly shot up; now what do you suppose made the krauts so energetic all of a sudden? By 0100 hours, the Companies were telephoning in, to say that they could hear motor vehicles and track laying vehicles moving on the other bank of the river. Usually everyone slept soundly in these parts but now it sounded as if the circus had come to town. At 0300 hours, German artillery opened up on the crossroads near Battalion headquarters, and H Company motor park was pounded. Wounded started to walk back to the Battalion aid station, a trickle of slow shadows. By 0400 hours, the outposts and the front line positions were being mortared with deadly intent and the wounded increased. The field telephones carried steady reports from the front: we can hear boats, they're shouting at each other, they've got bridging material. . . . The observer at the Battalion OP was in the middle of saying, "Tanks, trucks, I don't . . ." when his voice was cut off. Fox Company announced they could hear tanks, coming this way and very soon now: and that voice was cut off. Lieutenant Colonel Smithers, calling Regiment to beef up the artillery concentrations, found himself talking into a dead line. The German artillery was working like a giant scissors on the telephone wires, or else the Germans were already swarming over the sector. The last order from Division was to hold; but they could not hold.

Lieutenant Colonel Smithers had spent the night and the

blurred incomprehensible day trying to extricate his troops, set up a defensive line two ridges back, and keep in touch with his right and left flanks and Regiment. It was a bitter, new experience to see his Battalion mauled into retreat. Now, twenty-six hours after the night patrol had been shot up, Lieutenant Colonel Smithers was sitting on the floor in a cheese factory that was the latest Regimental Headquarters, listening to a Division Intelligence officer. The Intelligence officer seemed breathless and at the same time indignantly surprised. He was explaining that the Germans had spearheaded their attack all along the front with soldiers dressed in American uniforms and driving American vehicles. These masqueraders, the officer said, wore red and blue neckscarves to identify themselves, painted white balls on their jeeps, as a recognition signal, and also on farmhouses and trees to signify rallying points. In this shambles, ordinary passwords were not adequate: suspicious characters should be asked questions about Big League baseball. Lieutenant Gaylord muttered that he pitied the poor guys who didn't follow baseball, they'd be shot like dogs. Lieutenant Colonel Smithers listened, in a stupor of fatigue. He was thinking of the ride back, and wondering whether by now the Germans had pushed in behind his Battalion and if so what Hardcastle was doing about it. He wanted to leave: they had their orders, he wanted to get back to his outfit.

Then they were in the jeep, crawling along without lights in the steadily falling snow. They were listening and tense, for no one knew where the Germans might be. Here today and more of them here tomorrow, Lieutenant Gaylord had said. That's the worst, Lieutenant Colonel Smithers thought: you couldn't believe how much worse the German weapons sounded when the noise was coming from behind you. The three officers and the radio operator and Jacob Levy listened, and felt this uncertainty in their backs. Suddenly a man's back had become very large, very cold and very vulnerable. The orders were clear enough, Lieutenant Colonel Smithers thought, though nothing else was. They would hold this east to west line they had fallen back to and protect Luxembourg City: they were to contain the German penetration, as the phrase was. He was planning how he could divide and shift around the force remaining at his disposal. He would send Bill Gaylord to command G Company since Paul Willcox was now dead; two squads of the Ammo and Pioneer Platoon would go to F Company: all the battalion clerks, cooks and cooks helpers would be some use to E Company, and Luke Hermann would replace Rod Blackmer who was hit in the lungs. Doc Weber told him he'd been getting bodies in at Battalion aid station that froze to death before the aidmen could load them on jeeps; he had to do something about that if he could, though with the amount of transport they'd lost in the first night's shelling it was hard to know where you'd pick up enough vehicles. Considering how big this war was and how much it cost and the millions of people who seemed to be milling around in it somewhere, it was goddam peculiar the way you always had to fight it on a shoe string, with not enough men or materiel when the chips were down. They better raise a new army from those goldbricks in Paris, Lieutenant Colonel Smithers thought, and they better do it fast.

But he had something more to think about than his work and how to manage it: the phrase "women and children" kept coming to his mind. He'd forget and then, before he knew it, there they were again, and for once they had faces, he had seen them, they truly existed. Luxembourg City was only nine miles away. This army had liberated the place. And now maybe the krauts would re-enter Luxembourg City and all those poor miserable women and children, who had thought the Americans were the second coming of Christ, would have to think again. They'd get a dose of artillery and bombs, too, while they were thinking. And furthermore, how about Dotty? Why by God, the krauts would take Dotty prisoner.

They had not spoken in the jeep and they stumbled out, rigid with cold, and walked to the farmhouse that was now their CP. The place looked different, abandoned and dead, as if they had already left it. In this silence, you could feel a prickling doubt: who was here now, we or they? Lieutenant Colonel Smithers had opened the door and for a moment a line of light stood like a wand in the darkness. An unseen sentry shouted at them. It was reassuring to hear that voice. Jacob Levy drove the jeep behind the barn, where he would hide it under the trees. He had a feeling of affection for that sentry, doing his job, loud and mean the way they usually were.

Bert Hammer brought a pot full of coffee into Lieutenant Colonel Smithers' office.

"Thanks, Hammer," Lieutenant Colonel Smithers said, "we can use that." With coffee and benzedrine tablets, you could keep talking and moving long after you were really asleep. But the sudden warmth made Lieutenant Colonel Smithers drowsy and he hurried to give his orders, while he was still sure of himself and would know that he wasn't making mistakes from fatigue.

Lieutenant Gaylord was elated to take over G Company. He went to collect his bedroll and when he came back Lieutenant Colonel Smithers said, "Have fun, Bill."

Lieutenant Gaylord grinned; he was already inventing a splendid dream for his new command. His men would rise from foxholes in the snow, and kill Tiger tanks with grenades; they would surround superior forces and annihilate them; they would hold the front no matter what and be awarded the Presidential citation, for heroic conduct above and beyond the call of duty; and they would have their pictures in Life and he would get a leave in Paris, for reasons not yet determined.

Sergeant Postalozzi brought in the runner who was to lead Lieutenant Gaylord to his company and as they left, Lieutenant Colonel Smithers said, "If you meet any krauts on the way, just shoot them. They got no business around here."

But he hated to see Bill go; he hated to think what Bill would do when he wasn't around to clamp down on Bill's imagination. And now he would have to worry alone, for there was no one besides Bill to whom he would dare admit doubt. The field telephone was buzzing again, and he forgot Bill Gaylord. The benzedrine tablets kept him awake, and all night he moved and directed men who were groggy with sleeplessness and numb with cold and hungry and desperately uncertain, and who accepted this condition without complaint. As always before, in the bad times, Lieutenant Colonel Smithers' pride in his Battalion grew in him, and drove from his mind any other emotion. He had only one duty: he must see these men through the night. The night was the limit of all time, and what he felt for his men was the strongest and richest passion of his life.

Jacob Levy crawled into his bedroll, in the hall outside Lieutenant Colonel Smithers' office, and worked himself into the shape of a doughnut so that he could massage his feet. They weren't cold anymore, they were white bloodless lumps. He was thinking of the map: Bleifall-Luxembourg City, nine miles. The krauts would probably bomb Luxembourg City, it was an Army Group Headquarters, and just the sort of target they'd want. And there was Kathe, on the third floor, alone in her cold little room with no one to look after her. Nine miles was nothing: he wished he had never spoken to Kathe. If the krauts came back they would find out she'd been going with an American soldier, he had brought danger to her; the krauts would take it out on any of the natives who had been friendly to Americans. She'd never know enough to light out on the roads and walk south.

Bert Hammer stepped over Jacob Levy's circular body and pushed into his bedroll, farther down the hall.

"Jake?"

"Yeh?"

"You hear anything at Regiment?"

"No."

"Are we cut off?"

"I don't know."

"It's kind of like the movies," Bert Hammer said.

"What is?"

"The way it is up here. You know, when the white men were in a fort or something and the Indians riding around outside shooting at them."

"I guess so."

"The Colonel don't seem upset."

"No." But the Colonel didn't know about Kathe; he didn't

know what it would be like for a young girl to look after herself if all hell broke loose and the army had to retreat and leave the people alone.

Oh God, Jacob Levy whispered, keep an eye on her, see nothing happens to her. Then he was so surprised that he stopped rubbing his feet and straightened out in his bedroll and lay on his back, staring into the dark. I'm praying, he thought, I never prayed before; it don't make sense, I haven't got any arrangement with God, I don't even know whose God I'd be talking to. I must be goofy, he told himself, if I think that's going to help Kathe. But Kathe was religious and had her own God and believed in Him and worked at it. Allright, allright, he thought, funny things happen, how do I know how it is with God, it can't hurt to put in a word for her.

· · · · · · · · · · · ·

At daylight, shrunken into themselves with cold, Lieutenant Colonel Smithers and Jacob Levy and Dave Penny, a radio operator, got into the jeep and set out for F Company. F Company had reported it was having a fire fight but the account came in, excited and garbled over the radio, and they seemed in a bad way, so Lieutenant Colonel Smithers decided to go and check for himself. The rutted mud road curved around a small hill and straightened out, flanked on one side by a frozen field and on the other by a tight diamond-shaped wood. Lieutenant Colonel Smithers was thinking about F Company, far understrength, and strung out above the base of a hill where two roads intersected; Jacob Levy was thinking that to drive the jeep over this cowpath was like riding a bronco and they'd sure as hell knock off the oil pan before they got through; and Dave Penny was thinking that it was a funny feeling to have your nose full of icicles, and maybe that was because snot froze on all those little hairs. The road was ominously empty and still. They did not notice this, being deceived by the quietness that falling snow lays on the earth.

From the diamond-shaped wood, a machine gun cracked out three short bursts and snow rose in puffs from the road and the bank of the field, ahead of them. Jacob Levy skidded the jeep to a stop, tilted over the side of the ditch away from the wood. They were out of the jeep and in the ditch, as fast as breathing. They waited and nothing happened. Snow fell; the wood appeared to be harmless and deserted; there were no tire tracks or footprints on the fresh snow of the road.

Lieutenant Colonel Smithers focussed his binoculars on the wood and could see nothing except the thickly planted black trunks of the pine trees. There was also a screen of under-brush and second growth; behind this any number of krauts could be lying comfortably, waiting for them to move from their ditch. They had better get away from the jeep. He turned, using the binoculars on the road, and thought he saw a disturbance in the snow some forty yards ahead. The light was poor and this downward whirl of snowflakes marred his vision.

"Follow me," Lieutenant Colonel Smithers whispered. "Keep down and quiet."

They crawled along the bottom of the ditch until they were safely distant from the jeep; then Lieutenant Colonel Smithers kneeled and stared again at that unsmooth portion of the road. It showed up clearly in the lenses now: tank tracks, with snow settling in them and hiding them. So the krauts had moved into that wood, sometime during the night, and there they were, hidden and happy, with a tank to keep them company.

From deep inside the wood, they heard the cough of a mortar and after the interval of silence, they heard the shell landing behind them in the direction of the Battalion CP. The mortar coughed again. Well, Lieutenant Colonel Smithers thought, that makes a mortar, a tank, an undecided number of krauts and God knows what else besides. This kraut-laden wood now separated him from F Company. You couldn't have a front like a sieve.

The sky sagged over them, solid with heavy grey cloud; the gluey snow stuck and then froze on a man's face, his gun, his clothes. The snow deadened sound too; it was bad enough to be half blind in this watery light; not being able to hear was like being blind twice. Lieutenant Colonel Smithers thought of calling for artillery; but he could not risk it. F Company's position was immediately south and west of this wood, it might even be in the far edge of the wood for all he knew. Nothing to do but rassle those krauts out of there, Lieutenant Colonel Smithers decided.

"Going back," he whispered and Jacob Levy and Dave Penny flattened themselves against the side of the ditch so he could pass and take the lead.

When they had crawled far enough so that Lieutenant Colonel Smithers judged they were safe from observation, he stopped and said, "You stay here, Levy. I'm going to send back to the CP for a platoon. Join up with them when you see them. Keep your eyes open so you can report what happens."

Then Lieutenant Colonel Smithers was gone, and Dave Penny with him, and Jacob Levy had the road and the wood and the cotton-soft daybreak to himself.

This was something you could never understand; it always happened and it was beyond understanding. When things got bad enough, so bad that you knew here was a place where it could be decided for you one way or the other, there was no one around. There was this special silence, in which your own heart beats sounded like a drum and the world—which usually crackled or moved or did something; there was always some kind of noise, even if it was only a rooster or a man talking or a truck passing on a road—sank into this tight stretched silence. And you were alone. Even if there were guys anywhere around you didn't feel them; you were alone and they were alone and this silence was the sure sign of your danger.

Now time stopped, for that always happened too. It did not stop and cease to be; it stopped and settled on you, all the time of your life, hours of time, years of time in which you could hear the silence and be alone.

Where in the hell is that platoon, Jacob Levy thought, those krauts could be moving in a whole Division. He raised his head, slowly, over the side of the ditch and saw a gentle winter landscape: fat snowflakes falling on a peaceful wood. His heart pounded inside him, so that he felt shaken by it and alarmed as if he were calling out his position.

The platoon, crossing the field behind him in single file with the hill as protection, looked at first like an extra thickness of the snow. Jacob Levy climbed out of the ditch and ran, in the bent shamble that no one needs to be taught, and joined them. Sergeant Postalozzi was leading the platoon.

"Anything happen, Jake?"

"Nothing I could see."

"Okay, fall in."

Sergeant Postalozzi got his men across the road as fast and as silently as possible. The fuzz of snow and ground mist, blurring the road, helped them. Inside, the wood lay in evening shadow. The men advanced slowly, in a loose column. At the end of this line, just ahead of Bert Hammer, Jacob Levy walked with exceeding care. He only felt natural in combat when driving a jeep; being on his feet felt like being naked. The platoon had orders to hold their fire until they were fired on; the first bazooka team had the task of taking on the German tank.

Before they had gone fifty yards into the black trees, the blast of a mine broke the silence. It was easy to lay mines in that blanket of pine needles and rotting leaves, dusted over with snow. Afterwards, the whole wood seemed to burst apart with noise; the column was well scattered. Jacob Levy and Bert Hammer, alone now, crouching behind round snow-covered bushes, saw Sergeant Postalozzi being carried out. His face was wet and grey, and his eyes were crazy. There was, where his leg or legs had been, a dirty blackish mush. Sergeant Postalozzi had discovered the mine field.

"You'll be allright, Sarge," Jacob Levy whispered. The sight of those legs had taken his voice away. This was what happened when you left a jeep and started walking. He had to move ahead, that was all he knew. A curious momentary silence fell on the forest; this frightened Jacob Levy even more. Breathing through his mouth, he heard only himself, making a muffled roar like a sea-shell. He turned and saw Bert Hammer flattened against a tree. Bert Hammer's face

looked gaunt and old, frozen in attention. Bert looked the
way he felt but Bert had done this before, he must know
something about it.

"What do we do now?" Jacob Levy whispered.

Bert Hammer shrugged and the expression of his face did
not change.

Any noise would be better, Jacob Levy thought. This way
you felt someone was watching, you only had to move and
you'd be clipped.

From the right, and deeper in the woods, the noise broke
out again, the hot clattering of a machine gun, the short hammer of burp guns, and the explosion of hand grenades. Jacob
Levy, bending low, ran towards the noise. He wanted to be
where there were a lot of men.

He saw Lieutenant Colonel Smithers directing the bazooka
team. The Colonel looked angry which was an unusual way
to look. How did he get here, Jacob Levy wondered. The
bazooka men looked blank like Bert Hammer, attentive and
sort of stupid. The noise of the hand grenades was still farther
away. Then Jacob Levy fell flat and began to crawl; even the
Colonel ducked and stayed down. That kraut machine gun
was too near; the Colonel and the bazooka team showed up
very black against the snow.

Lieutenant Colonel Smithers saw them and called and when
they reached him he said, "Levy, take three men and get
that machine gun."

Christ, Jacob Levy thought. He started off, bowed over,
running, with Bert Hammer behind him. It had not occurred
to him to get three men; anyhow where were three men;
anyhow how could he tell three men what to do when he
didn't know what to do himself. Now he stopped and tried

to isolate the sound of the machine gun. He began to make a wide detour, walking lightly and hoping there were no mines. All you could do about mines was hope. It seemed to him that he and Bert Hammer were again entirely alone in this enormous forest. He had never done a job like this; he wished there was someone who knew the pitch to give him orders. Then he thought he saw a flash coming from behind a mound of snow. The forest floor was lumpy with fallen branches piled over with snow; this mound looked no different from any other. Jacob Levy's mouth was so dry he could scarcely swallow, and his heart made sloshing bangs against his side. He crawled farther on, keeping the mound to his left, and then risked kneeling behind a tree. That was it allright; he saw their legs, the krauts would be lying on their stomachs in the snow, feeding and firing the gun. Now what do I do, Jacob Levy thought.

He stood up, with his nerves screaming to him to get down, and stepped out from behind his tree, and threw a grenade on to those grey legs lying in the snow. He did not remember throwing the second grenade, nor did he hear either of them explode. He heard a thin one-note cry, and then he saw a man rise from behind the mound and stagger like a drunk, away from them. All this happened very slowly and very fast. He watched the man with interest. The noise of Bert Hammer's rifle made him jump. There were four shots and the staggering man fell. Maybe he was dead; maybe the one who yelled but did not run was dead.

Jacob Levy turned to Bert Hammer and said in a flat voice, "What next?"

"Get the hell out of here!"

Bert Hammer was running down towards the edge of the

woods. Jacob Levy followed him; it was good to follow anyone. Bert Hammer jumped over what looked like a natural
barricade of logs, and squatted in the hollow on the other
side. Jacob Levy sat beside him. They did not speak.

That's the first German I ever killed, Jacob Levy thought,
if I killed him. He drove a jeep; the Germans almost killed
him twice but they were far off, they didn't know who they'd
get, you couldn't fight back with a jeep. Or maybe I mushed
up his legs, like the Sarge's. He hoped he had killed the
kraut; it didn't matter about killing him but he didn't like
the idea of mushing up legs. He felt very sleepy. He was
exhausted too, as if he had been marching all day with a
heavy pack. He could not stop yawning. Then he took a
handful of snow and began to eat it, to get that bitter dry
taste out of his mouth.

"We ought to go somewhere," he said to Bert Hammer.

"Yeh."

They did not move.

They heard a noise like a stampede of iron cattle, crashing
through the trees. It was not coming their way.

"Tank," Bert Hammer said.

Jacob Levy nodded. He felt too tired to speak.

"Taking off," Bert Hammer said.

A Mark IV tank, dun-colored, ornamented with a square
black cross, plowed out of the woods, waddled over the field
to a fold in the land, turned, and began to fire into the trees.
The noise came in a lightning pointed cone and then exploded.

"That's no good," Bert Hammer said.

"It's allright here." The shells were passing over them. "I
could go to sleep right now."

"Don't do that! Hey! Wake up, Jake! You'll freeze to death."

"Why?"

"That's the first sign. When you feel like sleeping. After that you freeze."

"We ought to find the Colonel," Bert Hammer said.

"Allright."

They did not move. Presently, behind them, they heard men running and they peered over the top of their barricade. Bert Hammer called out, "What's up?"

"F Company," someone answered. "Joined up."

"Okay," Jacob Levy said.

"I guess it's in the bag," Bert Hammer said.

Lieutenant Colonel Smithers, reconnoitering the edge of the wood, found them.

"Stay here and dig in," he said.

"Yes sir." That was just about what he and Bert Hammer had planned to do. My God, it's long, Jacob Levy thought. I wonder when we'll ever get out of these lousy woods. The action had lasted fifty-six minutes.

> *16* <

SERGEANT POSTALOZZI lost his left foot and his right leg to above the knee. Royal Lommax was wounded in the stomach by a shell fragment from the tank cannon. Dan Thompson's hip was smashed by a machine gun bullet. Marvin Busch had been killed by a mortar two days earlier, so he did not count. Aside from these, eight men whom Jacob Levy saw every day, talked to, called by their names, and did not know, were killed in the little wood. That night the Divisional front was withdrawn 1100 yards, leaving the wood open to the Germans who entered it in the morning.

Jacob Levy realized that he had never thought about the war before. Now he was concerned for every foot of this grey snowscape. If they kept on giving ground to the krauts, what would happen to Kathe? This was not a battle like other battles, where you did your job and tried to stay alive and wanted to win so the war would finish. This was the way men must feel when they were fighting at home.

And besides he had personally contributed to cleaning out the wood; it was the first real part he had taken in the war. What was the use, for anybody, if they threw your work away? And how about Sergeant Postalozzi's legs? It was a dirty deal for a man to lose his legs for life, doing a job that didn't matter. To say nothing of the eight guys who might as well be alive if they were just going to hand that wood right back to the krauts.

Lieutenant Colonel Smithers was bitter too. He had believed it was essential to link his front and hold it; if they had all been killed doing this, and failed, that would be hard but reasonable. Had he known they were only putting on a delaying action, he would have used his men differently. An unwanted, eating doubt returned: did the big brass know what it was doing? They don't pay me to worry, he thought, they got to take the rap if it goes bad. Still it seemed easier to take the rap for mistakes if you weren't around where the mistakes could kill you.

.   .   .   .

They were back where they had started. The whole thing disgusted Jacob Levy. The krauts kicked them back fifteen miles and then they kicked the krauts back fifteen miles and what did it prove? For seven days the Battalion had counterattacked through brilliant unmarred snow, which piled deeper and deeper until they were wading in it. The Battalion had been ahead of the front, and cut off; and behind the front and shot up by Germans who were behind them. Everyone had heard, closely, the grinding rumble of German tanks, since short tank battles developed, anywhere, anytime. They had been dived on, strafed and bombed, with the greatest daring and precision, by their own planes. They had constantly met wandering soldiers who were separated from their units, and had themselves unceasingly wondered where they were. They huddled, freezing, through the nights in foxholes that were scarcely more than dents in the iron ground; exhausted, hungry and tormented by the wind, they had fought their way north through the endless days. Now the fields sprouted dead Germans in dark swollen lumps. The American dead were carted off in trucks to be buried decently. In the burned villages, German bodies were thrown into jeep trailers like cordwood and taken away somewhere, and half-frozen soldiers would dig a hole for them in soil like stone. Who could find any sense in it? It was enough to drive you crazy just thinking about it.

The snow had fallen over the garbage of battle, covering smoothly tank tracks and shell holes and dirty papers and tin cans and live mines and excrement and all the other by-products of war. The ruin of Hackenthal was softened by the snow. A German self-propelled 88 tilted against a low stone wall; its treads were ripped off. In the disturbed snow, the possessions of the gun's crew were blown about it; a pair of bedroom slippers, a diary, two helmets, a first aid kit, rations, and a woman's embroidered handkerchief. Nearby an old farmer was shovelling grain, from split burned sacks, into a box lashed to a child's sled. Two dead horses, bloated and greenish black, lay with stiff legs in the doorway of another barn. Some soldiers were trying to clean up Lieutenant Colonel Smithers' old command post; a shell had fallen through the roof and the rooms looked as if a wind machine had stirred up this thick stew of broken glass, papers and the torn pieces of furniture.

Down the street, a woman stood before her house, crying and shouting. Her house looked better than most of Hackenthal; it was standing, the second floor windows were not even cracked, but it was roped off with white mine tapes. A red-haired soldier, a runner from the message center, was arguing with her.

"You can't go in there, lady. If it's got mine tapes that means it ain't safe, see? Go away now, lady. Go on and visit with one of your friends for a while."

The woman understood nothing and went on crying and talking to herself. Suddenly she turned on the soldier and raised her arm to strike him.

"What goes on here?" the soldier asked. "Somebody get the interpreter."

Jacob Levy called to Sergeant Black, who was coming out of the CP. The woman had started to run up and down before her front door, with short steps like a frightened dog. Sergeant Black sent Pfc Wedemeyer across the street and Pfc Wedemeyer, speaking German, calmed the woman so that she would talk reasonably.

"She says you stole her sheets," Pfc Wedemeyer announced to the red-haired soldier.

"I stole her sheets?"

"That's what she says."

"When in the hell would I steal her sheets? What in the hell would I do with her sheets? Why goddam her anyhow,

I been fighting around here, I ain't got no time for stealing sheets. You tell her for me she should of been here when the fighting was going on and she wouldn't stand there talking about her goddam sheets."

"Maybe she's crazy," Pfc Wedemeyer said.

"You're damn right she's crazy." The red-haired soldier turned and walked up the street. "She can go back in her house," he called, "and blow her ass off for all I care."

Pfc Wedemeyer spoke to the frantic crying woman. She listened in silence, and rubbed her sleeve over her face. Then she walked down the road away from the village, empty-handed and alone. She looked very strange to the soldiers who had gathered to watch.

"The poor old dame," Bert Hammer said. "I guess it's pretty rough on them when you think about it."

Two little boys, who had been hiding in a barn, climbed over the dead horses and went up to the nearest soldiers. "Gum?" one said. The other shook his head, correcting. "Manger," he said, and made chewing gestures and pretended to put food into his mouth. "This way," a soldier answered, and herded the two in front of him towards the Battalion kitchen. There seemed to be no one else in Hackenthal except the silent old man, who went on shovelling grain.

"It's sure beat up," Bert Hammer said.

"It wasn't much, before," Jacob Levy observed.

"I wonder where the civilians get to? Does anybody look out for them?"

This was what he had dreaded for Kathe, all during the confused fearful days. This might have happened to Kathe. They had been bad days but if you had to fight, it made you feel better to know you were doing it for a good reason. If nothing else had been accomplished, anyhow they kept the Germans from Kathe.

. . . .

The krauts had either given up Luxembourg City or it was always a sideshow; their real business lay elsewhere. They were headed for Antwerp and the battle went on, roughly in the shape of a great triangle pointed towards the sea. The fighting was hard and costly: to live in such weather was a trial of strength. The Battle of the Bulge, as the newspapers named it, continued with the Germans still on the offensive, and Christmas was just another ominous day of it.

But at Hackenthal and along this short southern front the krauts had been pushed back. One shoulder of the penetration was contained. Comparatively speaking, they could take it easy.

At Christmas, the army made a serious effort to get turkey to whatever troops were not too occupied to eat. If a man was homesick, bored, cold and liable to danger at any moment, give him turkey and he'll feel better. Probably the army was right. It was rumored in the Second Battalion that turkey had reached as far as Regiment. The Regimental C.O. came over on Christmas morning and gave Lieutenant Colonel Smithers a bottle of whiskey.

The Catholic chaplain arrived in Hackenthal at 0930 hours and celebrated Mass in a barn. At 0940 hours, the krauts sent in some shells which gouged holes in a nearby field and worried no one. Jacob Levy wanted to go and watch the Mass; he thought it would be a good idea to get all the pointers he could on Kathe's religion. If possible, he would like to straighten out religion before they married so it would be easier for Kathe. He straggled behind the other soldiers, across the shining snow, and stopped twelve feet away from the barn. It didn't seem right; they might feel sore about an outsider sneaking in on their church. Now that Sergeant Postalozzi wasn't around, he did not know anyone to ask.

The chaplain was an officer and you never went to an officer about something until you knew the angles and besides the chaplain was busy, he had to look after the Catholics in all three Battalions so he wouldn't have time to chew the fat with a fellow who didn't belong to his crowd. It'll work out, Jacob Levy thought, I better leave it a while till I see some guy I can get the dope from.

He went back to the CP farmhouse and found Bert Hammer sitting on a bench in the sun. Bert had pulled the bench against the wall of the house, out of the wind, and was whittling another boat for his sister's kid.

"I bet I'm home this time next year," Bert Hammer remarked, "drunk."

"I guess that's right."

Bert Hammer inspected the roughly carved hull of his boat. "You know something, Jake, I think I'm going in the ship building business when the war's over."

"That's a good idea."

"You got any plans? You figured out what you're going to do?"

"I don't know yet, Bert." Don't know, hell, he thought with great and secret joy, I'm going to live is what I'm going to do.

IT WAS CLEAR that the winter would never end and neither would the war. They were still in Hackenthal. Like a taunt, Luxembourg City lay just over the squat hills, full of beds with sheets, hot water, square meals, liquor, movies, shops, girls. The Battalion held a stationary front, along a frozen river, from Hackenthal to Merk. Across the river the tank teeth and the green concrete pillboxes of the Siegfried Line coiled over the bluffs. By day, nothing moved. At night, patrols operated from both sides of the river. There was a reasonable amount of artillery, outgoing and incoming.

The soldiers adjusted to this icy, motionless life as they had adjusted to everything else. They shot rabbits and occasionally cows, to vary their diet; those units holding wooded areas lived hopefully with the notion they would one day bag deer. They made handsome snow men and shot tin cans off their heads; they liberated children's sleds from the abandoned houses and used them for transport; they constructed fancy improvements for the holes they lived in; they talked and talked in the meandering way of men who are bored to insensibility; they trained, worked, ate, slept and endured.

January was a winter in itself.

"Sometimes I just don't believe that Luxembourg Officers'

Club can really be there," Lieutenant Colonel Smithers said. He had climbed into his bedroll, fully clad and wearing three pairs of socks for warmth, and was now lying, like a khaki mummy, on the boards of a scratched fourposter which had been salvaged from the debris of Hackenthal.

"I wonder if Havemeyer still has his apartment?"

"Oh sure," Lieutenant Gaylord said. "Probably Lucille's in bed with him this minute."

Lieutenant Colonel Smithers thought of Dotty; he could not talk about her now with anyone. There had been time, these last weeks, to build a memory suitable to his needs and his desires. He had no other raw material for memories at hand. Yvonne of Paris was too remote and had existed too briefly. Mary Jane Cotterell and Elise Rathbone, the purest dreams, always ended by stinging him with shame. The Honorable Anne Northway, though real, seemed the most fanciful of all: London was even farther away than Paris, and the Limeys, even female, were more foreign than all other foreigners. Slowly, for the last three weeks were the slowest time on earth, Lieutenant Colonel Smithers invented with love a girl named Dorothy Brock. He promised himself that he would find her again, if he had to search the entire ETO and the USA. But his plans did not extend beyond finding her, and taking her in his arms, the dark girl who knew what this war was like and would never be a stranger.

Lieutenant Gaylord began slapping and rubbing his hands together.

"My handwriting looks like I was drunk," he observed. "I wouldn't want to give anyone the impression we have liquor in this Battalion."

It was unusual for Bill to be writing a letter especially at night in a room where your fountain pen would freeze to your fingers, given half a chance. Lieutenant Colonel Smithers had noticed that Bill was upset about something, the last three days, but he decided not to ask questions. If it was Battalion business Bill would talk when he got ready.

Boy, I'm high, Lieutenant Colonel Smithers thought. He had not taken his clothes off for over a month. If it was hot weather, he would barely be able to stand himself. It was never hot weather in Europe, only in Georgia. The sun shone exclusively on Georgia. Lieutenant Colonel Smithers felt warmer due to the Georgia sun.

"I'm writing my wife," Lieutenant Gaylord said. "Seems she's divorcing me."

So that's it, Lieutenant Colonel Smithers thought, recalled from sleep. The good old home front again.

"I'm sorry to hear it, Bill."

"I'm not. Let some other sucker keep her for a change." The indifference sounded too studied. Lieutenant Colonel Smithers knew there was no law which forbade a man to love a woman just because she was a bitch and grabbed all his money and treated him like dirt.

"That's that," Lieutenant Gaylord said. "Look at the dough I'll have to spend if we ever get a leave." He made a great deal of noise, settling for the night.

Lieutenant Colonel Smithers could think of nothing to say. Maybe this was how people talked, when they were getting divorced, in those books Bill always read. Maybe, if anyone said a kind word to him, Bill would break up. They ought to shave their heads, Lieutenant Colonel Smithers thought, the goddam whores.

"The chaplain hasn't been around in a long time," Lieutenant Gaylord remarked from the darkness across the room.

This startled Lieutenant Colonel Smithers. Did Bill want to mull it over with the chaplain? He must be taking it hard if he needed religion.

"I'm out of books," Lieutenant Gaylord went on. "There's nothing to do in this ice factory but read."

He had found that the books would not bear reading twice. The bloom was gone; you looked at them with a knowing eye. He sought refuge, only; and he did not want to lose the last one. Everything panned out badly, war and peace; nothing was ever enough, shiny enough, fast enough, never as gallant, exciting and stylish as he wished. How could you be interested in a life which led straight to the career of desk clerk at the Lincoln Hotel in Harrisburg, Pa.? How could you keep your illusions in a two room apartment with a woman who sulked and quarreled and lived like a slut and blamed you for not being rich?

And this war was the final sell. Those movies, Lieutenant Gaylord thought, it's a wonder I don't believe in Santa Claus too. When he was a child he had been dazzled by the screen romances of another war, and even years later he did not doubt them entirely. War, as he had seen it in the moving pictures, had its points and he thought he had missed that glamor as he missed everything. When he enlisted, he still remembered the haggard young actor-pilots, flying planes with open cockpits and their long white scarves waving behind them in the wind. At night they returned to dine in a mess, lighted by crystal chandeliers. They were reckless and cynical, alternating between single combat high in the sky, gay conversation that concealed meaningful undertones in their châteaux billets, and swift but tragic love affairs with sequin-covered girls in Paris. I bet, Lieutenant Gaylord told himself. That war was probably no better than this one.

Unlike Lieutenant Colonel Smithers, he had never been able to see Paris as the promised land. For he wanted so much more: streets of silver, houses of gold, and himself another man, a sure, casual, polished man who had been born to the pleasures of the world. Nothing was good enough and everything became worse; life was stifled in boredom. He needed books to keep his mind from it.

"People make too much fuss about being knocked off," Lieutenant Gaylord said. "Why in the hell do they care?"

Lieutenant Colonel Smithers listened. He did not like this at all. He had seen men blow their tops before and if they didn't do it suddenly—in action, screaming or crying or passing out—they often started with a darkness in their voices and in their minds. I got to get Bill another job, Lieutenant Colonel Smithers thought, back at a Headquarters somewhere.

. . . .

Jacob Levy had cut a hole in the beaverboard that covered their window. Through this hole, he was now attempting to ease a bent length of stovepipe. This was a private operation of his and Bert's; they had been engaged on salvaging, repairing and cleaning a stove, and on scrounging pipe, for six days. If there was nothing else in Hackenthal there was at least plenty of wood to burn.

"We'll have this room fixed up nice and comfortable by spring," Bert Hammer said. "How's it going?"

"It looks okay to me."

"Let's try it."

They piled in paper and wood, lit the fire, shut the rusted iron door, and waited. When they heard flame crackling inside their lopsided stove it was a moment of triumph like launching a ship.

"Pull up a chair," Bert Hammer suggested. "If we had something to drink, this would be as good as home."

Jacob Levy dragged a stool, made of mortar shell containers, close to the stove. The heat relaxed them; the heat spread a pleasant evening atmosphere, ripe for confidences.

"You got a girl, Bert?" he asked suddenly.

Bert Hammer flushed and stared at the stove as if it were likely to get up and leave the room. He did not have a girl and he had never had a girl; he was too shy to start; and he was ashamed of being, as far as he could tell, the only virgin in the U. S. army.

"Not right now," he said. His voice sounded gruff or angry. Bert must have had some trouble, Jacob Levy thought, maybe his girl gave him the brush-off.

"I guess you fixed yourself up all right in Luxembourg," Bert Hammer said, "driving the Colonel in, every night."

Now they would talk about women, technically, and he would pretend he knew it all. He would laugh at the right time and make wise remarks and wear an experienced, conniving look. And all the time he would feel nervous of his turn to lie, and try to avoid it.

"Pretty hot jobs, those Luxembourg girls."

Jacob Levy was distressed by this turn in the conversation. It wasn't like Bert either; he had imagined Bert was faithful to a girl at home.

"I don't know about that," Jacob Levy said. "I didn't run around any. I didn't see anybody except my fiancée."

There was that wonderful word again. Jacob Levy smiled at the stove. My fiancée, he said to himself.

"Say, congratulations, Jake! I didn't know you planned on getting married."

"Yeh, that's about it," Jacob Levy said with calm pride. "We're going to get married as soon as the war's over and then she's coming home to the States."

"Well, congratulations! You got it all fixed up."

"Yeh, her folks agreed and everything. I guess it's all fixed. We're going to live in a little house I got down in the Smokies."

"I never knew you lived down there."

"I don't. It's just a little summer place but me and Kathe plan to fix it up."

"Well, that's really nice," Bert Hammer said. "It's really nice to have everything settled for after the war."

The words had surprised Jacob Levy, even as he spoke. He felt he had talked for hours and that Bert now knew everything about his life. It was allright for Bert to know; it was good; it sort of gave him and Kathe a family friend. And he hadn't been telling lies exactly and someday he would explain to Bert. It was a little previous, but not lies. Saying it like that, out loud in words, made it true.

"I didn't have a chance to get her a ring," Jacob Levy said. "That's the only thing. I sure wish I could get back to Luxembourg so I could buy her a ring." A fiancée wore a ring with a diamond; you could buy it on the installment plan if you had to.

. . . .

February was no better.

They had returned, through waist deep snow, fighting their way in the similar villages, across the narrow rivers and over the ugly wooded hills. They were back in the forest, though far to the east of where they had gratefully left it. Time had not improved the forest; and now in February you could feel how it would be when the snow melted and the mud came back.

"What's the name of that measly little river?" Lieutenant Gaylord asked.

"Klemm," Lieutenant Colonel Smithers said.

They were kneeling in the Battalion OP, a slit trench on a bluff above this river. Below them lay the river, no more than a stream by decent American standards, and a plain, and a brownish town, carved by artillery fire into a strange stalactite formation.

At the other end of the trench, the artillery forward observer was carrying on a conversation, over the field telephone, with Fire Direction. This conversation consisted almost entirely of numbers. Occasionally the artillery observer would say, "no!" in an exasperated voice, and occasionally he would say, "okay that does it." From the ruined town, the sound of the shells he was adjusting travelled back, round and muffled, and they could see thin grey smoke from the explosions.

A corporal from Lieutenant Gaylord's section, who had been shivering up here since daybreak, offered the information that there wasn't a damn thing to see.

"What do we do?" Lieutenant Gaylord asked.

"Sit," Lieutenant Colonel Smithers said.

No matter how bad a place had been, you always had reason to grow homesick for it. Obviously Hackenthal was preferable to the freezing twilight of this forest. The war seemed to be congealing; it was too cold, the winter was too long; maybe everyone would get enough energy to fight again, in the spring.

. . . .

"There comes a time," Lieutenant Gaylord said, "when a man has to take matters in his own hands."

Lieutenant Colonel Smithers had finished checking over the supply situation with his S-4 and had decided to shave, as the night seemed quiet enough.

"If we don't look out," Lieutenant Gaylord continued, "we'll get in a rut."

"Me for a nice deep rut," Captain Martinelli said.

"Colonel," Major Hardcastle said, "if you haven't any objections to moving the CP, there's a pretty good kraut pillbox about 100 yards west of here, we could take over. It would be drier than this."

Lieutenant Colonel Smithers looked around the crowded dugout and thought, I ought to say yes right now; but he did not care enough to decide. Maybe they wouldn't be here much longer. It was a lot of trouble to lay the telephone wires again.

"I'll think about it," he said.

"Goodnight, men," Lieutenant Gaylord remarked and stepped over their legs and set out in the drizzling dark.

"He's full of pep, all of a sudden," Captain Martinelli said.

No one bothered to go on with this; it was also too much trouble to talk.

Lieutenant Colonel Smithers did not know whether he approved of Bill's new cheerfulness. On the other hand it was better for morale, even though it irritated everybody, for Bill to act so energetic. No one at Regiment seemed interested in getting Bill a job out of the line, so probably he should accept Bill's good humor and hope Bill had pulled himself together and was going to be allright.

Bill was going out every night with the patrols; it wasn't his business to take them that often but Bill was good at the job and the men had confidence in him and felt the work was more important if Lieutenant Gaylord handled it himself. Lieutenant Colonel Smithers had a suspicion Bill was up to something especially fancy: if he wasn't out on patrol, he was up in the OP studying the town of Griesling across the river.

At three in the morning, Lieutenant Colonel Smithers waked, cramped and short-tempered, and saw Lieutenant Gaylord coming in the dugout door.

"Where've you been?"

"Out with the boys," Lieutenant Gaylord said. "We had a fine time. They've relieved that Regiment over there; we got two prisoners. It's the 540th Volksgrenadier now. Nothing much."

"Casualties?" Lieutenant Colonel Smithers asked.

"Oh no. Easy as rolling downhill. We had a little fight but nothing came of it. They screwed off."

Lieutenant Colonel Smithers was not satisfied. But he was tired, and he was not supposed to be Bill's nurse, and as long as Bill did his regular work there was no reason to order him to stay away from patrols.

"Let's get some sleep around here," Lieutenant Colonel Smithers said.

. . . .

The Intelligence Sergeant, Louis Black, knew more about Lieutenant Gaylord than he had ever known about his own wife, and perhaps more than he knew about himself. Sergeant Black was a year older than Lieutenant Gaylord. Sergeant Black thought of himself as a balanced responsible older man of twenty-six, committed to the service of a brilliant but unsound young officer. Sergeant Black was proud of Lieutenant Gaylord and he hid his pride, because it would have been ridiculous for a sergeant—the only important rank in the army—to go around bragging about his officer. Sergeant Black permitted himself to say, to his closest friend, Sergeant Follingsby in the message center, "That guy Gaylord tickles me." He never said the things which you could think but which would sound sappy in words. Right now, he was thinking: I'd die for that goddamned man. And he was deeply worried, for he knew what Lieutenant Gaylord planned.

Sergeant Follingsby, as usual, had arranged his message center with an eye to comfort and social life. True, the place was small, being a hand-hewn mud cave; and it was also true that there was not much visiting in this forest. Still Sergeant Follingsby had acquired, who knew how, some extra blankets which were nailed to the mud walls and so diminished the dampness; the floor was covered with pine boughs; there was a working kerosene stove and at night Sergeant Follingsby kept a pot of coffee boiling for any chance callers.

Sergeant Black had stumbled his way in the darkness from the Battalion CP, to pay a visit. He hated this forest for many reasons, but above all he hated the way you never walked through it, you fell through it. He had cracked his knee on a tree stump, sprawled over a blown-down branch (and been challenged by a sentry who was only a voice), and he was wet from the snow and winded and in need of advice.

"I don't see how I can go and rat on the guy," Sergeant Black told Sergeant Follingsby. "And the Colonel would probably throw me out if I came around snitching on my own officer. But you see my position, Mart."

"You can't do a thing," Sergeant Follingsby said, "except make damn sure you're not along. Where did he get such an idea?"

"He says any fool can see we're not getting anywhere. We pound Griesling flat about four times a day and the krauts are still there and they relieve their units when they feel like it and we'll be here till next year the way it is now. What the artillery needs is specific targets, he says, not just a whole damn town."

"He's crazy," Sergeant Follingsby said.

"He's the best officer in this outfit."

"Okay. Sure. But he's crazy."

"What do you think then, Mart?"

"I think it's none of your business, Louie. Don't act like a screwball, now. You stay away from that little party."

"Oh hell, he won't take me. If he goes anywhere, I'm the one stays behind to look after things."

"Well, what do you want? A medal, for Christ's sake?"

Four nights later Sergeant Black returned to the message center and said, "You can't see your nose on your own face. I must of fallen flat on my butt ten times in ten yards. It's going to rain. He's gone, Mart. I feel sick, honest to God. I should of squealed on him."

"Who's working it with him?"

"The artillery observer. He's down at G Company now."

"Whereabouts?"

"In an outpost by the river. I can't sit still from thinking about that guy."

"There's nothing you can do, Louie. What could you do anyhow?"

"I don't know."

"He's done crazy things before now."

"I guess I'll go on down to G Company. I can't just sit around up here, waiting."

The forest seemed, to Sergeant Black, a huge gruesome practical joke. It was planned so it hit you in the face, caught you behind the knees, or yanked your feet from under you. He could see nothing except different shades of darkness. He walked with one hand before him, trying to hurry, and trying to lift his feet above the gripping flotsam of the forest floor. The forest was still dangerous with old mines, for it could never be properly swept; and he did not think of this. It was useless to run. If you ran, the practical joke only worked better. You would probably get around faster, at night, by crawling.

There were, everywhere, the low threatening voices of sentries.

"Allright," Sergeant Black kept saying in answer to the whispered challenges, "banana split." It was the silliest password for a month. It enraged Sergeant Black. This was no night for jokes of any kind. "Banana split, for Christ's sake. It's me. Black. Take it easy."

Suddenly, overhead, there was the whirling, incredibly fast, loud, round wind of outgoing shells. Through the forest, men became silent to listen.

The officers in the dugout CP had raised their heads as if you could see the passing shells through the mud roof, the mangled tree tops and the smoky night.

"What goes on?" Captain Martinelli asked. "I didn't know we planned anything for tonight."

"Those Div Arty boys are probably too cold to sleep," Lieutenant Hermann said.

"It's a good idea," Major Hardcastle remarked, "to shake up the krauts at night. We ought to do more of it."

Lieutenant Colonel Smithers said nothing. Without reason he began to know and to get ready. He listened to the shells as if they were falling here. Eleven, he counted, twelve, thirteen. . . . After the twenty-second salvo, there was silence.

"Nice little barrage," Captain Martinelli said. "Must be Griesling. It sounds like they all landed in one place."

When the first shells passed over him, Sergeant Black started to run. He ran and fell and ran, knowing this was insane, and cursing the forest. He had torn a long strip loose on one trouser leg and scraped his hand raw on the bark of a tree. He almost plunged through the hanging blanket that was the door of G Company's CP. Sergeant Mullins, on duty by the field telephone, raised his head from the comic book he was reading and said, "Did you have a fight with a bear, Louie?"

"Where did Gaylord go through?"

Sergeant Mullins could tell at once that this was no time to make bright conversation with Sergeant Black.

"You'll never find it. I'll send a runner to show you."

Then Sergeant Black was following the runner, who had

owl or cat blood for he moved with such assurance through this trap of a forest. You could not see the bluff, nor know that here the land fell steeply away, but the air felt different—freer, more open. The runner said, "Sam? It's me." And from an invisible place in the ground another voice answered, "Nice to see you."

"From Battalion," the runner said, in explanation of Sergeant Black's body, and Sergeant Black, just in time, noticed the open short rectangular trench before him.

Sam was standing at one end of this outpost position, staring down the bluff towards the river and Griesling. At the other end, a man wearing earphones sat hunched over a radio. Sergeant Black knelt beside this man and touched his shoulder.

"Lieutenant Bayer?"

"Black?"

"Yes sir."

"I can't raise him."

"Did he say he was coming back?" Sergeant Black asked.

"No. He called in a position. That's the last I got. We laid on five more rounds to cover for them. We sent them wide, on the south edge of the town."

"Was it the Lieutenant talking all the time?"

"Yeh," Lieutenant Bayer said. "It worked, Black! We must of put those shells in on street numbers."

They're all crazy, Sergeant Black thought. He'll never get back. It's a fluke he even got down there. Sergeant Black stood up so he could look over the edge of the hole. The darkness of the sky was thinner than the darkness of the land. Below them the river gleamed like wet tar. Griesling could not be seen, even as a silhouette or a shadow. Let them get back, Sergeant Black thought. Give them one break and I'll squeal on him afterwards.

At the base of the cliffs across the river, Sergeant Black saw short flashes of light. They heard the cracking of rifles, very personal and man-made noises after the locomotive roar of the big shells.

"They must of run into a kraut patrol," Sergeant Black said. His lips trembled so that he sounded as if he were talking with his mouth full. "Should we go on down?"

"No," Lieutenant Bayer said. "Gaylord left men on both sides of the river. We'd get in their way."

The river banks were again dark and absolutely silent. It started to rain and they could hear nothing but the slur of water against the trees.

A head, which was only a big solid ball of shadow, appeared behind them at the edge of the trench.

"Bayer?" it said.

"Come on in."

A man jumped into the trench; the mud slapped as he landed.

"What goes on down there?" It was Captain Latham, now commanding G Company. He was the third new commanding officer in a month. You hardly learned their names before they got hit.

"Gaylord's patrol," Lieutenant Bayer said.

"What was all the artillery?"

"Gaylord."

"What's he doing? Running a private war?"

"Just about," Lieutenant Bayer said.

Let him come back, Sergeant Black thought, I'll tell the

Colonel he's crazy; I'll get him locked up where he'll be safe.

Now they heard movement on the down slope beneath them. The patrol would have scattered, on the near bank of the river, to make their way back through the line of friendly outposts. Still, you never knew: Sergeant Black and Sam had grenades ready.

A voice called softly, "Banana split," and Captain Latham said, "Okay, okay," and the blurs crept nearer.

Then two men were rolling over the side of the trench; they all had to stand packed upright against each other. Sergeant Black could feel the wetness of the newcomers' clothes. They must have waded chest deep in the river.

"That you, Mike?" Sergeant Black asked.

"Louie?" a voice answered. "Christ, I'm sweating."

"What happened?" Lieutenant Bayer said. "Did we get them in where you wanted them?"

"Some," Mike said, "not too many."

"What do you mean?"

"What I said, that's what I mean. About eight, I figure. The rest must of killed a lot of cows outside the town."

"Those bastards at Fire Direction!" Lieutenant Bayer shouted. "Can't they do one thing right?"

"I guess not," Mike answered. "It was a pretty big sweat for eight rounds. They'd probably of done that much, by accident."

"Mike," Sergeant Black said, "where's the Lieutenant?"

"He got it right through the neck, Louie. We couldn't bring him back. There wasn't a thing we could do."

"Louie?"

"That you, Hank?"

"Yeh. Louie, we got in allright. It was the damndest thing you ever saw. They were holed in so you'd never hit them if you didn't know where they were. We'd of made it out too, if we didn't run into that kraut patrol. I guess they use the same ford."

Sergeant Black did not speak.

"The Lieutenant was just behind me, Louie." The voice was tired, almost toneless. But something had to be explained now. There was something Louie had to understand. "We were coming out along the river and I swear I could hear him laughing. Then we were lying right down there, you must of seen it when they jumped us; we were waiting to see if it was okay to cross and he said to me, 'That's the most fun I had in this war.' If we hadn't hit that goddam patrol we'd of made it, Louie."

"Let's get going," Lieutenant Bayer said. "No use hashing it out, here. Thanks for the office space, Captain."

Sergeant Black was the last to climb out of the trench. I should have stopped him, he thought, they should have carried him back anyhow. You worked with a man from the beginning and you got so you loved him and then they just left his body, out in the open on some river, for the krauts to find. Sergeant Black walked slowly through the rain and the close trees, feeling his grief tight in his throat, heavy in his chest, hot in his eyes.

.   .   .   .

Major Hardcastle took the message over the field telephone. He tripped on Captain Martinelli's sleeping body and picked his way to the corner where Lieutenant Colonel Smithers was lying.

Major Hardcastle kneeled on the damp mud floor so that he could whisper more easily. He was nervous. This was the worst news he could give the Colonel and he wanted to break it gently.

"The patrol's in, Colonel."

"Allright."

"They took an SCR 610 with them. They got into Griesling and cased it and then they called in the artillery."

Lieutenant Colonel Smithers said nothing. He had guessed this, when he heard the first shells going over.

"Called the artillery in on top of themselves," Major Hardcastle said with enthusiasm. Then he remembered what he still had to say and his enthusiasm faltered. "The patrol reports we could take Griesling right now, they're so disorganized."

The patrol had reported that the krauts in Griesling must be a pretty low-grade outfit, they scared easy. They were running around hollering as if Div Arty had laid all the shells in, as directed, where they were supposed to.

"Except we're not meant to take Griesling," Lieutenant Colonel Smithers said. "We can take Griesling any time this front is ordered to move."

Major Hardcastle scratched the stubble on his chin; then he took off his glasses and began to clean them. Maybe he could skip it and wait for the Colonel to find out by himself in the morning. Maybe he could say Div Arty was pleased with the job; which they claimed they were because they didn't like to admit they'd boxed it. Any sort of stall might be the best way out.

A man at the other end of the dugout moved in his sleep and knocked over a canteen which rolled, clinking, and stopped. Captain Martinelli coughed or groaned and then took a deep snoring breath. The dugout was quiet again.

"Is that all?" Lieutenant Colonel Smithers asked. He had started to hope.

"Bill didn't get back, Colonel." Did I say that, Major Hardcastle thought, like I was spitting it up and couldn't stop? Now what'll I do? He watched Lieutenant Colonel Smithers' hands, creasing a fold in the cover of his bedroll.

"Wounded?"

"No sir. Killed instantly. They had to leave him. Fording the river. . . ."

"Allright."

"It's tough luck," Major Hardcastle began.

"I'd have courtmartialled him if he got back. He had no orders to risk his men that way."

"Yes sir," Major Hardcastle said and waited and could not think what to say or do. Then he stepped across the crowded floor and took up his place again by the field telephone. He thought Gaylord deserved the D.S.C. for trying, though you could never get very worked up about posthumous awards. You couldn't kid yourself the poor guy gave a damn one way or the other.

Later, Lieutenant Colonel Smithers stopped at the door of the dugout and said, "I'm going out to check the Companies. You take over, Hardcastle."

Lieutenant Colonel Smithers replied to the challenge of a sentry and walked farther on, into the forest. He felt his way around a solid mass of underbrush, fallen trees and splintered telegraph poles; he skirted a burned armored car and an open latrine ditch. He was not thinking, merely moving in search of what he wanted. The forest was enormous but it did not offer what every other forest always provided: a place to rest in. Then he came to a widening between the trees, fairly clear of underbrush, and found a pine tree whose branches curved down close to the ground and crawled in under this shelter. The snow lay thicker here. He sat with his back against the tree trunk and his legs stretched out before him. Rain fell steadily, seeping down through the pine needles. The shoulders of his overcoat were sodden with water. He felt nothing and sat without moving.

He was arguing with Bill. He blamed Bill, as for a suicide. He explained to Bill that what he had done was wrong and stupid. You had to have patience, you had to wait. The war wouldn't last forever; afterwards they could go into business together, some kind of business, how did Bill know, maybe everything would be fine after the war.

He could talk himself blind now, for all the good it would do. Bill was lying out there across the river, looking the way the dead look. You never even stopped to notice the dead; they weren't men any more. They lay along the roads, in the fields, in the streets of villages, under the trees, like old dirty laundry sacks, nothing, just dead. You never knew how much of nothing dying was until you saw the shapeless, nameless, meaningless dead.

You should have waited, Bill, Lieutenant Colonel Smithers said in silence.

He thought he knew everything about war but he had not known this. You read the letters that came in to the chaplain because you had to, you were supposed to answer them personally; you read the desperate confused letters from parents or wives asking where their men died, how did it happen, what did they say at the end. And you thought, truly, that the civilians were horning in where they didn't belong and making a lot more noise than was decent. You watched the people in the destroyed villages following a cheap funeral through the streets or fixing up a new, poor grave. You saw them crying behind a wooden coffin or beside a wooden cross and you thought: they ought to take it as it is, they ought to get used to it. It was easy enough to be cold about dying, if you only considered your own death. It was easy enough because, being your own, you didn't believe it. He had not imagined what dying meant when you had a share in it; when you went on living, with the hopeless regret and the long loneliness. He had believed that dying was each man's own affair, and concerned no one else.

We could have gone into business together, Lieutenant Colonel Smithers thought, we'd have had a fine time if you'd only given it a chance.

Daylight seemed to come up like grey mist smoking from the ground. Lieutenant Colonel Smithers saw his legs, black as tree trunks, heavy and scarcely part of him, and his boots like black stumps rising from the snow. His body was fixed in its numbness and its pains. He tried to think clearly about the daylight and having to move.

After a while he stood up, holding the wiry branches of the tree for support. He rubbed his arms and his hands and his back that was iron stiff. Slowly and wearily, he beat and stamped and shook himself alive. Then he walked back to the CP. He still had a Battalion to command whether his heart was in it or not.

> *18* <

BELGIUM WAS all brown. The sky was brown above the stringy brown trees that lined the mud road. The stone houses, rain-streaked, mud-spattered, rose in square pale brown blocks against the sky. Khaki trucks, mud-caked, parked almost bumper to bumper on the road and the soldiers climbed into them slowly, as if their bones hurt. At the open rear end of each truck the soldiers stood, staring at nothing, and did not speak. These were the young men, returning from battle. This was how they looked when no one took their pictures; old before their time, going from one place to another, indifferent, in the trucks. The rain of March was no less cold than the rain of November. It always rained in Belgium. Belgium was where you got in and out of the trucks.

Major Hardcastle held a map board on his knees and Lieutenant Colonel Smithers leaned against the side of the jeep, tracing the route of the convoy on the map.

"All clear?" Lieutenant Colonel Smithers asked.

"We're certainly going the long way round." Behind his glasses, Major Hardcastle's eyes were sick with fatigue. The skin around his eyes was white and soft and pleated in tiny lines. He managed still to look neater than any of them but he was shrunken with weariness, as people shrink with age.

"Then you'll meet us at Rouvier?" he said.

The Division convoy was circling wide to the west, to avoid the crowded roads that fed the front. Then the convoy would curve back into France and head south. The Division was being attached to another Army. Major Hardcastle hoped this meant a rest but he doubted it. He did not think the 20th Division was a highly favored outfit; maybe the General wasn't a good politician or had no powerful friends. The 20th seemed only to get the dirty unglorious jobs. Now the Rhine was the big job, and Berlin was the big goal. Whoever got to Berlin first would be somebody. So they were shifted south, where there was no glory at all but only mountains and lots of fresh krauts.

Lieutenant Colonel Smithers looked at his watch. It was 1330 hours.

"I'll be at Rouvier at 0500 hours tomorrow," he said, "waiting for you with the Rouvier band. You better get going."

"Have a good time, Colonel." Even in a dirty jeep, with a bullet hole through the windshield, Major Hardcastle looked as if he were sitting at a bookkeeper's desk. His back had that pinched, rigid look; he always seemed to be wearing a green eye shade though in fact he always wore a steel helmet and his thin neck bowed beneath its weight. He was a very good officer, unappealing, unimaginative, and reliable.

"Good luck, Hardcastle," Lieutenant Colonel Smithers said and slapped the bookkeeper's back. Then Major Hardcastle's jeep was moving on the outside of the line of trucks, like a sheepdog herding the flock, and Lieutenant Colonel Smithers turned and said, "Let's get started, Levy."

Jacob Levy had felt guilty, telling Bert Hammer goodbye. Bert Hammer leaned out the back of one of the Headquarters Company trucks and said, "Enjoy yourself, Jake."

"I wish you could come, Bert."

"A dog robber like me? What call have I got to see the world?"

"I'll pick you up a bottle of cognac."

Since, to Jacob Levy, this trip to Luxembourg City was a six hour pass to paradise, he imagined Bert's sorrow to be intolerable. Paradise was right there, down the straight highway through Belgium, and the whole unlucky Battalion would circle it, cheated, going to no city at all but only from one brown village to another, without stopping.

"Next war I'm going to be a General's driver," Bert Hammer announced.

Jacob Levy stood in the rain and looked at his friend and, unknowing, his face mourned. This distressed Bert Hammer who now felt guilty in turn.

"I don't mean it, Jake," he said. "I don't grudge you."

But Bert Hammer was forgotten, the tired deprived Battalion was forgotten. Jacob Levy watched the road, easing the jeep around holes, almost raising it over ruts, weaving fast and light through the traffic. He thought of nothing save the need for haste. The brown country, which to all the soldiers was so uninteresting that it became invisible, rolled past. He drove, counting the kilometres that remained between him and Kathe. They had a total of seventeen and one half hours, which belonged to them personally. The better he drove, the more he would have of Kathe.

The jeep was wedged between a tank carrier and a truck loaded with jerrycans of gasoline, while on the left a convoy of troops proceeded towards the front. Jacob Levy used this forced delay to light a cigarette and did not realize that his hands were shaking. I'll get her a ring this time, he thought. Joy steadied him as rest would have done. He saw the ring and the marriage and the gentle future all together, as one. In a few hours he would find Kathe and she would see it as he did. I got to keep my mind on driving, he told himself, and pulled the jeep from behind the overhanging cliff of damaged tanks on the carrier, swung it out and through the froth of mud on the road, and ahead as fast as he dared.

Lieutenant Colonel Smithers looked at his watch. If Levy kept on driving like this, they would make Luxembourg City by six o'clock. He ought to clean up before he went to Dotty's club; he could feel the dirt on him like an extra, evil skin. He felt it even on his teeth, on his scalp, under his fingernails. He could smell his itching clothes. But he could not bear to waste time; Dotty would forgive him, knowing no one would choose to look this way. He could pick her up and bring her back to Major Havemeyer's apartment and she could sit in the bedroom with a drink and he'd leave the bathroom door open a crack so he could talk to her while he washed. Otherwise he'd lose about forty-five minutes and he felt he would not be able to get everything said, even if Levy held this speed and he had a full seven hours with her.

They would go to bed later and that would be what he'd

dreamed of; holding her and feeling again the softness of her skin. But first, he needed to talk. Dotty had known Bill and he could tell her of the fine life, magically brightened in memory, they once had together. He couldn't remember it by himself, unshared, any more. Dotty would understand: you couldn't just lose your friend in the accident of death, and bury him in silence and forget about it; you had to have company in this lousy war. Dotty would like to hear all about Bill; after Bill, he was closer to her than to anyone.

"Christ, it's cold," Lieutenant Colonel Smithers said.

"We'll be there in a half hour, sir."

They had not eaten since dawn; they were shivering, wet, exhausted; the skin of their faces stretched over their bones; their eyes seemed fallen deep into the sockets; and they were fortunate and full of hope for they were going towards women who waited for them and would greet them with tenderness. It was all any man could ask for, it was what everyone wanted. They would not speak of their sorrow and weariness and disgust; the women would not know what happenings of what hours had so marked their faces. They went towards their women as towards water in the desert.

"Here we are, sir," Jacob Levy said. His voice broke with excitement. Coming in from the open country, the streets in the outskirts of Luxembourg seemed narrow slits between the towering houses. After the ruins of villages, like sores all along the road, this standing city had the rare beauty of permanence.

"Where to, sir?"

"We'll go to the Red Cross Club," Lieutenant Colonel Smithers said. He could feel his heart beating. He wanted to jump out of the jeep, slowed now in the city traffic, and run ahead. "I'll go in for a minute and get Miss Brock. I won't keep you, Levy. I know you'd like to get started yourself."

Jacob Levy had barely stopped the jeep on the drive leading to the Red Cross Club before Lieutenant Colonel Smithers was out and walking with steps that were almost running, up to the glass and iron porte cochere. Jacob Levy searched until he found a wadded filthy handkerchief in his trouser pocket, and licked a corner of it and tried to scrub his face. This wouldn't do much good but he would like to be as clean as possible for Kathe. It was still raining. You got used to rain. You probably wouldn't know how to act if the sun came out.

The hall and the big room of the club were full of soldiers. They stood around the bulletin board and the ping-pong tables and the billiard table; they lined the cafeteria counter; in another room a juke box played loud familiar homesick music. It was very bright in the club and steaming hot and all the men looked extraordinarily clean and sleek to Lieutenant Colonel Smithers. He turned from the hall, meaning to go and ask for Dotty in the office. He felt self-conscious about the stubble on his chin and the mud on his clothes; the signs of where he had come from seemed like a boast or a reproach to these dolled-up warriors. A Red Cross girl came through the crowd in the hall and noticed at once the silver oak leaf on Lieutenant Colonel Smithers' helmet, and his alien dirt.

"Can I help you, Colonel?" she asked. She had, somehow, a professional voice: it was dutifully sweet and officially cheerful. The Red Cross girls always wore their uniforms as if the uniforms were their personal choice; they looked stylish, pretty, or sloppy according to the wearer. This woman wore her uniform as if she had never worn anything else. She was older too, a new category altogether.

"I'm looking for Dorothy Brock."

"Oh, she's not here any more," the woman said, almost chidingly. "She left weeks ago with the Headquarters. They're all at Namur. We're an entirely new staff. Luxembourg's becoming quite a rest center now."

Lieutenant Colonel Smithers stared at this woman. He heard what she said and he could not believe it.

"She's not here?"

"Goodness, no. She must have left in January."

Still he did not move. He was too tired to move. There was no place to move to anyhow. His throat felt choked and throbbing and it was not safe to speak.

"Is there anything we can do for you, Colonel?"

He did not answer.

This Colonel's behavior was really most awkward. He might be getting ready to make a scene of some sort. It would be best to hurry him out of here; this was an enlisted men's club anyhow.

"The Officers' Club is just across the bridge, Colonel. You go right down this street and across the bridge and straight on. It's just opposite the railway station. It's a very attractive club."

"Yes," Lieutenant Colonel Smithers said.

"The Namur Red Cross is APO 613," the woman added, "in case you want to get in touch with Miss Brock. I'm sure she'll be awfully sorry to have missed you."

Lieutenant Colonel Smithers, moving as if his boots were made of lead, walked back through the hall and out the door. Some soldiers turned from the bulletin board, with its announcements of ping-pong tournaments, conducted tours, lessons in French, cameras for sale, lost and found, and watched him curiously. The Red Cross woman shrugged and went towards the office. He might have said thanks, she thought; Dorothy Brock wasn't after all the only Red Cross girl in the world.

When Jacob Levy saw Lieutenant Colonel Smithers coming towards him, alone, slowly, as if walking was a hardship and an effort, he knew what had happened. It was the army again; the army did its best to ruin people's lives. They would have shipped Dotty out, just to cheat and hurt the Colonel, just to steal from him the only thing he wanted. The dirty bastards, Jacob Levy thought, what do they know what it's like for a man not to find his girl.

Lieutenant Colonel Smithers climbed in the jeep. "I'll go to the rue Philippe," he said. "You can pick me up there, Levy."

They drove in silence through the familiar streets.

Lieutenant Colonel Smithers lifted his musette bag from the back of the jeep. "You've got until 0100 hours, Levy. I hope you fix yourself up allright."

"Thank you, sir."

He did not drive away at once. He watched Lieutenant Colonel Smithers crossing the pavement and waited until the door of the apartment house closed behind him. He could not help the Colonel or even say anything to him. He was worried; the Colonel was so dead beat, after that forest, that you couldn't tell what he would do when his plans were sunk. Major Havemeyer ought to look after the Colonel; maybe the Major could fix him up with another date or anyhow enough liquor so the Colonel could tie one on, and forget.

It was all the army's fault. He was lucky he didn't love someone the army could ship around until they got you so hopeless you wouldn't know where to turn.

Lieutenant Colonel Smithers stopped outside the door of Major Havemeyer's apartment and listened. He could hear girls' voices. They were having a party. They sounded as if they'd been having a party for quite a while. He heard a glass break and someone squealed with laughter. They were playing "Sentimental Journey" on the victrola and talking so loud they couldn't possibly hear it.

Lieutenant Colonel Smithers laid his musette bag on the floor beside the door, and turned and walked down the stairs. It would only be worse, to have to drink and jabber and act like a good fellow. He was too tired. None of them knew anyone he knew; none of them had been where he'd been.

The streets were bare, under the rain; the city was all stone, dead and dark, with strangers' lives going on secretly behind the blacked-out windows. Much later he could come back and ask if they'd loan him a bathroom; hot water would be nice anyhow; and then it would be 0100 hours and he would go to meet his Battalion.

. . . .

Jacob Levy had not meant to burst through the door. The door slammed back and Madame Steller looked up, from behind the nickel coffee urn, and saw Kathe's soldier standing there, smiling; and she took in at once the lined hunger of his cheeks and the darkness around his eyes and the filth of his clothes.

"Bong jour!" Jacob Levy said. He crossed the café to her counter and reached out a dirty cracked red hand and smiled and smiled. This restaurant was practically his home, a rooted known place where you returned to cleanliness and warmth and the faces of friends. Madame Steller had given Kathe the afternoon off, long ago. Madame Steller was a fine old lady.

"Mon pauvre petit," Madame Steller said.

"Kathe?" Jacob Levy asked. Kathe must be in the kitchen getting an order filled. He had forgotten that he looked like a tramp. He was waiting for Kathe to come through the pantry door; it made him laugh just to think of her funny loved face when she saw him. In advance, he could hear the torrent of pattering French that would flow from her. And he'd damn well kiss her, in front of everybody.

"Elle n'est pas ici," Madame Steller said. "Sa mère est malade. Elle est allée à Müllerhof, il y a une semaine, pour soigner sa mère."

Jacob Levy did not understand this. He imagined Madame Steller must be making friendly conversation with him. Maybe she was asking him how he was or where he'd been all this time. Jacob Levy went on smiling. He could wait. He wanted to see Kathe's face when she came through the door. But probably he ought to answer Madame Steller. He thought hard, to find words.

"Très bieng," he said. "Beaucoup guerre. Très bieng."

Madame Steller looked at Kathe's soldier, helplessly. He was alive; there was that to tell poor little Kathe when she came back. Maybe Kathe would eat more, knowing her soldier was alive; she had grown very thin and sad, fearing for this young American. But here he was, not beautiful now, looking old and scoured-out like a burned tree and he did not understand that Kathe was gone.

[222]

"Elle n'est pas ici," Madame Steller said again. She dreaded telling him, yet she had to. And then he would stop smiling that marvelous smile. "Vous ne voulez pas vous installer un peu? Nous allons vous offrir un grand bon dîner."

Jacob Levy began to feel impatient and a little puzzled. He didn't want to stand here all night, gassing with Madame Steller, even though she was a nice old lady. A shabby grey-haired man, who had been nursing a bock of beer to make it last and make the warmth and the light of the café last with it, rose from his table alongside the door and came to the chromium counter.

"Je connais un peu l'anglais," he said to Madame Steller. She nodded.

"Sir," the man said, "Madame Steller say Mademoiselle Kathe is with the mother in Müllerhof. The mother of Mademoiselle Kathe is sick. Mademoiselle Kathe is gone from here since one week."

Jacob Levy stepped back, away from the man. He looked at this stranger with hate. Who asked him? What did he mean, pushing in where he wasn't wanted and saying some sort of lying stuff about Kathe?

"Tell Kathe I'm here," Jacob Levy said.

The man lifted his hands, in a gesture of pity.

"Monsieur Wallach," Madame Steller said, "dites-lui de bien vouloir s'asseoir, qu'on lui offre le dîner."

"Madame Steller say please to take place, she offers you the dinner."

"No," Jacob Levy said.

The three of them stood by the counter in silence.

"Where is Kathe?" Jacob Levy said.

"In Müllerhof, sir. She must go since one week. Her mother is very sick."

"Where is Müllerhof?"

"It is south, sir, forty-fifty kilomètres."

There was silence again.

"C'est affreux," Madame Steller said to the interpreter. "Il faut faire quelque chose."

"Rien à faire," the man said.

"I won't see her then." Jacob Levy was talking to himself. He expected no answer and the others did not speak. "I won't see her at all."

"Donnez-lui un verre de bière," the man suggested.

Madame Steller was glad to do anything. She drew a glass of beer from the faucet, and cut off the thin foam with a wooden spatula. Jacob Levy did not see her hand, outstretched with the heavy glass stein.

"I don't know when I'll see her," he explained slowly to himself.

"Il ne veut pas boire?" Madame Steller asked. They had to do something for the boy, they had to give him something.

"Non. Paraît que non," the man said.

"Tell her I came," Jacob Levy said. His voice was heavy with grief.

Madame Steller watched Jacob Levy go through the curtained glass door of the café and then she put her hand over her eyes. The shabby grey-haired man was still looking at the door.

"Les jeunes, Monsieur Wallach," she said, "quelle misère pour les jeunes."

She gave the unwanted stein of beer to Monsieur Wallach, who thanked her and went back to his table. With this free beer, he could stay another half hour or even three quarters of an hour. It was brighter and warmer in the café than in his room and he did not like to spend the evenings alone. It was too bad the little waitress wasn't here but surely later the soldier would meet another girl. All the girls were very fond of Americans.

Jacob Levy left his jeep before the café, and walked down the street to the park by the river. The river was there, as he remembered it, gleaming in the dark at the bottom of the ravine. This was their park. He stood, looking at the river, and thought: I used to love this city. Forbidding and empty, it was only another strange city in another strange country. The night would be long, and colder and colder. I won't see her, he thought. He might as well go. There was nothing to wait for, anymore. He could sleep on the hall floor at the rue Philippe and when it was time the Colonel would come and they would return to the Battalion and to the never-ending war.

> *19* <

THE RHINE was not nearly as big as you'd expect after all
the talk. And it was certainly no trouble to get across. They
drove over a pontoon bridge as if the Rhine were any old
river. It looked dirty, a green scum color. But it gave Jacob
Levy a strange feeling, anyhow, to be across the Rhine. The
Germans were really licked now. After the Rhine, he knew
it.

"I guess we'll be home soon, sir," he said to Lieutenant
Colonel Smithers.

"Maybe so."

These were the first four days of April and in any other
year or any other country, it would be spring. It was not
spring but it was not winter either; the snow was finished and
the mud did not have the settled here-to-stay look of all previous muds. It was capable of drying. Though the sky was
too pale, it was clean and only lightly streaked with wind

cloud and could be expected to brighten and warm with sun.

For four days the Regiment rode slowly into Germany, not called upon to get out and fight. The tanks were up ahead; another Division preceded the 20th, combing the countryside behind the fast advance of the armor. This was a nice interesting way to make war. Lieutenant Colonel Smithers and Jacob Levy and Dave Penny, the radio operator, had time to look around them and take note of this incredible world. They were wedged in a solid khaki river of vehicles that seemed to wind back behind them all the way to the Atlantic. The endless transport was covered with soldiers who stared like sightseers on a conducted tour. For none of them had ever seen a country in the act of defeat.

This country, coming apart before their eyes, spewed out people. War, as they knew it, was lonely work; the citizenry vanished somehow, the landscape always emptied where the war was in progress. But now civilians cluttered the roads and the villages. It was as if the Germans, and the millions of strangers they herded with them, had been locked inside these frontiers and a giant jail-break was taking place.

On one side of the road a steady line of men and women walked west to the Rhine. They pushed baby carriages full of household goods, or wheelbarrows, or pulled small carts, or shoved bicycles garlanded with their possessions tied into packages. The Germans had not bothered to clothe them during their long exile, so they had recently stolen a few useful odds and ends. A man would be wearing a cloth cap and a gleaming swallow-tail coat; a woman would be stumbling along in oversize rough boots and, above a burlap skirt, a green satin blouse. They were all scrawny and fierce, hanging on to what they owned and walking to the Rhine. They made the V-sign to the American soldiers and sometimes shouted jokes and laughed, and sometimes they sang. They were mostly French and they were going home. They had waited for no help or guidance, at night they slept by the roadside curled around their belongings. They knew where home was and they were going there.

On the same side of the road, driving west to the prisoner of war enclosures, were American army trucks loaded with German soldiers. The French, straggling along the soft shoulder of the road, never looked at these. The German soldiers stood packed in the trucks and the sharp April wind brought no color to their faces. Even their skin seemed different from that of all other men. It was grey and thick and their faces were without curiosity. They, apparently, saw no one. Their uniforms still appeared more soldierly than those of the Americans; their bodies did not wear any special pitiful sag as you might expect from the defeated. You did not notice that some were very young and some were too old to have been fighting men at all. They looked alike.

"The bastards," Lieutenant Colonel Smithers said. Why couldn't they all climb into P.W. trucks and go on back to wherever prisoners went? They were whipped. Why wouldn't they admit it and stop harassing sensible people with their stinking war?

The convoy moved slowly on, past prosperous farms undamaged by the war. It seemed that all the chickens and geese and pigs and cows of Europe must have been collected inside Germany. In other countries, the farms had been bare and the farmers were always engaged in cherishing one bony cow or one old sore-scarred horse.

"In Georgia," Lieutenant Colonel Smithers said, "there's plenty of people right now would be proud to own these farms."

Then the road would rise over a smooth hill and below in the hollow they would see pointed church steeples, rosy tiled roofs, narrow gabled houses with gleaming window panes, crowded together into a gingerbread village. These villages too were intact; and from every window, clean white sheets hung in token .of surrender.

"They sure got a lot of sheets," Lieutenant Colonel Smithers said. One or two would have been enough. They didn't all have to surrender, for God's sake.

Dave Penny stopped chewing gum long enough to say, "Can you beat it?" On the outskirts of another pretty village, blonde children waved little white flags, as if to surrender was a festive occasion.

A line of Germans stood outside a high, redbrick, sharp-roofed building; they carried shot guns, hunting rifles, pistols and old army rifles. A few brought duelling swords. They were waiting to deposit their weapons in the Town Hall, as directed by the conquerors. Seeing these obedient krauts, waiting their turn to disarm, Jacob Levy said, "Look at the werewolves."

And there were plump girls everywhere, riding bicycles or watching from the fields or the doorways of houses. They wore stockings that shone in the sun. In England, the women's legs got red from the cold; in Belgium they seemed more purple and were embarrassing because of the dark down on them.

"I guess these krauts weren't hurting for anything," Jacob Levy remarked.

Lieutenant Colonel Smithers looked at the gliding hills with the fields spread on them in rich various patterns and thought: what the hell did they do it for? They had all they needed. You could have understood the war better if Germany had been a lousy starving ugly country, as imagined.

Then the perilous game of leap-frog, which was being played across Germany, caught up with them; it was their turn; the Division ahead went into reserve and they got out of the trucks and became infantry again, fighting on their feet. That four days' tour had been too good to be true anyhow. The Battalion cleaned out roadblocks, and emptied villages of snipers; they pushed the krauts off small, strategically placed hills; they crossed bridgeless rivers and protected the banks while the engineers strung pontoons for the armor; they patrolled the woods like men collecting dirty trash in a park, driving out the scattered German Volkswehr. It was brisk, mean work and men got killed doing it. This was unnecessary death; the German army was busted up, the country eaten into on every side, there was no war left to fight. So you could only think these goddam krauts had decided dying was a good idea and meant to take as many Americans with them as possible.

· · · · · · · · · · · ·

The Regiment rode into a town called Hildenwald. It was one of the towns the P-47's had worked over. You had to hand it to those P-47 boys, when they set out to mash a place they mashed it. Riding through Hildenwald was like riding on a roller coaster; you climbed up and down over mountains of rubble. Here they learned that the tanks were held up;

[231]

the routed and divided Germans had again solidified up ahead and were giving battle. The Regiment went into Division reserve and the Battalion found itself camping in the park of a great house, unsuccessfully copied from a French château by some wealthy, now absent, Hildenwalder.

The Colonel set up his CP in the bare grandeur of the house: as always he sat behind a kitchen table and as always there appeared before him the papers that seemed to multiply by themselves in war. He wore his usual paper-work frown and talked with his usual paper-work snarl, and Jacob Levy decided the Colonel would be stuck at that table for some time. Jacob Levy found Bert Hammer, who was trying to sort out a jumble of bedrolls, and suggested they visit the town.

"We could ask Sergeant Hancock," Jacob Levy said. "Just a couple of hours."

Sergeant Hancock, who had replaced Sergeant Postalozzi, said they could go weave daisy chains for all he cared, but you never knew when the Battalion would move and if they got left behind that was their tough luck and they'd be AWOL in his books.

"Not a chance, Sarge," Bert Hammer said. "You know this Battalion can't operate without us."

It was the end of the afternoon; they had two or three hours of daylight. It was nice to walk around in the spring air, with nothing on your mind.

"I wish we had time to go fishing," Bert Hammer said. They had passed a stream before they came to this town. It flowed pleasantly between grass banks. Fishing with grenades, you couldn't miss; though if you had a pole it was still better to fish in the old-fashioned way. They had no time for this. They decided, therefore, to go looting.

They did not want anything; looting was only a sport. It was also curiosity, to learn how the Germans lived, what did they own, what did they keep in their houses? That was how Americans always judged people and at last you had a chance to see what the enemy was really like.

There were sharp characters who looted with intention, who found jewelry, valuable cameras, or pictures, and saved their loot and would later sell it. These were the businessmen. Most of the soldiers picked up junk, not believing it belonged to anybody (the houses were empty), and they would carry this worthless stuff a few miles along the clogged roads and dump it out.

Some soldiers were frightened of looting because they had heard about the booby traps. The Germans were famous for booby traps. It was alleged that you'd pull open a bureau drawer and it blew up on you. This had always happened to some other fellow, who was blind, hand-less or dead as a result. These stories had a very wide circulation; no one had time to prove or disprove them. They kept a certain number of men law-abiding.

Jacob Levy and Bert Hammer found their house at the edge of Hildenwald. This was a suburban street and had escaped the bombers. The house was made of tan stucco, new and unscarred. You would not be surprised to find the family in the parlor, waiting for supper They broke the lock on the front door, kicked it open and jumped back down the steps. This was when they expected something to blow up. Nothing happened. They went inside and found the house as undisturbed as if no army had passed. The town was evidently so rich in pickings that the preceding soldiers had not stopped to rifle this place.

They went into the living room. The furniture was shiny, dark, and modern; there were bookcases full of books bound in sticky leather with much gold lettering; there were small statues, a bronze head of Hitler looking noble, a Greek maiden and a stag; ornamental beer mugs; and crossed duelling swords on the wall. The leather chairs had brown velvet cushions with lace doilies pinned to them. On a small table, spread artistically, were handsome picture books showing the Führer in every public act and mood.

Bert Hammer picked up one of these. It opened at a picture of the Führer simpering on a crowd of young women in dirndls. Bert Hammer closed the book. The picture made him sick; he didn't know why. The look on the girls' faces was something you felt ashamed to see, there was something dirty and sexy about it.

Jacob Levy had opened a desk drawer, out of curiosity. The papers were neatly ranged inside. There was a pile of calling cards with "Dr. ing. Paul Schemmerkling" printed on them.

"The guy was a doctor," Jacob Levy said.

They walked through the dining room, all matching pieces of heavy carved oak, and a hanging chandelier of green glass, into the white tiled kitchen.

"It's like home," Jacob Levy said. They had nowhere seen such houses. Bert Hammer did not say that it was a lot better than his home.

There was a little dust in the house but otherwise it was in perfect order. The family could move back anytime. The main bedroom upstairs was filled with another set of furniture, brown and shiny and with chromium handles and knobs wherever possible. They opened a high mirrored cupboard and saw the clothes hanging there, the man's suits on the right, the woman's dresses on the left. Bert Hammer pulled out a white satin wedding dress and they stared at it. There was a set of blue glass toilet articles on the dressing table.

Next door was the nursery. The furniture was small and pale blue, trimmed with a design of white rabbits. There were two blue cribs.

"That's cute," Bert Hammer said, smiling.

The bathroom was also white-tiled and had a shower.

You could not help respecting people who had such a fine clean house. You could not help being a little sorry for them, knowing what they had lost. You could not really believe a doctor would be a Nazi and a bad guy; he probably had to have those picture books and the statue of Hitler so he wouldn't get in trouble. They were admiring the bathroom when they heard feet on the stairs.

"We found it open," Bert Hammer whispered. They had touched nothing; if it was an officer they would say they were only looking.

"Hey!" said a voice in the hall.

A soldier was standing there. He was not from their outfit.

"Nice little joint," he said. "Found anything good?"

He walked into the bedroom and said scornfully, "What're you waiting for?" He jerked open a drawer of the dressing table and dumped its contents on the floor. He stirred these around with his foot.

"Junk," he said. "Not much jewelry in houses anyhow. You mostly find it in stores. If the armored boys don't get it first."

He pulled out another drawer and dumped it.

"Snot rags," he said. "I can use some of them." He picked up four handkerchiefs and put them in his pocket.

"Listen, Mac," Bert Hammer said, "this here is our house. First come, first served. I didn't notice anybody invite you in."

"So," said the soldier.

"Right," Bert Hammer said.

The soldier looked them over; the little guy who gave orders would be easy but the other was a big man. And there were two of them. Anyhow there were plenty of houses.

"Have it your own way, pal." He stopped to take a silver trimmed comb from the dressing table.

"So long pals," he said.

They followed him downstairs to make sure he left, without disturbing the living room.

"Son of a bitch," said Bert Hammer.

They looked with regret at the once orderly bedroom. Jacob Levy felt they ought to pick the stuff up and put it back in the drawers but that was foolish. It was funny how much you knew about people, seeing what they kept in their house. It was sort of wrong too; it wasn't right to snoop on people when they couldn't help themselves.

He went over to the bedside table where he had seen a picture in a fancy silver frame. It was turned sideways towards the bed. Maybe this was the man or the lady who lived here. The little blue room for the kids made you think they must be good friendly people.

The photograph showed a man of about thirty-four, glaring pop-eyed at the camera. He was grinding his teeth together in an expression of martial ardor, so that his jaw muscles were ridged. He wore the black uniform of the S.S., complete with cap and skull and crossbones insignia. At the bottom of the picture, in ornate script, was written: Für meinen geliebte Lotte, herzliche küssen, Paul.

The man looked to him like a blown-up, full-sized bastard, and mean.

"Take a look at our doctor," he said.

Bert Hammer studied the picture. "You mean to say this doctor was in the S.S.?"

"Seems so."

"You mean to say this guy had this fine house and the two kids and was a doctor and went and joined the S.S.?"

"I guess so."

"Well screw him, is what I say. Screw his house, too."

Bert Hammer went to the dressing table and pulled out the remaining drawers, as they had seen the other soldier do.

"Want anything?" he said, kicking at a collection of gloves, scarves, stockings, socks, handkerchiefs, hairpins, and cuff-links.

"No."

Casually Bert Hammer brushed the blue glass toilet articles off the dressing table; they broke on the floor.

"I want to steal me something big out of this place," he said, "something that son of a bitching S.S. doctor will really miss."

They could find nothing and contented themselves with tearing the house apart as much as possible. They felt they had been made fools of, believing he was a nice guy and looking after his home for him, the way they had. Jacob Levy threw the bronze bust of Hitler through the living room window, and they left whistling. They hadn't gotten any loot but it had been a useful afternoon anyhow. This would show those crooked krauts whether they could get away with being S.S. on the sly or not.

* * * * * * * * * * * *

They met the new cook, Leroy Backley, on what was almost a street. A bulldozer had pushed the towering rubble off the street and down a bare slope so there were cobbles to walk on and bits of curbstone to show where the borders of the street had been. On the right a row of housefronts stood, with nothing behind them but rubble-grey, churned-up holes. The housefronts were old, pretty and fantastic, pale candy colors, coated with plaster ornament and decorated with crossed timbers and fragile balconies. They would collapse any day. They were a reminder that once Hildenwald had been noted in the guide books for its medieval charm.

Below the climbing street lay a flat semi-circle of land: this was what the airforce called marshalling yards. The airforce was attracted to marshalling yards everywhere, and the open expanse showed how thoroughly the airforce worked. Tracks rose in the air like weird flower stalks; the ground was pitted with bomb craters; locomotives and freight cars had been blown about in every position, on their sides, upended, piled together like kindling; the railway station was crushed through in three places; no switch tower remained upright.

"I guess they'll have to do without trains here for quite a while," Jacob Levy said.

In the midst of this perfect destruction, one long line of freight cars stood as solid as new. It had the appearance of a miracle.

"I just came from that train," Leroy Backley said. "You ought to see those Russians."

They liked Leroy Backley allright; he was a good man though a terrible cook. But he wasn't Royal Lommax, he didn't have the authority and style of old Roy. They didn't want to get stuck with Leroy Backley for the rest of their one free afternoon.

"What Russians?" Bert Hammer asked.

"The d.p.'s or the slave laborers or whatever they are. They're down there collecting back pay. You ought to see them. There's some nice stuff in that train. I got me a vanity case for my girl."

That sounded more like it.

"What's up that way?" Leroy Backley asked, pointing the way they had come.

"Some pretty good houses," Bert Hammer said, knowing Leroy would take the bait.

"I better go and look them over," Leroy Backley said. "See you later."

Jacob Levy and Bert Hammer considered the bombed wilderness and the miracle train.

"Should we go down?" Jacob Levy asked.

"I better get back, Jake. It's near chow time. I got to bring it to the staff. I better not take a chance. If you see anything good, get me one."

The train was very long and the Russians swarmed like ants, in and out of the cars. There were Russian women too. They all looked thin, sick, and determined. They did not talk to each other. The way they were going about this, you could tell they really needed whatever they were after.

Jacob Levy climbed through the door of a box car and

saw that the Russians had been there before him. The Russians broke open everything, spilled everything, looking for what they wanted: food. After food, they wanted clothes. This car was full of pharmaceutical scales: thousands of boxes held little gilt metal trays and stands and the graduated kilogram weights. The Russians were not interested in these, but had kicked the place over on the chance there would be food in some of the boxes. Jacob Levy did not care about the scales either until he thought his father might like a set as a souvenir. He sat on the floor trying to find one untouched box. Then he heard the scream of an incoming shell and he jumped from the car and ducked down by its side.

The shell was long. Now a fast little barrage started. What an ugly sound an 88 made, the coldest, fastest, dirtiest sound of all. The Russians went calmly on, picking over the train. They must be crazy; didn't they know these things killed you? Or else, Jacob Levy thought, they don't give a damn. Or else they think artillery is a nice change. With complete unconcern and in purposeful silence, men and women continued to climb in and out of the freight cars, looking for food.

When the car behind the engine was hit, Jacob Levy decided it was time to leave. He had a wooden box with the scale and weights, for his father, and this was no place to linger in. The krauts knew what they were aiming at and pretty soon, unless these Russians learned some sense, there would be a lot of spattered Russians around this train.

Jacob Levy crawled under a freight car, waited, listened, and ran fast across the tracks to get in the lee of the crushed railroad station. There he found another nonchalant group of Russians, treating this shower of steel as if it were no worse than a heavy rain. A young Russian, with a bony face, advanced to Jacob Levy. The Russian wore a red satin necktie though he had no shirt, and two suit jackets. He held a box of thin malevolent German cigars and these he offered with the greatest friendliness.

"Ich komm' aus Stalingrad," he said and laughed and slapped Jacob Levy on the back. Then he shook hands formally.

Two Russian women were trying on brassieres, which they had looted from the train, over their clothes. They did not seem to know what these articles of clothing were meant for. The brassieres looked formidably strong, as if they were made of tough pink canvas. They were bright and new and the Russian women seemed delighted with them. They're all cracked, Jacob Levy thought, and who can blame them. He did not like 88 shells; the Russians could be brave for him too.

That night lying side by side in their bedrolls, he told Bert Hammer about the Russians and the train. Bert Hammer said, "You're making it up."

"No, honestly. They just don't give a damn for 88's."

"They must be funny people."

The floor of what had once been the ballroom appeared to be covered with large misshapen khaki sausages. The men slept noisily in their bedrolls, grunting and twisting, and one man snored like a teakettle. It took a while to get used to the air in this room which smelled as the men did. Jacob Levy lay in the dark and began to think about all the people who had been held and misused by the Germans, during these long years. They hated the krauts but they didn't seem to take them seriously. Like the French who didn't even see the Germans, they kind of walked through them, they wouldn't bother to notice them. Like the way the Russians didn't move for the German artillery. They acted as if the Germans were dirt, you couldn't get excited about them, they weren't people. But he had taken the Germans seriously; he had known they were dangerous; he had been painfully afraid of them. Maybe the Russians and the French and all were right: look how the Germans hung out big white sheets to surrender, and how they bowed and scraped now. Maybe they were just dirt. They're all through pushing people around, Jacob Levy thought, and they are stupid-looking. They're a stupid-looking race. It was a big change to look down on the Germans, and it felt fine.

. . . .

The cellar shook from blast. There was nothing small and chinchy about the bombs we were using. The airforce was running a regular bus service over Nürnberg; the noise of the planes was so constant you stopped hearing it. Lieutenant Colonel Smithers sat on the floor beside the field telephone and thought that Bill would have liked this show. It seemed that the entire Seventh Army had come together here and was now pounding Nürnberg with everything they had. Even in this cellar on the northern outskirts of the town, your ears rang and ached with the explosions. Bill would have got a big kick out of it. Something new had been added. They now fought all around the clock, with antiaircraft searchlights pouring thick blue-white shafts of light on to the vast rubbish heap that was ancient Nürnberg. If the Germans enjoyed going down in a blaze of glory they were getting the blaze anyhow. I'm bored, Lieutenant Colonel Smithers decided. It's all stupid. There's nothing different, even with searchlights.

Jacob Levy and Bert Hammer huddled in the corner of a house which had retained, beside this excellent safe angle, one wall and a set of steps leading to nothing. Jacob Levy did not know what they were supposed to be doing, but Bert seemed to have a rough idea. Jacob Levy guessed they were defending this house as if there was anything to defend. He hoped that no one would come and tell them to move. He would just as soon keep these bricks against his back.

"Seems they call this place their sacred city," Bert Hammer explained. He was always one to pick up information. "Maybe they got a church here or Hitler was born here or something. Maybe it's kind of like the White House to them. Anyhow that's why the bastards are hanging on."

Sacred city, Jacob Levy thought, why did they have to put it here? Why not up north somewhere? In the dark, he took his calendar from his breast pocket. He did not dare make a light to look at it and he had already crossed out this day, because it was officially finished. He rubbed his hand over the greasy paper, for comfort. If ever they needed luck, it was now. It made you stiff and cold to think about your chances, when any day there would be peace: peace and the sunlit certain life by his stream, with Kathe.

A rifle bullet ricochetted against the wall above their heads. Goddam them, Jacob Levy thought, and their sacred city.

At dawn, F Company reported via the field telephone that they were held up six blocks away. There were krauts in a three storey house, with a good field of fire around them. F

Company wanted mortars to blast the krauts out. Lieutenant Colonel Smithers said he would be right over. He could no longer wait for an action to develop as he ordered; he had to hurry it along in person. And each day he understood Bill Gaylord better, and what drove Bill. He told Major Hardcastle, who disapproved, to take charge; and he climbed out of the cellar and picked his way through the wrecked back yards, to F Company. Dave Penny with a walkie-talkie, and Corporal Schwarz of Milwaukee, an interpreter, followed him.

The house full of krauts stood, as reported, among the stumps of other buildings; the krauts had clear observation on all four sides. Lieutenant Colonel Smithers crouched behind the broken window of a house diagonally across the street, and watched.

"I'd like to kill them all," Lieutenant Colonel Smithers announced. "Men, women and children."

Captain Huebsch did not look at his commanding officer. The Colonel oughtn't to talk like that, where the men could hear. His voice didn't sound right, he didn't act the way he used to. He blew up nowadays; he ran around more than he had to. The officers had noticed; pretty soon the men would too. The Colonel's nerves were bad.

I'm so bored I'm just about nuts, Lieutenant Colonel Smithers thought, I got to watch what I say.

This was the eighth fair-sized fight they'd had in this rotten country. He couldn't even remember the names of the places they'd fought in. These krauts had now tried his patience as far as it would go. Lieutenant Colonel Smithers called for the interpreter and Corporal Schwarz advanced towards the window, on hands and knees.

"Schwarz, tell those krauts they can give up or we'll kill every last damn one of them."

Corporal Schwarz, keeping in a safe angle, shouted this news to the house across the street. A machine gun answered him.

"If that's how they want it," Lieutenant Colonel Smithers said.

He took a certain satisfaction in that house, finally. It looked like gang warfare in the movies. Everything was smashed and dead men lay in most of the rooms.

"They only had to keep their noses clean," Lieutenant Colonel Smithers observed. "I got no sympathy for them."

And he thought: this is the last time. It has to be.

He was sick and tired of the whole business. So was everyone else. Everyone walked lightly, looked in all directions, held his breath and hoped. It was so near the end. A man could honestly believe now that he had a fine chance of getting home.

> *20* <

IT WAS NICE, driving in the jeep. It reminded Lieutenant Colonel Smithers of when they were young and had roared across France. Not that they roared anywhere now; they were again wedged in the endless convoy. They crawled along and then the traffic would halt, for no reason you could see. The officers would get out of their jeeps and hurry up the long line of khaki vehicles, saying: what the hell's holding us up, who's responsible, look alive there, get a move on. The soldiers relaxed, for they were trained in patience and they did not care where they went nor when they got there. Usually an accident—a driver fallen asleep at the wheel, a truck crashing in from a side road, a side-swiping tank—or a balky, conked-out engine, had caused the delay. The halts were always short. They shoved the blocking vehicle off to the side of the road and the parade went on.

Lieutenant Colonel Smithers was content with this pace. Whatever had harried and driven him before was worn out, as the war was worn out.

And it was finally spring. The lovely tended land lay under a green mist. Above the exhaust fumes and the reek of gasoline, the air was sweet with the smell of this growing. The sun smoothed warmth over your shoulders, your face, your hands.

Lieutenant Colonel Smithers looked at the distant snow mountains and knew that when they reached them the war would be over for that was the limit of Germany. From La Harpe, Georgia to the Bavarian Alps, he thought, the hard way. Hard it had been, nobody could deny it: hard in the hedgerows and hard at St. Lô; never easy except for one brief spell when all they did was burn up gasoline in France; hell hard both times in the forest, harder than anyone wanted to remember; plenty hard in Luxembourg in the snow; and hard enough at all these worthless German towns. It tired you, there was no question about that. And it made you old. He knew he had lines that weren't there when he left La Harpe, in some other life, a smiling young man, everybody's pal Johnny, who liked his job because it gave him a chance to drive the new models and show off to the girls. And he had grey hair too, alongside his temples and streaking the brown up from his forehead. This grey hair alarmed him, yet it seemed to belong to another man. You looked at it and wondered what had happened to the guy that would give him grey hair at twenty-eight. You weren't ready for grey hair yourself. It was some other fellow, showing these signs of strain and anxiety.

It had been hard allright and plenty of good men were dead. He had known many of them and gotten on with them all, but Bill Gaylord was the only one he cared about. He felt that no one would notice much that Bill was dead; he was also the only one Bill had, to do the remembering and the caring.

Perhaps Bill had never been happy; the war didn't explain it. Bill didn't give a damn for his wife, or how could he lay anything he got his hands on. Looking back, Lieutenant Colonel Smithers decided Bill wasn't hurt by the divorce, he was just sort of ashamed because divorce was a cheap business, something like being caught in a raid on a gambling joint. And Bill never talked about his parents, as if they didn't hit it off or they weren't his kind of people and meant nothing to him. Bill said that if anybody thought he was going back to the reception desk at the Lincoln Hotel in Harrisburg, Pa., they were crazy. He was a funny boy, Bill Gaylord, he always sounded cheerful enough but he seemed to be disgusted deep down into where he lived, war or peace.

But after the war it might have been better. They'd have been together, it would be easier when there were two of them. It wouldn't mean returning alone, a stranger where you came from, a new man that no one knew or wanted to know. Because nobody's going back the same, after this, Lieutenant Colonel Smithers thought. Bill was dead. Bill was not going back anywhere.

The past was safe territory, he felt at home in the war, so he began to think of the way Bill operated in combat. Bill's bravery was peculiar too. He wasn't brave like the people you read about who don't feel fear, in case there really were any people like that. Bill acted fine, always cool, even joking, but his eyes said something else. Bill would have liked to see himself written up in the papers, though he sneered at that stuff. But he would have liked it. And so would I, Lieutenant Colonel Smithers thought. You know I would.

If he, Johnny Smithers, had been written up in the papers

and become famous in this war, as some men had, perhaps he'd be a different person when he got home. He was different but how would anybody in La Harpe know that? He could almost hear how it would be: "Why Johnny, hello boy, when did you get back? It's been a long time. Well, happy to be home, I reckon? Back at your old job again?" He couldn't tell them all that had happened to him and all that he had become. He could tell them nothing of the real war, they would never understand and he never wanted to speak of it. It was too serious to shoot the bull about with people who had not seen it and felt it. But he couldn't tell them, either, about the trimmings, the excursions. He couldn't even say that he had been invited twice for the weekend at an English house that was so old it was like a museum, and the people who owned it were a Lord and Lady and he had been the big shot because the Lady thought he was the stuff. But that didn't mean he'd get asked to dinner at the Cotterells or the Merrills or the Rathbones in La Harpe. In La Harpe, he was Johnny Smithers and that was that.

He couldn't kid himself; his people were not the ones who owned and ran things; they weren't even the second new batch that had money and was starting to horn in. Maybe if Lord and Lady Rayne could have seen beyond his uniform, with the silver oak leaves on the shoulders, to his family's house on East Magnolia Street by the mills, they wouldn't have been so wild for him. But he had the uniform, he earned it, he deserved it. And in it he had commanded nine hundred men from the English Channel to the Bavarian Alps and you couldn't be a complete slob and do that. And in it also, he had seen London often, the best hotels, the best night clubs, and several fine houses in the English countryside, and

Paris once and Liège, Belgium, though it was shot up at the time and he had no social life there. And he was almost a resident of Luxembourg City. Anyhow, he had been a lot more places and seen a lot more people than anyone in La Harpe. But would they know? He could have married that crazy English girl, with her picture in the Tatler and all the rest, the Honorable Anne Northway. But Mary Jane Cotterell and Elise Rathbone wouldn't think he was worth marrying.

How would they know, in La Harpe, that an American officer, a Lieutenant Colonel, lived in a world where everyone called him sir, where he gave the orders, where he had special separate clubs and messes and billets, and was treated with respect as an officer and a gentleman? He was Johnny, was all, he had started as Johnny and if he came home wearing his uniform and his ribbons and anything else, they wouldn't forget that his father was a retired post office clerk and his mother said Ma'am to people like Mrs. Cotterell and Mrs. Merrill and Mrs. Rathbone, and he didn't go to college, he studied at a filling station. I'll make money, Lieutenant Colonel Smithers thought. If I can command a Battalion all through this frigging war, I can goddam well make money and be somebody at home.

He was as good as they were any day of the week. What did they do in this war? What did they have to show for it? But he knew that would not matter. The war's almost over, he thought, and a war record isn't going to mean a thing in La Harpe. I ought to bring home a wife that would show them I could have anyone I want. But what would the wife think? Take Dotty. Maybe Dotty would marry him; she seemed pretty stuck on him at the end. And he was the same man out of uniform, he wouldn't be any less good because his clothes were different. But what Dotty knew was an officer, with the strength of his Battalion behind him. There wasn't a combat officer in the army who wouldn't hold his head up and be proud to anyone, including the President and the King of England and John D. Rockefeller. Dotty had perhaps, he hoped, a little, at the end, loved Lieutenant Colonel Smithers—not a salesman for the Meredith Agency in La Harpe. How would she feel when she took a look at his house and saw the town's big shots being nice enough to him, but keeping their distance at the same time. Her old man was a rich lawyer; she was a society girl. Thinking this way, Dorothy Brock whom he had invented to warm his heart, whom he had longed for and trusted, became another girl and he lost her. He began to feel trapped, beating against an unseen destruction. It isn't true, he protested to himself, Dotty's not that way, Dotty's one of us. He could not bear to lose Dotty, too.

He could never go back to being the boy he was, the cheerful boy, getting ahead slowly and pleased with any small success. I've had everything, he thought, I am somebody now. I can't, I can't. Maybe that was why he didn't make close friends with more men. He could tell whether they were people like him, or better off than he. He didn't want the ones like him; he didn't want to be pushed back into what he came from. And the others, the ones you knew were brought up in wealthy homes and had everything their own way, well, you thought it might not work out just right. You didn't feel too sure. So in the end, he belonged nowhere; he wouldn't be any worse off in a foreign country.

Just about the only friend he had now was Levy. That seemed a funny idea, on the face of it, but he'd been with

Levy as much as with anyone and though they never really talked, Levy always seemed to know what was going on. Levy didn't ask questions or put in wise remarks but he would bet Levy knew about Dotty and understood about Bill. He'd like to see Levy again, after the war, and talk over the old days. He knew Levy wouldn't change, when he got out of uniform, and turn into some sort of show-off punk. Levy would be the same close-mouthed decent guy, all his life.

Then Lieutenant Colonel Smithers thought: that's all I'd need in La Harpe; meet my old war buddy, Jacob Levy. He could just see Mary Jane Cotterell and Elise Rathbone and Mrs. Merrill and that old snake-tongue Mrs. Buckley. Well, where had they been when Levy was at the war: driving their cars around La Harpe, visiting and gossiping, the same as always. Levy was a damn sight better American than they were. But he felt a little chilled, a little frightened; they'd laugh about it among themselves; Johnny Smithers brought a war friend home with him, name of Jacob Levy. . . .

Money, Lieutenant Colonel Smithers thought, that's all the hell it is. I'll get money if it kills me.

He looked at the distant mountains and they came nearer and they were the declaration of peace. And he thought, I ought to be blind happy it's almost over. He turned back longingly to the safety and the pride and the grandeur of Lieutenant Colonel Smithers, and he felt cold and sick as he imagined La Harpe and people saying to him with friendliness, "Hello, Johnny, good to see you home."

·   ·   ·   ·   ·   ·   ·   ·   ·   ·   ·

Jacob Levy had taken off his hot, unnecessary steel helmet and the pleasant spring wind lifted his hair. This was a marvelous feeling, the feeling of a free man who was through with helmets. Good comfortable sweat stuck his shirt to his back and he held the wheel with easy hands and forgot the Colonel and the convoy and Germany and the war. He was repeating the same stories and the same plans. He smiled as if Kathe were already here beside him and any minute he could lean close and put his arm around her.

The great mountains ahead were beautiful, but he was loyal to the Smokies. The mountains also meant the end of the war to him, and he looked at them with love, for when they reached them his life which had never started would start at last. As soon as the war was over he would send Kathe the letter. It was written and in his pocket. Sergeant Postalozzi wouldn't have wanted his dictionary anymore and if he ever saw the Sarge he would pay for the dictionary and explain why he needed to take it. He could not send the letter before the end of the war, because he had to be sure. But in his heart he was sure; he had come through things he never hoped to come through, and the Colonel and his luck were always there.

He had worked hard on the letter. His system had been to write it first in English and then look up the words in the dictionary, but his English letter was too complicated, so finally he made it short and direct: Cherie petite Kathe; Voulez vous epouser moi? Je revenir quand possible. Attendez pour moi. Je vous aime. He signed it Jawn, since that was the way Kathe said it. He had to sign it something, it wasn't really wrong to sign it Jawn, it was more like a nickname. Kathe could call him Jawn all their lives if she wanted to, it was only a nickname.

He had puzzled how to get this letter to her and then he

thought of Dotty. The Red Cross girls would get mail just like anyone in the army, and he could ask the Colonel, as soon as the war was over, for Dotty's address and he would enclose the letter to Kathe. Dotty would do this for him; even if she had left Luxembourg she could send the letter to the club there and ask one of the other girls to handle it. The Red Cross girls were supposed to do things like that for soldiers. So Kathe would know and she would wait.

He did not try to guess how long they would stay in Europe before they were shipped home but he knew the Colonel would give him a few days leave to go to Luxembourg City. The Colonel and he were friends now, they'd been together a long time, and he'd say how he wanted to marry Kathe and the Colonel would let him go. Then they'd get married in Luxembourg City because once you were married to a girl the army couldn't laugh it off. He imagined they'd go home on a troop ship the way they came but that was allright because Kathe would be his wife and an American and as soon as he got home he'd ask Poppa for the money and bring her over and go to New York himself to meet her.

Then they'd visit in St. Louis so Momma and Poppa could see her, but while he'd been waiting for Kathe to come, he'd already have got their piece of land by the stream, and he'd already have started building their shack. If it was good weather when Kathe landed, she could come and camp with him while he was finishing it; otherwise she could stay with Momma until he had a warm place fixed for her. And then they would live together in their own house.

Jacob Levy did not feel it was reckless to hope and plan this way. They hadn't killed him and he knew now that he would never get killed. He almost ought to be grateful to this war, for Kathe. And he would tell her he was a Jew and she would not mind, because he loved her so much. Where they were going to live it would not matter about being a Jew. There would be no one but Kathe and him, alone, with the clear, fast stream and the peaceful days, and their home to build, and their life. No one would envy them or hurt them; they would be happy.

It seemed to Jacob Levy that his whole life had been shadowy and pointless and always waiting for something bad to happen. Ever since the war began, he had been waiting for the worst, which was to die. And before that he had waited, in resignation, for the careless insults and the injustices that he inherited simply because of being born. But that was finished: Kathe stood between him and all pain. I'm alive, he thought, and from here on out, I'm going to have the finest life there is. He looked at the mountains with longing, for every mile brought him nearer to the beautiful future. It was only a question of days now, and the future would begin.

> *21* <

Jacob Levy had driven the jeep into a street like a grey canyon; high heavy apartment buildings rose on both sides. It was all stone, cold looking even in the spring sun. But it was in wonderful condition; behind the front walls there were still rooms and floors. Unlike the center of Munich, you could live here without expecting it to fall on you.

The Battalion was to take over this street.

"I got a hunch," Lieutenant Colonel Smithers said, "we won't be moving for a while."

The street was full of trucks, for Captain Huebsch's Company had already arrived. More trucks rumbled in, the street was not blocked but moving solidly with transport, with men. Signs went up on the outsides of the apartment buildings, wires were strung, the efficient apparently chaotic business of settling in had started.

"I'll take that one," Lieutenant Colonel Smithers said. There was no difference he could see between any of these hunks of grey cement.

He entered the musty hallway of the apartment building, and with Sergeant Hancock forced open the door of a first floor flat. They found a middle-class home: stiff matched furniture and hard uncomfortable chairs, all arranged like a doctor's waiting room; family photographs; vases holding dried grasses and gilded cattails; bookcases with locked glass doors and imposing leather-bound books; and scenic views in oils. Lieutenant Colonel Smithers had seen so many of these by now that he felt as if he were constantly returning to the same drab hotel room. There would be nothing a body could sit on, with pleasure.

"Major Hardcastle and I'll keep this one. I'll check the others."

The other apartments were so similar they might have been owned by the same family or furnished by the same furniture dealer.

"Set up the officers' mess on the second floor here, all Battalion officers," he instructed Sergeant Hancock. "I'll have my office on the first floor, for the telephone. Use the rest of the place as billets for the Battalion staff. Put Headquarters Company next door."

He went downstairs to find Major Hardcastle experimenting with a radio in the living room of their quarters. Major Hardcastle turned a dial and they heard American jazz.

"The AFN," Major Hardcastle said. "It's nice to have a radio that operates. How about the bathroom?" But that was too much to expect; the water did not run.

"I don't guess the water works anywhere," Major Hardcastle said. "We'll have a bad situation in this block, with the cans not working."

They went out to reconnoitre behind the apartment buildings and Lieutenant Colonel Smithers gave orders for latrines to be dug in all the back yards. "Got to get a good water point," he said.

"You act like we're going to stay here, Colonel."

"I got a hunch," Lieutenant Colonel Smithers said. "Man, what I wouldn't give for a bath." He had not had a bath since March in Major Havemeyer's apartment in Luxembourg, and it was now the beginning of May.

"Water and a shower unit," he said to Major Hardcastle.

He went into the apartment he had chosen, picked out the least painful of the chairs, found another for his feet, and sat down. He knew they would find him when they wanted to ask questions. There was the sign on the front door, which showed where he was. I can't get worked up anymore, Lieutenant Colonel Smithers thought, it's all over.

. . . .

Washing hung from twisted iron balconies at all the windows. The Battalion was cleaning up. Lieutenant Colonel Smithers had issued a general order to get the scum off everything. Men were standing in line at the mobile showers, scrubbing clothes in buckets and helmets, washing jeeps and trucks, cleaning rifles. The street was full of sun and the concentrated and not unjoyful effort of the soldiers to wash away five weeks of Germany. It was a nice day. It only lacked the voices of women, calling the things they did when they were cleaning a house. It did not lack children; towheaded little Germans had wandered in to stare, to fraternize, to beg for chocolate. The soldiers made the children welcome. It was a perfect day for peace to come.

It came, in the most unspectacular manner, after lunch over the radio.

Lieutenant Colonel Smithers was in his office; Jacob Levy had just asked whether he could take the jeep back to the Service Company because there was something wrong with the steering gear.

Peace was announced with not nearly as much excitement as goes into the advertising of breakfast food or hand lotion.

Lieutenant Colonel Smithers and Jacob Levy stared at each other.

"Did I hear right?" Lieutenant Colonel Smithers said softly.

They waited, not speaking. Peace was announced again.

Lieutenant Colonel Smithers and Jacob Levy laughed and shook hands and laughed some more and did not know what to do. Lieutenant Colonel Smithers went to the open first floor window and called to some soldiers in the street, "The krauts surrendered! Declaration of Peace!" The soldiers looked stunned. No one seemed to know how to take it. Some laughed and shook hands; realists talked of Japan and said it was too early to get excited; and others, suddenly seeing what the war had been because it was now ended, cursed without purpose, since they could find no other words to explain their feelings. By now the news had been shouted to the other apartment buildings and soon men were leaning from every window, whistling and cheering. The realists and the ones who felt cheated and baffled went away from the street so they could think of the peace, alone. The jovial fellows at the windows threw their caps down and then they threw toilet paper and shredded newspaper in imitation of the New York paper storms they had seen in newsreels.

Someone thought more noise would be better and started it off by throwing his helmet, which made a fine clanking sound, and followed this with a flower vase and a china teapot. This idea met with general approval and now men were throwing down anything that would break or rattle. A soldier decided this was still inadequate so he fired his rifle. Major Hardcastle rushed out of his office and arrested him, and presently the street became quiet again. Sergeant Hancock detailed men to sweep it up.

Lieutenant Colonel Smithers had shut his window. He felt an enormous relief, that he had never guessed he would feel, a great slow weight-lifted relief; and he felt tired.

"I guess we won, Levy," he said.

Jacob Levy could not look at the Colonel because his eyes were full of tears. He couldn't help it. This long hopeless journey was over, and he was alive. There were a lot of people alive. It had stopped in time. The world was going to be decent and people were going to live. The worst thing there could be, ever, anywhere, was over. This was the future; it had finally arrived, and from now on everyone had the chance of being happy. Well for Christ's sake if you're going to bawl, he thought, clear out of here.

"I'll get going, sir," Jacob Levy muttered.

Lieutenant Colonel Smithers had seen the shine in Levy's eyes and heard the hoarseness of Levy's voice. It made him feel ashamed to see Levy taking the peace like this, ashamed of his own doubts and dreads. There must be millions of guys like Levy, trying not to cry for happiness, guys aching sick crazy to get home.

.   .   .   .

The Battalion officers were celebrating the victory in the second floor mess and the sound of the celebration could be heard in the street. They had listened, on the radio, to accounts of celebrations happening in Paris and London and they meant theirs to be a good one too for they had certainly earned it. They brought whatever liquor they owned or could buy during the afternoon, to this rigid dining room, and all were drinking freely from their pooled resources. It sounded fine; it sounded lighthearted and triumphant the way you ought to be, at the victorious end of such a war. Yet there was something wrong with it. They had got drunk too fast and too intently; they were making almost too much noise. The noise covered a silence. For, out of those who started, only eight remained. No matter how they laughed and smashed glasses and took ringing pot shots at the chandelier with salt cellars and table napkins, no one could forget this. The party ended early, dwindling off into quietness.

Jacob Levy had just mailed his letter to Miss Dorothy Brock, with the letter enclosed for Miss Kathe Limpert. The soldiers were celebrating as and where and with whatever they could, due to the regulation which forbids liquor to be rationed to enlisted men. This forced them to acquire, at rare prices, the drink called everywhere in Europe cognac. Bert Hammer had heard of a hole in the rubble where a kraut sold cognac and they directed themselves to this place. They planned to get very drunk; no one was likely to celebrate a peace twice.

The hole in the rubble had once been a bakery. You entered through a blasted door and scrunched over the splintered and plaster-strewn floor and found a back room, airless, smoky, and full of soldiers drinking cognac from any sort of container.

Bert Hammer was excited and happy. "We ought to get up a snake dance or a torchlight parade," he said.

Jacob Levy agreed to this, but he was not interested. His own happiness was too private to share.

"I guess that's where you get a drink," Bert Hammer said.

They pushed through the crowded soldiers towards a door at the other end of the room. In front of this door, the proprietor had set up a bar which was a chipped mahogany sideboard from some wrecked dining room. The proprietor, a round-shouldered, glum, elderly man, wearing a cloth cap, came through the door and gave Jacob Levy and Bert Hammer two handleless white china cups. Inside these cups was a thick liquid looking like cough syrup.

Bert Hammer began to drink his cognac in short revolted swallows. With half a drink down, he was ready to consider this room. He still wanted to organize some form of celebration, like New Year's Eve or the Fourth of July, he thought, trying to find a suitable model. But the soldiers here did not look promising. A lot of them were drunk already, only they were not celebrating-drunk; they slumped against the walls or at the few rickety tables, in silence. Maybe the cognac was poison so it worked on them like that. If the stuff didn't make you sick right off, you could always be sure you'd wake up the next day with a pain like a corkscrew in your gut. The soldiers who were not drunk were talking loudly but not as Bert Hammer had imagined they would. If you could believe it, they were talking about the war, remembering this river, that town, a roadblock, a minefield. It seemed a pretty poor way to greet the peace.

Two soldiers edged in beside them and hammered with their fists on the sideboard.

"Kraut!" one of them shouted. "Move your fat ass out here and bring some cognac."

"I'd just as soon shoot him as pay him," the other said.

Jacob Levy recognized, on their sleeves, the patch of the 12th Division.

"Hey," he said, "we sort of lost you guys. Where you been?"

The two men turned. Bert Hammer noticed they had trouble focussing their eyes. This cognac must be the worst and quickest kind of poison.

"Dachau," the tall one with glasses said.

"Where's that?"

"Listen, brother," the tall one said with slow carefulness, "That's hell, that's where that is."

"We threw those S.S. bastards over the wire and we let the prisoners tear them apart," his friend said, swaying a little. "That's what we did. I seen one of our fellows kill one of them S.S. bastards just beating his brains out."

"Say, what is this?" Bert Hammer said. What kind of talk was this, for a night when you were supposed to be happy and dance in the streets and have a good time?

"It's about twelve miles from here," the man with glasses explained.

"It's the biggest one of these kraut death prisons," the other one said. "Believe me, you're goddam lucky you're here, is what I mean."

"And smell," the tall soldier said, "I still smell it."

Bert Hammer pulled at Jacob Levy's arm. This was not the way he intended to spend the first night of peace, glooming with two drunks who didn't have a cheerful word to say.

"Be seeing you guys," he said. Jacob Levy, who had scarcely listened to the conversation, followed him. He was willing to do whatever anyone wanted.

Bert Hammer found an empty space against the wall which was almost as good as finding a table.

"What's the matter with everybody?" Bert Hammer asked. "You'd think this was a funeral."

Even Jake wasn't behaving right; why didn't somebody get up enough pep to start something? He wished Marv Busch was here; he'd eat glass; Marv was the best one to have on a party. Suddenly Bert Hammer thought, with real surprise: Marv is dead. Goddamit, Marv was dead and Dan and Roy were shot up bad and the Sarge didn't have any legs.

"Here's to Victory," he said, without conviction.

"Here's to going home," Jacob Levy said.

"Now you're talking."

Bert Hammer finished his drink and shuddered. It was the worst cognac yet. Marv's dead, he thought. It counts now. We might as well go to our place and hit the sack. This is the most disappointing peace I ever saw.

Jacob Levy did not propose his last toast aloud. Here's to Kathe, he said, and our life. Then he drank his cognac as if it were good.

> *22* <

"IT's ABOUT twelve miles from here. Seems it's the biggest concentration camp the krauts had. You hear a lot of talk about it," Jacob Levy said. "It won't take more than a couple of hours, sir."

He wanted to be alone so he could talk with Kathe. And he wanted to be out in the country, to remind himself of what spring would be like by his stream. But he could not suggest to the Colonel that he be given time off for these purposes. He had been trying to invent some reasonable excuse for two days, when he remembered the 12th Division soldiers and their death camp. The Battalion had not liberated any such place; a death camp was legitimate business; everybody talked about them; you had a right to be curious. Anyhow it was the best scheme he could think of and he watched to see how the Colonel took it.

Lieutenant Colonel Smithers was not permitting his men to get the idea they were civilians, just because the war was over. He had tightened up on discipline the day after the celebration of victory, and he meant to keep them working until their backs broke, so they'd be too busy and tired to get in trouble. The war had only been over three days, and it felt like three months, or three years, and that was the way everybody acted. He did not know Levy was crazy about prisons, but everybody was coming up with cockeyed notions. He'd make an exception once, because Levy had earned a morning off and it wouldn't do any harm.

"Okay," he said. "I'll want you here at twelve."

"Thank you, sir. I could stop to see the Motor Sergeant on the way back." This would show the Colonel he had his mind on his work. "They didn't have time to go over the jeep right the other day. He says maybe it needs new pins."

This was the first time, since coming to Europe, that he had had a chance to get in the jeep and go off for his own pleasure. It was almost like getting into the car at home and going for a drive. I guess I ought to go to Dachau, he thought, the Colonel might ask me about it; he was tempted to take a risk and just mooch out into the country and lie under a tree. But he decided he better not pull a fast one like that on the Colonel.

Once he was out of Munich the road was nice, not crowded and with a respectable hard surface. This was sweet country, rolling away in cultivated fields. I got to learn a lot, Jacob Levy thought, about crops and vegetables and all. High lacy trees, whose names he did not know, stood up from the green fields. The farmers must have thought they were too pretty to cut down. The wind blew them about gently, as he remembered the wind blowing his silver-leafed trees by the stream. And there were flowers growing in the fields, round fresh specks of pink and white and yellow. The farmhouses looked very fine to him; his own shack wouldn't be a big white place with a red tile roof. For a moment he resented these krauts who had better houses than he had, then he forgot this. Let them have their houses; he had plenty of luck of his own.

I'd like to stop right here, Jacob Levy thought, and the hell with Dachau. Across a green wheat field, he saw a double row of poplars and sun shone on the narrow band of water flowing between them. He wanted to make himself comfortable under those trees and think of home. If I hurry, he decided, I bet I can see plenty in a half hour to tell the Colonel about it and afterwards I could come back. He located the poplars in his memory because there was a building here with Gasthaus in gold letters over the door. Then he pushed the jeep to an almost legal forty, so he could get to Dachau quickly and finish with it.

It was no distance at all. He had been wondering whether you had to go to school to learn about farming and fish hatcheries, or maybe you picked it up as you went, like combat, and suddenly there was a big black and white placard at the side of the road, saying Dachau. He had imagined something like Sing Sing in the movies, but Dachau was a little village with sharp-roofed houses, and the krauts all leaning over their front gates and gossiping together in the sun. The women looked clean and bright, compared to the tattered women of Italy and the dingy women in the villages of France. Of course it was spring and that made a difference, but these women wore good clothes, for Europe.

[269]

The houses had window boxes with flowers, and flowers in the yards, and the windows shone like diamonds, with starched curtains behind the polished glass. The bombers had not troubled this place: it didn't seem as if the war had bothered them any way. They were well-off, lucky people; they'd had it easy. He could not speak German and he did not know how to ask for this prison but he thought if it was so big it would show up by itself. Then he saw, from the main road, a group of buildings and a high wall and he turned his jeep from the sunlit prosperous street, and found himself driving alongside the wall.

Behind the wall were square cement houses, painted grey. They looked very pleasant with trees all around them, and Jacob Levy thought: I don't figure that's a bad prison. Farther on, there was a gate and much traffic milling about the sentry box. There were too many officers. He parked his jeep opposite a red brick apartment which was full of soldiers, and hoped he would see his 12th Division friends of V-E night coming out of the building. He waited a few minutes and decided this would not get him anywhere. He was wasting time; the morning would not last forever; so he walked across the street and opened conversation with the sentry, standing outside the arched prison gate.

"How about getting in here, Mac?" he asked. He had noticed a great deal of paper being flourished around: passes. The army couldn't do a thing without a ton of papers. Behind the gate he saw a sunny yard, a big white stone building, and trees. It looked like a pretty good prison to him; those 12th Division guys were just drunk and shooting a line.

"Wait a sec," the sentry said. Jacob Levy moved off and lighted a cigarette.

Presently the sentry beckoned to him and he came over and the sentry said, "That slob of a Major we got is running this place like he was working for the Nazis. Two days ago he turned away some correspondents. The war's over, for Christ's sake, and anyhow they ought to let people go in there." The sentry seemed like the serious type, pretty old too, maybe thirty. "They ought to see what the krauts did to those Jews."

Jacob Levy's eyelids flickered; he looked at the sentry and saw he was not a Jew. "Is that what they got in there?"

"Jews? Sure, I guess so. That's what they look like. That's who Hitler wanted to bump off."

Jacob Levy stood aside as the sentry saluted two captains, walking past with brief cases under their arms. These captains carried more fat and had smoother faces than Jacob Levy was accustomed to seeing on officers. They must be that new kind, the military government ones.

"You want to get in?"

"Yeh," Jacob Levy said. He felt nervous now, and strange. He did want to get in and he would have given anything never to have come here. This was what he had heard about, and now he was going to see it: what Hitler did to the Jews.

"Wait till these guys get through."

The place was overrun with indoor officers. He certainly didn't want to tangle with them about not having a pass.

"Now get on in, and turn to your right the other side of a big brick building. You'll see the barbed wire. They stop you and dust you for typhus first but the soldiers there'll let you in allright. If you run into some snoopy officer, say you have a message for Sergeant Sweeny, he's inside there somewhere. Tell him Harold sent you. The Sarge is okay."

"Thanks, Mac." Jacob Levy walked fast across the prison

yard, keeping his eye out for brief-case captains. Above all, he didn't want to get in trouble and be delayed, and lose his morning under the trees. He turned right as instructed and saw at the end of the prison street the high barbed wire fence, and behind it, dimly, a mass of greyish people. Then he was at the gate, beneath a watch tower, opening his shirt and unbuttoning the top of his trousers, and getting sprayed with DDT against typhus.

"This'll give you a nice itch later on, when you start to sweat," the soldier with the spray-gun said. "But don't let it worry you. If you get any lice, after what I've done to you, I hear you don't take more'n three days to die."

"Thanks, pal," Jacob Levy said. Then he was through the gate.

He started to turn and go back. But the entry in the barbed wire was blocked with a bunch of medics getting the DDT treatment and he couldn't push past them without calling attention to himself and probably being asked for his pass. Maybe it was the feeling of the barbed wire, the prison feeling, that alarmed him; maybe it was the thought of typhus; and maybe it was the prisoners. Either their faces were floating before him in the sun, or he could not force himself to look straight at them. They moved about in a way that was almost like crawling even if they were walking, slow and aimless and sick. Their eyes were all the same: too big, black and empty. There was no recognition or curiosity or anything in those eyes, just sick dead eyes in yellow or grey faces. Their bodies moved, without reason, as there was nowhere to go; and they stared at him. He had never imagined people could look like this.

They were all bald, too. No, their heads were shaved and

the skin was so tight on the bone they seemed like bare skulls. Their teeth were rotten, with black holes where teeth were missing. You almost saw the grey striped rags that covered them, creeping with lice. Jesus, their hands were enormous too, or maybe it was only because their wrists were thin as sticks. Jacob Levy stood, feeling the sweat come out on his face, and stared back at them: thousands of starved mindless men, weaving in the sunshine. Some of them sat on the ground and from time to time scratched themselves.

He had no pity for these men: he had only fear. He was afraid of them, afraid of everything they showed in their eyes and their dragging bodies. He was paralyzed with fear.

A little grey man drifted up to Jacob Levy, like a piece of paper blowing along a gutter. The little man did not seem to have a body; he was a bundle of rags that walked. His eyes had a look of intelligence in them: the intelligence was bitter and cold and not at all human.

"Shall I help you please?" he said.

Jacob Levy wanted to brush this man away, he did not want to stay here talking with anyone. He could not think of an answer. Help me how? he wondered.

"Shall I show you? At your service, sir." He had a muted soft voice. Perhaps people talked like that in their sleep.

Jacob Levy followed the little man; at least he had a plan, this place did not freeze him to one spot. They passed through the still or swaying bodies; and Jacob Levy did not look at them. He looked at his feet. The crowded prison yard was as quiet as if it were empty; occasional voices seemed to come from some other place. They were American voices.

"My name is Heinrich, sir," the little man said, stopping at the door of a long discolored wood building.

"Levy," he murmured and shook hands. He supposed it was the right thing to do. The little man's hand was as small as a child's, and bony and cold.

"This is the infirmary of the prison," Heinrich announced. They went into a hallway that was fairly clean to look at and smelled more horrible than any place Jacob Levy had yet been. The smell of these bodies was not dirt, it was decay. Down the hallway, in silent patience, the prisoners sat waiting to see the doctor. No doctor could do anything for them. Jacob Levy held his breath to keep out this smell.

Heinrich led him into what looked like a doctor's office; there were cabinets against the walls and a few medical instruments. You could guess anyhow what the place was meant for. A doctor in a white jacket was bending over a man, seated on a chair. The man himself did not look at the doctor; he seemed to be absent. There were great sores on the man's legs. The doctor said something and the man rose, slowly, and shuffled away.

Heinrich effected the introductions. The doctor smiled politely. His smile amazed Jacob Levy as if the man had hit him. A smile seemed impossible here. The doctor too had intelligent eyes; like Heinrich's, his intelligence had grown so bitter and so weary that it made his eyes cold.

"The doctors here are all Polish," Heinrich explained. "The Nazis put them here because they wish to finish the Pole peoples. They attacked the educated mens."

The doctor did not look like a Jew, but how did he know what a Polish Jewish doctor would look like. The doctor was a little fatter than the others; in ordinary life, the doctor would have seemed a very thin man. Anyhow, there were not cavities like wounds where his cheeks were meant to be; his hands did not strike you as deformed. He had more hair on his head; it was grey as his skin was. Something about the way the doctor held himself impressed Jacob Levy. He took off his cap and stretched out his hand.

"Glad to meet you, Doctor."

"I speak not so much English," the doctor said.

"You would like to know of the experiments, sir?" Heinrich asked.

The door opened and a man came in; he was as tall as Jacob Levy, and weighed possibly ninety pounds; his knees, showing in the gaps of a khaki blanket, looked big and gnarled on the dirty stalks of his legs. He wore, as clothing, this blanket like a shawl, and a pair of unlaced black boots. He stood staring about him with wild reddened eyes, and then he began to cry. He babbled something, and clutched his blanket around him. The doctor smiled. My God, Jacob Levy thought, the doctor's crazy. The doctor smiled with a remote hopeless indifference, and spoke to the man. The man went on crying. The doctor called some words in Polish, and turned back to Jacob Levy.

"Aren't you going to do something for him?" Jacob Levy asked. They could give this awful thing a chair to sit on, before he died standing there.

"He will be fine," the doctor said and responded to the anger in Jacob Levy's face by making some explanation in German to Heinrich.

"The doctor says this one comes from the last death transport. You know the Americans dug these peoples out. It was on the tracks for the peoples to die. This one lived. Now his brain is not very good. The doctor says in two or three weeks he will be better."

Jacob Levy heard the words without understanding them. "How old is he?"

Another doctor or assistant in a white jacket had come in, received orders in Polish, and was now leading the blanket-draped man away. Heinrich asked a question; the Polish assistant repeated it; the man in the blanket mumbled something. He had stopped crying; his voice sounded so weak that Jacob Levy was sure he would faint before he crossed the room.

"Twenty-two," Heinrich said. "If you come in the operating room, the doctor will show you."

Twenty-two, Jacob Levy thought. He had thought it was an old man of sixty. His hair was matted and filthy but there was grey in it; his beard had hardly grown on the waxen skin of the face; it looked like the wispy hair of the very old. Jacob Levy followed the doctor and Heinrich into an operating room. In his experience of hospitals, he had never seen an operating room as bare as this. They kept it clean, but they had nothing to work with. There was a table, and some cabinets, almost empty. Where was the lamp, where was all the stuff he remembered? He waited for the smell of ether. There was no smell of ether. He needed to sit down, and when Heinrich saw him looking for a chair, he brought one. The others stood. I can't sit down if they're standing, Jacob Levy thought.

"Here is where they do the castrations," Heinrich stated in his amiable dead voice. He sounded like a guide, too. "All who touch German womens, gypsies, Polish priests and Jews."

What's he talking about, Jacob Levy thought, does he mean on live men? It couldn't be; he didn't believe it.

"These Polish doctors do not make such operations. But they have the record."

A big book was thrust before Jacob Levy. They pulled his chair to the operating table and made inviting gestures for him to sit down. They opened the book and gathered around the table to watch him; Heinrich and the doctor and the two younger men, also Polish it would seem from their talk, also in white coats, also with inquisitive yet lifeless faces. The book appeared to be a neat accountant's ledger. It was full of the names and ages of men whom the German doctors had mutilated.

"Yeh," Jacob Levy said. Unaware of having moved, his hand slid down to protect himself. In Italy, that was why the guys were so scared of mines; they were scared they'd catch it there. It had happened to two men he knew and afterwards he only wanted to forget about them; it was the very worst; it was the oldest, deepest fear. But to do it to men on purpose, to have it done to you in an operating room: Christ! shooting was too good for those Nazi doctors. He wished Heinrich wouldn't stand so close. Heinrich smelled like the people in the hall, though not so strong. He wished they wouldn't all look at him the way they did. What were they waiting for? He was damned if he was going to show them how sick he felt.

The doctor watched with that polite smile; his cold eyes watched to see how an outsider would receive news from this world of darkness where they all lived. For years he had watched the Nazi doctors, seeing the operations, the implanting of disease, the experiments. He could do nothing except keep a record for the future, if there was a future. He had accepted the torment and humiliation of his own body, but he feared madness. If he went insane he would be taken away with those who raved and those who stumbled, the ones no longer useful to the Nazis as work animals. And though he did not want to live, he did not want to die as the Nazis made men die. The prisoners, knowing he was like them and their friend, turned to him as the sick had a right to turn to the doctor charged with their healing. And he could not help them. He had come to dread this welcome in the eyes of the prisoners; it reminded him of what he once had been, and the honorable practise of a profession he loved. Finally he had learned to observe everything, dispassionate as the dead. He had not spoken to the American camp commandant about leaving Dachau, or trying to find his family if he still had a family. He had not tried to change anything. He lived because it was a habit. Meanwhile there was some interest in studying these newcomers.

Heinrich, speaking with a grey unexcited contempt, went on to tell of the experiments which killed hundreds and hundreds of prisoners in vats of freezing water or strangled them in airless boxes, and Jacob Levy listened, unable to make sense of what he was hearing. He looked at the doctor and the two assistants and Heinrich, and they frightened him, they had seen too much, they couldn't be right in their heads. Then like a repeating victrola record, Heinrich started to explain it all over again. Heinrich checked himself, and his eyes blinked with doubt, as if he too wondered about his sanity. The doctor stood by, smiling.

"Shall I show you the boxes where the prisoners collapsed their lungs, sir?" Heinrich asked.

"No!" He had not meant to shout at them. What did

Heinrich have to bring him here for? If Heinrich hadn't grabbed him, he'd have been away long ago.

"Tell the doctor it was very interesting. I got to be going, I got to get back to my unit."

He stood up and shook hands with the three men in white jackets, and Heinrich said, "This way, sir," and led him into the evil smelling hall where the prisoners still waited on their chairs. They walked back through the prison yard and Jacob Levy watched his feet again, fearing those faces. Then he raised his head, and saw a group of women standing on the steps of a brown weatherbeaten barracks.

"They had women here?" he said.

"At the end, they bring some womens from other camps. Auschwitz, Ravensbruck." They had walked towards the women as they spoke.

The women looked at Jacob Levy silently and he looked at them. They wore rags of dresses, not prison uniforms, rags of flowered cotton and faded silk and torn woolen suits. Some had kept their hair combed and curled as best they could, clinging still to what they remembered of themselves. They had numbers tattooed on their arms. They seemed younger than the men and he could not understand why several of them were so repulsively bloated. You could not feel them as women. They were different animals from the ones in the prison yard, but not people.

A woman began to speak, then many spoke. They crowded around him. One of them plucked at him lightly like a beggar asking alms and then many touched him. Jacob Levy was seized with panic; he had to force himself not to raise his arm to push them away from him.

[279]

Heinrich tried to soothe the women. He translated pieces of their talk for Jacob Levy. "Poor womens," he said, "She says they will not let her die in the gas chamber with her sister, they kick her to let go and they take her sister . . . she says they broke her arms, yes, see, they are not straight; they did not heal . . . she says please help them, please help them . . ."

"I can't," Jacob Levy said. "What can I do?" He pulled money from his pocket and offered it to the women and they stopped talking and stood back from him. "Tell them to buy themselves something."

"There is nothing to buy. I do not know what they want. To go home, I think."

"Tell them the Army will take them home as soon as they can."

The women seemed quieter, hearing this. One of them smiled.

"Good luck," Jacob Levy said, and then he thought it sounded not only foolish but mean, as if he didn't know there wasn't any luck for them.

They waved, when he walked away. At a distance, when you could not see their faces and bodies clearly, they made a piece of attractive bright color in that grey place.

Heinrich had led him to another building; he was helpless in the hands of this insistent little man. He seemed to have no will any more, only a futile desire to escape.

"Here is the nacht und nebel," Heinrich said. "This is where the prisoners are put who must die alone. Secretly, so no one knows. I never understand the Nazis. If they want the mens to die why do they not shoot them? They shoot us every day. Shoot, gas, starve, beat; many ways. But here they have a special house for special people and they make them die slowly. I do not understand." He shrugged his shoulders, as if he had been speaking of a foible of strangers which was not worth discussion.

The hallway was long and narrow, broken by small thick wooden doors. The building was silent and apparently empty; it smelled clean, but there was still a prison smell about it. Heinrich led the way down the hall; he seemed eager and almost gay. Jacob Levy heard his own feet scraping on the cement floor. At the end of the hall, Heinrich said, "Look at this, sir."

Jacob Levy saw a small plain windowless closet. "What about it?"

"This is the punishment. Eight mens in here; see how little is the room? Eight mens stand up close together, touching each other, in the darkness. Is a little air from the top. Water to drink once a day. Cannot move. The filth, you can think of the filth. Two days, four days. The prisoners become crazy and then they are taken out."

Heinrich was smiling a little, nervously or apologetically. The American soldier could not understand what this prison meant; and perhaps he did not even believe what he, Heinrich, was saying; perhaps he thought this closet was stupid and not interesting or Heinrich had made it up. Heinrich had stood in the closet three years ago; he did not remember why or what he was supposed to have done; even now, looking at it, a kind of darkness passed over his mind. But the good young Americans, how would they understand? Heinrich suddenly felt ashamed, because all he had to show, the only world he knew, was this place. He had no other life and no other knowledge; he knew that he could not live anywhere now because in his mind, slyly, there was nothing but horror. He wanted the others to know; the sane, the healthy, the free; he wanted to infect them with his pain, or what had been pain. Now he had no feeling but he wanted them to know. They could never know; no one could know; you had to suffer it to know.

A woman's voice, behind them in the hall, rose from a groan into a high single screaming note. The scream stopped; the hall was perfectly silent; then the voice repeated itself, and the unendurable high note rang between the cement walls.

"Christ!" Jacob Levy said. "What is that? Why doesn't somebody do something? They're killing her!" He started to run down the hall.

Heinrich followed him; he could not run. Jacob Levy was trying to trace this voice. Heinrich went to a door and opened the sentry-slot in it.

"Here, sir," he said.

Jacob Levy saw a woman, thin, of no age, perhaps thirty or twenty or forty, with dark hair fallen across her face and down her shoulders, half kneeling and half lying on a cot in the corner of one of the solitary cells. She was silent now. Then the scream started again in a groan; and slowly she began to beat her head against the wall.

"Get a doctor! Can't you see she's killing herself?"

"Sir," Heinrich said, "she is crazy in her head. You see that. She comes with the other womens from their camps and now her brain has gone. It happens always, every day, sometimes many. What shall anyone do? She will die soon; it is the best."

Jacob Levy turned on Heinrich; he was alive wasn't he; he seemed to be doing allright; why couldn't he hustle around for somebody else; he seemed to take everybody else's troubles pretty lightly.

"How long have you been here?" he asked with suspicion.

"Twelve years."

"They had this place going twelve years?"

"I am one of the earliest," Heinrich said. "I am a Social Democrat. Here I have book-keeping work, I can sit down, I am lucky. I do not even remember what is Social Democrat politics. The food is so little, you see. The memory goes away from you. I try for two years to remember if my mother is dead; I cannot remember. It is funny."

They were all crazy. Now the woman took a rasping breath and began the patient insane scream.

"Let's get out of here, for God's sake!" Heinrich was so slow too, moved slow, talked slow, thought slow. Let everybody hurry; burn the place down would be best; send the people to real hospitals and pour gasoline on the buildings and burn it down now; quick, fast, so nothing would be left.

But he was lost, in the jumble of brown wooden buildings, and the crowds of grey prisoners. He did not know where the main gate was, and Heinrich said, "Yes sir, I take you out the quick way," and walked with infuriating slowness along a path, between the barracks.

"No no sir," Heinrich said, "you must not go that way, there is the barracks where all have typhus. We must stay here."

They now passed a beautifully arranged vegetable garden. Heinrich pointed to it. "Food for the officers. You see, over the trees in the big houses." Jacob Levy realized these were the backs of the grey, tree-shrouded houses he had seen beyond the outside wall. That was when I figured it looked like a pretty good prison, he thought.

"Very fine garden," Heinrich said, "See also the fine glass house for flowers. The Nazis love flowers. We work, they beat us, then they take home the lovely flowers to the lovely wife." Heinrich's airy colorless voice seemed never to stop. Jacob Levy had begun to hate him. He was doing this on purpose. They didn't have to walk all around the camp to reach the gate. Heinrich led him under a grove of pine trees; a big factory chimney rose above the trees.

"We stop here a little instant on the way for the gate," Heinrich said innocently.

Then they were on it, and Jacob Levy could not turn back. He could not, in front of this man who had lived here for twelve years, break and run.

On the right was the pile of prisoners, naked, putrefying, yellow skeletons. There was just enough flesh to melt and make this smell, in the sun. The pile was as high as a small house. On the left was a mound of S.S. troopers, dressed in their black uniforms, and looking like giants compared to the faggots of the Dachau dead. Alongside the low brick building were two big mastiffs.

"Their dogs," Heinrich explained. "They had many. We killed them all."

Jacob Levy followed Heinrich in silence. They entered a whitewashed room. Heinrich pointed out a square grille in the wall, a ventilator, you might think, but not exactly. "The gas comes from there," Heinrich said. Jacob Levy had his handkerchief over his mouth and nose, his eyes were stinging with the smell. He followed again, into the other side of the building. A disorder of bodies spread over the floor. "They had not time to burn these," Heinrich said, and showed Jacob Levy the great ovens, like old fashioned bakers' ovens. Jacob Levy could not take the handkerchief from his mouth and he was glad, because that way he did not have to talk. He was trying not to gag on the smell, and he hoped Heinrich would not notice. If he can take it, Jacob Levy thought, I can. But waves of heat flushed over his body and he felt sweat trickling down his cheeks. He couldn't let Heinrich see, that was all, that was what he had to do; keep going, and not let Heinrich know.

"It makes many ashes," Heinrich said, and gestured with his hand. "The ashes fall in the lovely gardens of the lovely wives and make the house dirty." Then he walked around to the back of the building, and Jacob Levy saw the neatly sorted prisoners' clothes, trousers in one pile, jackets in another, boots in another. "Can be used again, always," Heinrich said. "They take out the teeth for the gold fillings before they bring here the bodies, and also at the end cut off the womens' hair for the mattresses . . ."

"Get me out of here, God damn you!" Jacob Levy shouted, and suddenly Heinrich changed, and became a man used to threats, small and wary and quiet, waiting inside an old fear.

"Yes sir," he said, and started to move quickly along the path under the trees, past the vegetable garden, towards the prison yard. Jacob Levy caught up with him and saw the white sweating face, and heard the little man sobbing for breath.

"Heinrich," he said, "slow down. I'm sorry I said that. Take it easy, Heinrich."

"Yes sir," the little man said, but fear and wariness stayed in his eyes. At the gate he shook hands, keeping his head lowered. There was a clammy sweat on his face and his breath did not come easily; he could not move that fast. Jacob Levy offered him money and Heinrich declined it with thanks; then Jacob Levy pressed a package of cigarettes into his hand, and turned and stepped outside the barbed wire fence before the little man could return the cigarettes too. Jacob Levy forced himself not to run down the prison street to the main gate. As he passed, the sentry called, "How'd you like it, Mac?"

> *23* <

But Jacob Levy could not speak; he shook his head and walked through the gate, just not running. He forgot he had parked his jeep across the street, and walked fast along the wall, trying to put distance between himself and the sight and smell of that place. The smell went with him, he thought he could taste it. He felt it sticky and oozing and thick, on his hands, his clothes, his hair. He would have been warned of what he was walking into, had he not thought the smell went with him.

Then he turned a corner and found the street blocked by a long line of freight cars, with a sandy path beside them and feathery, newly green trees shading the path.

A train was being unloaded. The freight cars looked like any others; most of them were low open coal cars, there were perhaps ten box cars. The civilians, doing the unloading, wore masks over their faces, made of colored bandanas or white handkerchiefs. Also their clothes were unusual for working people; they seemed to have come here dressed for their everyday occupations, as if they'd had no time to change. Jacob Levy stared at a fat bald man wearing gold rimmed glasses, a stiff-collared shirt, black trousers and grey spats. Beyond these civilians, American soldiers, masked and therefore expressionless, policed the job with tommy guns. There were twelve of them, the length of the fifty car train, standing as far back under the trees as they could. No one spoke. The unloading went on in such silence that Jacob Levy could hear the flies buzzing over the train's cargo.

Bodies were handed down by a man standing in a freight car to a man standing on the path beside it. Open trucks, parked alongside the train, received these bodies; the trucks were now about three quarters full. There were also men with shovels, for the decomposing bodies nearest the floor could not always be lifted. A middle-aged German in a dark business suit threw a limp stinking bundle to another man, standing below him: the long hair of the woman caught on the buttons of his left sleeve. He cursed and tried to disentangle it. Below him, the other man said, "Was ist los? Mach' schnell!" in a voice of simple irritation.

Jacob Levy turned and started to run back the way he had come. He passed the corner out of sight of the train: the smell of the dead was everywhere. He coughed and stood still and vomited. He steadied himself against the wall and went on vomiting. Then he groped along the wall that hid the fine grey houses. On the other side of the houses were the ovens and the gas chamber. If you didn't get around to gassing them, you could pack them into freight cars. They would die allright, look at them. Or maybe one man was in a box car so he wouldn't die of exposure, and he fought his way to a crack where he'd get enough air, and lived because he was young and had once been strong; but then he went crazy afterwards. If the woman screamed enough, she would die; maybe the man in the blanket would start to scream soon. Or he might even get well and then he could sit in the prison yard with the others who had no place to go.

They were people, Jacob Levy thought, they lived somewhere. They were real people like anybody else. Like Poppa and Momma. He leaned against the wall and rested his head on his folded arms. The ground was moving under his feet; he felt cold. He pressed his forehead hard against his arms.

I never thought about them except it was pretty tough on them and they should of left Europe long ago. I never knew. They had their lives and their friends the same as me. They went to work and came home like Poppa and there'd be a wife there fussing around the house and trying to make things nice. They weren't bad; nobody said they did anything wrong. They were born. What gave these krauts a right to say who should be born and who shouldn't, and who could live and be let alone, and who would get caught and killed? What gave them a right to gang up and murder poor people who lived like everybody else and did no harm and only wanted their kids to have it good and go to college and get a start and have some fun? I never knew; I thought those goddam krauts had to fight like we did and I thought these weasling kraut civilians were sort of stupid and pretty yellow besides. I never thought; I never thought about anything. I went along and tried to keep out of trouble and make the best of it. And all the time this was happening. They were murdering people for nothing. For nothing, for nothing, for nothing. For being Jews. Who did they hurt? What did they do to anybody? I didn't hate the krauts. I didn't have the sense. I thought they must be pushed into it, like us, by whoever decides those things. And who caught all those poor people and who ran the train and who guarded the prison and who did the beating and the starving and the gassing and the burning in the ovens? That wasn't any big shots did that dirty work. That was krauts, just everyday krauts like anybody you'd meet on the street. And I hoped I didn't mush up that bastard's legs. I hoped he wouldn't have to go around like the Sarge. You had to kill them or they'd kill you but I didn't hold anything against them except that. And they knew; they knew about Dachau. They were here. By God, they must of liked it or they'd of stopped it. They must of laughed when they saw all those dumb Jews waiting around to get killed. Heinrich said they took the gold fillings. They wouldn't even shoot people and make it quick; they fixed it so everyone died slow, the longest hardest way, so you'd know every minute you were dying and every minute would twist in you. They're worse than murderers; they're something you couldn't ever have heard about. They're the dirtiest lowest things on earth, and they're getting away with it. The people are dead and the krauts are all over the place, acting friendly and not saying what they'd really done. They wouldn't say, not them. They'd murder the people and talk nice afterwards. They'd lie and say they didn't do it. But the people are here, you can smell them till you choke on it. The people didn't have a chance; there were too many krauts; they got caught slow whenever the krauts felt like it and killed slow. I hope to Christ I mushed his legs. And what did that count? One. When they should all pay for this, all the time they lived. Momma has black hair too, long black hair.

And I was only scared of getting hit a third time, Jacob Levy told himself, in terrible judgement.

Now he walked without plan and found his jeep and started it and drove back through the village, guided by memory. He was making a hiccoughing sound but he did not hear it. He held his arms straight before him, as if he were trying to push the steering wheel against the dashboard. The jeep lurched in and out of a pothole which he had not noticed, and a boy whistled shrilly to a dog who had run barking into the street and now slunk fast away from the left front wheel. The jeep had always belonged to him, he managed it as easily as his body, but he did not seem to feel it anymore or to remember his own old skill. His mouth tasted bitter and dirty and his teeth were clamped together over the words that shouted in his mind. My mother has long black hair, my mother has long black hair. He drove, blind and jolting, down the clean prosperous street where the Germans went about their business in the sun. Two men tipped their hats and stopped to exchange politenesses at a front gate. A woman called to her child who arrived, pig-tails bouncing, and departed again on some errand. Two girls walked along the pavement; they must have been discussing clothes, because the brunette paused and pulled her skirt to one side and held it so draped while the other considered this style. The shorter one carried a loaf of bread and a string sack with vegetables in it. Everyone looked healthy and occupied and cheerful. No one turned to watch the single American soldier driving his jeep in that erratic fashion along their street. No one remarked the set white face of the soldier, and the strange stare of his eyes.

Two blocks ahead, a group of civilians stood almost in the

middle of the street. As Jacob Levy drove closer he saw there was a man holding a bicycle and three other men and two women. He honked his horn. The road was wide. The Germans looked in the direction of the oncoming jeep, but did not move. There was plenty of room to pass them. They were talking together eagerly and they were laughing.

Jacob Levy saw them as he had seen no one in his life before. They strutted there, proud and strong as if they owned the world. Their bodies boasted how fat they were. The grinning pink faces dared him to bother them. They didn't have to move for anyone. They'd gotten away with it. Laughing, he thought, laughing out loud in the street to show me.

The people in the freight cars must have screamed a long time before they died. When the wind was right, the ashes from the chimney must have blown down this way. Not a mile away, not even a mile. They knew, they didn't care, they *laughed*. Hate exploded in his brain. He felt himself sliding, slipping. It was hard to breathe. He held his fist on the horn and pressed his foot until the accelerator touched the floor. At sixty miles an hour, Jacob Levy drove his jeep on to the laughing Germans.

> *24* <

Major Gordon Jarvis slumped even lower in his chair; he was now almost lying on his neck. Fine manners, Lieutenant Colonel Smithers thought, you can certainly tell these fat cats from Division. Major Jarvis held out a package of Camels and Lieutenant Colonel Smithers shook his head in refusal, because he disapproved of Major Jarvis' behavior. You would never get the impression from Major Jarvis that this was Lieutenant Colonel Smithers' office.

"Of course," Major Jarvis went on, breathing out smoke, "he mucked himself up pretty thoroughly too. His nose will need plastic surgery to make it look like a nose again. He almost tore off his left cheek and he knocked out a lot of teeth."

Major Jarvis talked as if he were going to fall asleep. That voice and that way of talking infuriated Lieutenant Colonel Smithers; it sounded like a Limey to him. Any mustache was foolish but a bushy blond one like that was a plain copy of those Limey officers who carried handkerchiefs in their cuffs. Pretty sure of himself, this lawyer character, Lieutenant Colonel Smithers thought.

"And two broken ribs and a broken shoulder and a compound fracture of the left arm and a fractured skull. He was lucky at that," Major Jarvis finished.

Lieutenant Colonel Smithers said nothing. Sun poured in the windows, shining on the glass doors of the bookcase and on the gilded cattails.

"I think he must have taken his hands off the wheel and closed his eyes. I don't see how he could have bucked that tree, otherwise."

There were many things Lieutenant Colonel Smithers wanted to ask, but they would not take shape in his mind. For eight days he had had Division and Regiment on his neck, about Levy. You'd think Levy was a secret weapon, so many people were stewing around in this business. If only I'd got there first, Lieutenant Colonel Smithers thought, I'd have hushed it up somehow. No one could hush it up now. Even the General knew about it. And Colonel O'Neal and the Chief of Staff and the Judge Advocate and the Provost Marshal and anyone else you wanted to name. He'd had a fine time trying to explain how Levy happened to go off alone in the jeep in the first place. The only person who was not talking was Levy. It seemed that Levy wouldn't open his mouth; either he didn't care what became of him or he was too sick to notice. So the Chief of Staff appointed this fancy G-4 type as Levy's defense counsel, and whenever Levy was well enough to walk they would hold a general court. He couldn't do anything about it now. The law had moved in.

"One of the surgeons told Levy that he needn't worry about his face. He said he'd fix up his nose so that Levy would be delighted with it. Levy said he didn't see any reason to bother. He expects to hang."

The word "hang" produced a knot in Lieutenant Colonel Smithers' stomach.

"I wouldn't have believed any man in my Battalion would be up for manslaughter," he said. "He might have killed one of the women, just as easy." This is where I came in, Major Jarvis thought; opening gambit, now repeated by the gallant Colonel. If Jacob Levy had not said, with difficulty through the bandages, "I don't want to cause the Colonel trouble. The Colonel's a fine man," he would not have stayed here more than five minutes.

"Well, there it is," Major Jarvis said. "I didn't have much success, talking to him. I saw him for the first time yesterday and I suppose that cracked skull isn't helping him to think. I tried to explain that the charge is manslaughter but he believes he committed murder and he sticks to it. He understood I was his defense counsel so he loosened up a little and I made him promise not to discuss his case with anyone else. The point being, if he'll keep quiet and let me plead not guilty for him, I know I could get him off. He won't touch it."

"What does he say?"

"He says that he regrets he didn't have a machine gun instead of a jeep. He also says that he is sorry the war is over because if the war were not over he could volunteer to operate a flame thrower. He said that he only killed one German in the war; being a jeep driver he didn't have a chance at them. That's the sort of thing he says."

"That's crazy talk."

"He doesn't sound crazy."

"I never knew Levy was like that. You couldn't have wanted a steadier man in combat. I always used to tell Bill Gaylord, that was my S-2, how solid Levy was. He never showed a thing. We all thought a lot of Levy."

Major Jarvis ignored these remarks, which he found both irrelevant and irritating.

"I haven't gone into this enough yet, but I understand there was something wrong with the steering gear of the jeep?" Major Jarvis said.

"The Motor Sergeant said maybe it needed new pins."

"It's broken now, all right. The pins sheared off, the jeep went out of control, Levy ran into a tree because he couldn't stop. That's the way it looked to me, straight off, and I know I can make a sound case out of it. No court would imagine a man smashed himself up on purpose. He was going too fast but we'll think up a reason. With that, and his record, I'd take a bet the court will be only too glad to call it involuntary manslaughter and recommend a suspended sentence. No one's got any sympathy for the krauts. Dachau was their idea. It's just that you can't allow people to wreak private vengeance all over the place. Discipline."

"Maybe that's how it did happen?" Lieutenant Colonel Smithers grasped this possibility, with hope.

"Not from what Levy says. I'll need you as a character witness."

"I'll be glad to do anything I can."

"He has also announced to me, about ten times, that he is a Jew. Which I could have guessed from his name."

"But you'd never think Levy was a Jew," Lieutenant Colonel Smithers interrupted. "I swear I forgot all about it. Ask anyone in the Battalion. They'll tell you there wasn't a thing like a Jew about Levy. I don't know how many times I said to my officers that Levy was a real white man."

Major Jarvis looked at Lieutenant Colonel Smithers through his cigarette smoke. His eyes were almost closed.

"I am not the one who is concerned about Levy's being a Jew," he said. "Levy is the one who insists on it."

Now what did this slick desk officer mean by that, Lieutenant Colonel Smithers asked himself.

"He was a little shaken," Major Jarvis went on, "when I told him that the prisoners in Dachau were not all Jews. In fact, practically none of them are Jews. There were similar places for Jews. They've got everything in Dachau."

"But if he thought they were Jews that kind of explains it," Lieutenant Colonel Smithers said. It explained Levy to him. Jews were different, you couldn't figure them out. Only Levy had never seemed different. "His being a Jew and all. The court would give him a break on that, wouldn't they?"

"I'm not going to bring it up. The steering gear is my story. Have you seen Dachau?"

"I haven't had time." And nothing would get him there if he could help it; not after this godawful deal of Levy's.

"I saw it two days after the 12th got there." Major Jarvis settled himself more comfortably in his chair. "People were still making noises inside that death transport. It was fairly cleaned up when Levy arrived. I felt the way he did. You will have to take my word that I am not a Jew," Major

Jarvis said and smiled at Lieutenant Colonel Smithers.

Lieutenant Colonel Smithers moved restlessly behind his desk.

"The difference between Levy and me is that I knew I'd get caught. You ought to go over there and see it, Colonel. It makes combat seem a pleasure."

Lieutenant Colonel Smithers stiffened. What in hell would Major Jarvis, of Division G-4, know about combat? He wanted to get rid of this smooth-talking citizen, and have a drink.

"Well, all I can say is, Levy was the best driver I had in the whole war, and he was mighty popular with all of us. He was a damn good man in a fight too. There was enough in this war to make anybody crazy, as far as that goes."

Major Jarvis accepted his dismissal. He rose, from the back of his neck, and said, "Thank you, Colonel. I wish you'd talk to Levy. It's the 113th Evac Hospital. They took over an empty asylum behind the Town Hall. You'll see the signs. Levy thinks it's a prison because they've got bars at the windows. You might persuade him to keep quiet and let me handle this. He thinks a lot of you."

"I'd be happy to." But he did not want to go, for he did not want to see Levy. He thought he knew Levy; he thought, aside from rank, that Levy was pretty much the same sort of man he was, anyhow someone familiar, someone okay, someone you could count on. But there was a difference and now Levy was a stranger. He would not know how to talk to him. It would be hard to see Levy again.

"I'm going to do my best to get him off," Major Jarvis said. His voice sounded awake and serious for the first time. Lieutenant Colonel Smithers looked up, puzzled by this change. "I like him. He's quite a man."

"Levy was always a good straight boy."

"I don't know what he was before," Major Jarvis said. This wooden-headed Dixie hero thought only of combat, as if combat were all of life. "But he's something now."

"How do you mean?"

"He's not asking any favors," Major Jarvis said, and stopped. Lieutenant Colonel Smithers would never know what he meant; he was not entirely sure himself. He thought of Jacob Levy, in bandages and plaster, lying on a cot in a room like a prison cell, and refusing to escape the consequences of his act. Whatever doubt or fear he might feel, he kept to himself. He was very quiet and very polite and he stood by what he had done, alone. As far as Major Jarvis was concerned, Levy's bag of three dead Germans mattered not at all. Hadn't they been patriotically killing Germans for years? Looking at the bombed towns, you could say with reason that they had been killing any Germans, including women and children.

"Got to be going." I'm talking too much, Major Jarvis thought, and into a vacuum besides. "Oh, I almost forgot this. A letter Levy gave me. He said you would see it was delivered for him. I haven't read it. I knew you could do the censoring."

Major Jarvis handed over a letter addressed to Miss Dorothy Brock. That's funny, Lieutenant Colonel Smithers thought, though he remembered now that Levy had once asked him for Dotty's A.P.O.

"I'll attend to it." And furthermore this Major did not have to teach him his job and his duties. "You know the way out, don't you?"

"Thanks. I'll keep in touch with you."

Lieutenant Colonel Smithers sat at his desk and looked at

the letter; it was not sealed. He did not want to read it and he took it out slowly. He felt as if he were prying into the affairs of the dead.

There was a single sheet of paper: "Dear Miss Brock, I'd appreciate it if you could get this letter to the girl it's addressed to. Thank you for your trouble. Yours sincerely, Jacob Levy."

The enclosed envelope was addressed to Miss Kathe Limpert. So that's it, Lieutenant Colonel Smithers thought, he's nuts for some girl he met in Luxembourg. He pulled out another single sheet and saw that this letter was printed.

"Cherie petite Kathe; Je ne revenir. No attendez pour moi. Je vous aime tout la vie. JACOB LEVY." The signature was printed twice as large as the rest.

The poor bastard, Lieutenant Colonel Smithers thought, he's really had it. He sealed both envelopes and put the letter on the corner of his desk. The girl would never guess what had happened to Jacob Levy. He opened a drawer and took out a bottle of gin. He disliked gin but it was all he could get. He swallowed two big mouthfulls of it.

This war's gone on too long, Lieutenant Colonel Smithers thought. First they got killed and now they went crazy and fell into the hands of the law. Had Levy been mulling over that business about Jews, all the time he was there in the jeep, looking and acting like anybody else? I don't want to think about it, Lieutenant Colonel Smithers decided. He didn't know what to think; he didn't know what the answers were. He took another drink of gin. I'll get over to see Gallagher tonight, he thought, we might fix up a poker game.

There was a knock at the door and Sergeant Hancock came in, without waiting for permission.

"Can't you see I'm busy?" Lieutenant Colonel Smithers said. This whole goddam Battalion was going to hell; they acted any way they felt like.

"Yes sir," Sergeant Hancock said. He started to sidle out the door.

"Now you're here, you might as well tell me what it is."

"The replacements have come, sir."

Again, Lieutenant Colonel Smithers thought. What the hell for? Who cares anymore? Or do they expect us to get all spruced up and fight in Japan? Okay, then; if it was going to be Japan it was going to be Japan. But he, John Dawson Smithers, was through with war; he'd go to Japan and he'd command his Battalion, but if anybody thought he meant to take an interest in it, they were wrong. Because he was not interested. He did not give a damn where he went, but he was not interested. He was sick of it, war and peace, he didn't understand it, nothing made any sense. You couldn't tell where you stood. You could just damn well get drunk and they could all screw themselves.

"Major Hardcastle sent them to the Companies, sir," Sergeant Hancock said, into the silence. He didn't know whether he was meant to stay or go. The Colonel was in a bitch of a temper these days.

"Right."

"Your new driver's here, sir."

Lieutenant Colonel Smithers looked at the letter on the desk.

"Is he?"

"Yes sir."

"Show him what to do and don't bother me again."

Sergeant Hancock closed the door quietly. He told the thin

freckled boy from Texas, who was the new driver, that there'd been some trouble with the Colonel's old driver, and the Colonel was pretty attached to him and just to take it easy for a while, if the Colonel acted mean. The freckled boy from Texas thought he wouldn't have to put up with mean or otherwise Colonels for very long; he'd be going home soon, they all would, this war was over.

Lieutenant Colonel Smithers got out the gin bottle again. He tipped his head back to drink. Here's to nothing, he thought, here's to what we all got, nothing, nothing, nothing.

> *25* <

Now in the dark, after they had all gone, he could rest. They were good to him; he had not expected them to be good to him. When he found he was in a prison hospital, he did not think they would ask if he felt better, and bring him magazines and cigarettes and handle his body with care. He was surprised that there was a Major who was going to be his lawyer, and he was surprised that the Major was interested and wanted to get him off. The Major was a nice fellow; the doctor was a fine man; the nurse was kind too. He asked nothing and he was grateful for what they gave him. But at night, when it was dark, he could rest.

He felt the pain in his head as something edged and sharp, yet always pressing like a clamped vise over his eyes. This made it harder to think but after he had been alone a while, he would try again. He was thinking, he knew, for no one but himself: there was no purpose in it. It was only for himself.

The Major said the prisoners were not Jews, or anyhow not all of them were Jews. Last night and the night before, this had confused him. It was allright now. The others who were not Jews had been brought down to being equal with the Jews; they lived and died as the Jews did. It was one case where men were the same. Now he was glad he had done it for the others too. He was glad he had been able to stop the laughing, once, for everyone.

I couldn't have done otherwise, he told himself gravely. He knew that too and he was not going to lie about it to anyone. He was not going to abandon the people. He had joined himself to his race and to all those who were destroyed as his own were. If I'd gone to college, he thought, maybe I could have figured out some bigger way.

But three Germans, who had laughed a mile from that merciless death, would not laugh again. It was all I could do, he thought; he could not have allowed them to go on, insulting the dead.

It would be necessary to write home. He would do that too, later, when his head did not bother him at all. Major Jarvis said he would get a picture of the gas chamber and the ovens and the dead people outside. He would send that picture to Poppa, so Poppa would understand. He was sorry for Poppa and Momma and he knew he had brought them terrible sadness. It would break his mother's heart when the army executed him. Then he stopped thinking about this: he accepted the knowledge of his death, but he did not want to think about it.

He thought the war was a good thing and he would write

and tell Poppa so. They did not make the war because of Dachau; if they had, he would certainly have heard about Dachau long ago. But in the end, they reached it. And the S.S. guards were there, piled up dead in a mound; and their dogs were dead. So the war was a good thing. He did not want to think about the war either, because then he had to remember he had done nothing in it. Only that one German, only one or maybe two handgrenades. And then too he had to remember how he hated the war and how he feared being hit and how he did not believe it was any of his business.

I will have time, he promised himself, I will have time to think of everything and fix it all up so I understand it.

He wanted to look out the window. He raised his head slowly; it felt big and heavy and burning. Then he sat on the edge of his cot and waited for all the jangling pains to subside so that, from his head down through his chest and arms, what was broken and cut would become one steady pain which he could manage. He stood up, again slowly, and walked across the cold floor in his bare feet.

He had also never known before how fine a window could be. The night sky was soft and clean with stars. The air was the air of spring, even if it came from a crumbling, foul-smelling city. He did not look down on the buildings and the street. He watched the sky with pleasure and held on to the bars for support. The bars did not frighten him anymore, he was used to them and they made it easier to stand.

This was the last thing he had to think about and this was not to be answered, never to be answered. He had to do what he had done, but he was two people and he had acted alone. The other one would have to pay too, without being asked whether the price was too heavy. What will happen to her, he thought. He could not imagine her alone, without him, anymore than he could imagine himself without her. This was where his heart failed him. He had believed in happiness, he had taken another person's life for himself, he had offered happiness because he was so sure. It was the only great mistake he had made.

"Kathe," he said, leaning against the bars, "Oh Kathe."

The nurse had left two sleeping tablets on the chair by his bed, with the water. The sleeping tablets were for later, when the night became long and lonely and hard. He walked back carefully and swallowed the tablets and lowered himself on to the cot. It is allright, Jacob Levy told himself in the night, I only have to wait.

> *26* <

SERGEANT HANCOCK knocked but did not open the door until he heard Lieutenant Colonel Smithers say "Come in," the second time. He was taking no chances. He had been chewed enough in three weeks to last a lifetime. When he told Louie Black he wanted to transfer out of this Battalion or anyhow away from this goddam Headquarters, Louie said it was because the Colonel didn't have Lieutenant Gaylord around to keep him reasonable. Plenty of other guys had lost their friends. The way Sergeant Hancock doped it, peace didn't agree with the Colonel.

"What is it, Sergeant?"

"There's a lady to see you, sir."

Another kraut, Lieutenant Colonel Smithers thought, another blatting kraut woman who would claim his men had stolen something or raped her or owed her money. This new policeman's job gave him a pain. There was no other way to describe it: they had become cops. Guard military installations, process prisoners of war, patrol by motor, enforce military government regulations, act like a conquering army and occupy the joint. He would have to see the woman.

"Send her in."

When Sergeant Hancock left he remembered he should have asked for the interpreter too, but Hancock, though not the man Postalozzi used to be, ought to think of that by himself.

He was frowning over a sheaf of papers which assigned extra duties, changed old orders and generally ruined his working arrangements, when a voice said, "Johnny darling!"

He stood up, his face stiff with surprise, and she ran across the room and flung her arms around his neck. He remembered the smell of her hair, or maybe it was her perfume. He remembered it with sorrow because this babbling embrace, this display of intimacy, was as impersonal as a handshake. She would never need to tell him. He got it. The sum of darling-it's-too-thrilling-darling-isn't-it-lucky-darling-isn't-this-heavenly added up to goodbye. They all said, we're through, we're noisy strangers.

Dorothy Brock stepped back from his arms which had made no attempt to hold her, and he was startled by her appearance. She looked as spotless and well-pressed as ever. She wore her uniform like a perfectly cut suit she had chosen for herself. Those Red Cross caps were the only pretty ones for women. She had on white gloves too. Her hair had been permanented, no doubt in some WAC beauty shop, and these curls did not specially become her. But it was the thinness of her face, the lines from her nose to her mouth, and a hot restless

shine in her eyes, that had changed her. She looked sick.
If he didn't know her, and if besides he hadn't been in a
position to check her breath, he'd think she was drunk or
suffering a hangover after long drunkenness. It was none of
this. It was something else, caused by something he could
not see.

"How'd you get here, Dotty?"

"From Wiesbaden, darling." This reminded her of the man
still standing in the door, who had refrained from entering
and interrupting a reunion of old war buddies.

"Johnny, this is Captain Lane. Colonel Smithers. Tommy
brought me. It's really too wild these days. I haven't got
orders or a thing. We're all just sailing off, anywhere we can
go."

The airforce captain shook hands and did not trouble to
smile. So he was the new one; useful fellow, he had an airplane. Lieutenant Colonel Smithers knew the signs well: a
certain stuffiness, a melting eye, small gestures to establish
ownership. Okay Lane, he thought, she's all yours, take her
away.

"Sit down, won't you? Have you got some time?"

"Darling! Of course. Aren't you surprised? I'd no idea you
were here. We only got in this afternoon. We were driving
to the Officers' Club for a drink, you know the one down
near that big arch thing, and I saw the Division road markers.
So I made Tommy stop and ask an M.P. and then we asked
about twenty M.P.'s and finally we found you. You'll come
to the club, won't you? I'm just staying overnight. We've got
a million things to talk about. Why, it's been nearly six
months since I saw you."

She's got a fine memory anyhow, Lieutenant Colonel

Smithers thought, and when you consider the turnover it's a neat trick to keep us straight.

"I'd love to, Dotty, but I can't leave now. I might join you later."

"That's it. We'll all have dinner together."

Lieutenant Colonel Smithers watched Captain Lane uncross and re-cross his legs. You'll have to get used to it, bud, he thought with pleasure, if you take this girl around in a plane I bet you'll meet a lot of former competition. As for him, he would rather eat boiled helmet liners than have dinner with Dotty. Attending wakes was not his version of a good time.

"How's Bill?" Dotty said. "Where's Bill?" The way these bloody men glared at each other like constipated bull dogs, she raged. Who gave them such rights? Who had promised them anything? All that was left to do now was rush around, at ever increasing speed, trying to sound merry. It was not much of a success but there was no choice. They could at least have some manners and co-operate.

"Bill caught one."

"Oh Johnny, I'm sorry."

"Yes." If she said anymore, he'd throw her out. He was not going to talk about Bill, now or ever.

"Levy?" she asked, with some hesitation. She did not want to force Johnny to make a roll call of the dead. That, and much else besides, was what she was running from in the airplanes of the abundant, chummy pilots.

Lieutenant Colonel Smithers lighted a cigarette and ignored the question.

"I'm his mailman, now," Dorothy Brock went on. "I got one letter and forwarded it to Janet Flaxman in Luxembourg.

She's at the club there. But I got another about a week ago and I had so much to do, I simply forgot it. To the same girl. Kathe something. It's too awful of me but I was up to my neck; we're making a huge club, it looks like a copy of Madison Square Garden, and I put Levy's letter away and forgot it. Could I see him, Johnny, and explain? I always liked Levy; I wouldn't want him to think I'd been careless on purpose."

"He's at the 113th Evac Hospital."

"No! What for?"

"He had a jeep accident."

"Oh dear, how did that happen?"

So he told her. Captain Lane listened, wondering how much more time Dotty was going to waste here. There must be better things to do in Munich than sit in a dingy parlor, with nothing to drink, talking about a jeep driver who'd gone off his chump.

"You'll fix it, Johnny, won't you? I'm sure Levy says all that just because he's had concussion. We can't let him go to jail for ten years."

"It's not my job to fix it. That's Jarvis's job, his lawyer. I don't like him but he's a shrewd operator. He's worked up a foolproof case and he's got witnesses to prove every bit of it. Levy'd be in the clear if he'd listen to reason. I'm sold it was an accident, myself. The way Levy sounds, I don't think he knows what he did. It strikes me he's got something like combat fatigue. I've been to see him twice and Hammer goes to see him and Hancock and I don't know who else. You can't even decide if he takes any notice. He says: yes sir, thank you for coming to see me, Colonel, I appreciate it. And that's about all."

"But *why?*"

Lieutenant Colonel Smithers shrugged. He didn't know; there was nothing more he could do.

"Waste!" Dorothy Brock said and stamped her heel on her cigarette. "My God, hasn't there been enough?"

"Maybe you could talk to him. Maybe he'd take it better, coming from a woman."

"I will. I will right now."

That's a good idea, he thought, and leave me in peace to be a cop.

Dorothy Brock turned, with the practised sweetness, the accomplished smile, and said, "You don't mind, Tommy, do you? You could drop me and go to the club and send the car back for me in a few minutes. That way you'd have a head start."

"Allright, Dotty, but let's get going." Captain Lane could not control the irritation in his voice. "We haven't got too much time, as it is."

"Where is it, Johnny?"

"Behind the Town Hall. You can't miss it."

"We'll see you later?"

"Sure thing."

She put her arms around his neck again, and kissed him on the cheek and said it was marvelous finding him, she'd worried about him, and Lieutenant Colonel Smithers doubted that she heard what she was saying. Then they were gone and for a moment he listened to that cool precise voice talking in the hall to Hancock and then on the street to some soldier probably, and then their car started. Carbon, he thought, testing the noise of the engine as they drove down the block.

He shut the door and went to his desk, opened the bottom drawer and took out a bottle. It was long, narrow, without a label, and contained cognac. If you drank enough of this you could later drink gasoline and not detect the change. He was not going to offer them a drink, even of this foul stuff, and have that airforce character go around saying the infantry was a bunch of drunks and kept liquor in their desks. But when he smelled it, though he needed a drink badly, he corked the bottle and put it away. You couldn't swallow it cold; you had to be stiff before you began.

He remembered how he had dreamed about her, from Luxembourg to the Hürtgen and all the way back; across Germany from the Rhine to the mountains; and here in this stone street. He had feared though, always, that the dream was false; and he could not say she had ever given him grounds for dreams of any kind. So that was over too. He was no worse off than when he started. In the beginning he didn't know any of them; not Bill, not Dotty, not Levy either. So if, at the end, they were gone, what difference did it make? He was no worse off than when he started. He hadn't lost anything except three years of his life. That was all: just three years of his life.

* * * * * * * * * * * *

Lieutenant Spalding, the nurse, put her head inside the door and announced, "You've got a caller, Jake. A lady." That ought to brighten him up.

"I've been trying to make the boy smile for three weeks," she told Dorothy Brock who was waiting behind her in the hall. "He's presentable. You can go on in."

For one moment, he thought it would be Kathe. Against reason, he believed the door would open and she would be standing there, very small in this big place and frightened because of the bars and the strangers, too frightened to say anything, and she would come over to the bed and he could hold her against him with his good arm and kiss her and be happy. How would she know where he was? How could she ever get transportation? He was ready for the disappointment when Dotty came in and he said, "Hello, Miss Brock," as well as he could through his bandages.

His head and face were covered with bandages, leaving only his eyes and mouth clear. The dressings around his head gave it a high squarish shape. Johnny had not warned her of this; he had not said what the accident did to Levy. Dorothy Brock imagined, under the white gauze, the fine bones crushed and that face, which would give any woman pleasure even if Levy meant nothing to her, ruined. She had not been prepared so she had no time to think and find a conventional expression of sympathy.

"I see you mashed your face, Levy."

He nodded. She was mad about something. Her eyes looked mean, she was so mad. Maybe it was because of the letters he sent her for Kathe; maybe he shouldn't have. He could recall nothing else he had done to Miss Brock.

"You might have thought about Kathe before you did that."

She walked over to the window. She hadn't said hello or shaken hands. He frowned and the ache in his head, which had lessened this last week, grew tight and sharp again.

The pigs, Dorothy Brock thought, the selfish pigs. They never think of anything but themselves. His face doesn't matter to him so he goes and runs into a tree. And his girl? Did he stop to consider her? It would make a woman feel beautiful herself if such a man loved her. But he'd take that away from Kathe, in a second, without a backward glance.

"Nice view," Dorothy Brock remarked. She pulled up the only chair and sat beside him, looking at the mound of plaster that held his left shoulder and enfolded his arm. "I hear you want to go to jail for ten years."

"It isn't that." He could not stand any more of this. He was stuck here in bed and they could come whenever they liked and argue at him.

"How do you feel?"

"I'm allright." His left arm hurt so much that he had to watch himself or he'd start crying like a fool. It began last night. The nurse, when he finally told her about it after lunch because he couldn't eat and she asked questions, said the doctor would look in later this afternoon. He had been waiting for three hours, while the fever burned him and the pain turned like a knife.

"Nothing surprises me anymore," Dorothy Brock said. "I don't suppose anything a man could dream up would surprise me. But I hoped, after the war, they'd get over it. I guess not. First heroes, now martyrs. My theory is that men like to die. If they can't manage that, they think of some other way to do themselves in."

Jacob Levy said nothing. He did not know what she was talking about.

"They're noble, men are. They're brave. They've got principles or loyalties or something. They go out, noble as hell and proud as punch, and get killed or smashed to pieces. But what about the women? What are they supposed to do?"

She sounds crazy, he thought; she looks bad too, maybe she's had the jaundice.

"I'm not sure I even care about the men anymore. I used to but I could have saved my pity. I think they enjoy it. I think it makes them feel good. Anyhow, it doesn't seem to me they pay. It's their women who get it. No one gives a damn about the women. Mothers, wives, what do they matter, anyhow? Let them rot."

"Would you like a cigarette?" Jacob Levy asked. He wished he could stop her. Her words fell all over the room, clattering like dropped china or tin pans, and the sound beat on his nerves and on the broken bones of his skull.

"Thank you." Dorothy Brock lighted a cigarette and went on, talking for herself. She did not look at him to see whether he was listening.

"Maybe it was allright the way they had their wars in the old days. But now women get mixed up in it and they can't take it. I don't mean the danger; I mean what you see. After you've seen enough of it you get frightened. What's the use of loving a man and having children and trying to make a life, if it's all going to be wasted? Men don't love women, you know," she said, conversationally. "Sex, yes, that's different. But not love them. Or else how is it they can always invent something that finishes any life a woman could be happy in? Like wars and concentration camps and whatever they'll think up next? I know the men get massacred while they're about it but I tell you, honestly, that's their nature."

As if the people in Dachau wanted a place like Dachau, Jacob Levy thought, trying to follow this hostile voice. She was crazy and stupid and mean, and he stared at her without friendliness.

"You're a good example," Dorothy Brock observed. "The person who censored your letter didn't close it, the one to Kathe, so I read it. Straight curiosity and I shouldn't have but anyway I did. So you ask a girl to marry you, you let her get her hope up and plan and look forward to a lovely life and then, as soon as you can, you fix it so she'll have nothing. See what I mean?"

"I'm sorry I sent you those letters," Jacob Levy said. If he wasn't lying down he wouldn't feel so weak and helpless, with her taller than he was and slamming words at him. "I shouldn't of asked."

"Oh that's allright, Levy. I was glad to do it. I haven't had a chance to forward the second one but I will when I get back."

Kathe didn't know. Kathe was waiting for him to come. He knew about hope. He knew how you paid for every day of hope, after the hope failed, with anguish. He had tried to spare Kathe that, but Dotty couldn't be bothered. He turned from Dorothy Brock then because, if he saw her, he would curse her out loud, to her face.

"Or maybe you're scared of going home. Jail's safe. You don't have to decide anything there. Maybe it's a good idea; maybe I could use it myself. Because God knows," she said softly, "I cannot see what I'm to do next."

She looked at her watch. Levy was not listening and she had stayed longer than she meant to. Levy had made up his mind and nothing she said would change him. Besides, she had spoken in anger because of his face and because she hated to see extra waste and suffering. There was no need for any more; the world was sufficiently spoiled without Levy adding himself to the disaster. But anger was wrong and she

[317]

had muffed it. She could help no one. One way or another, she thought, we're diseased. You could, perhaps, not expect to come out of a war fresh as a daisy and sound as a dollar. She ought not to keep Tommy waiting. What was the sense in trying to think, for herself or Levy; where did it get you? The best system was to flit about, chattering like a monkey, or else work until you dropped at some simple job like tacking paper streamers in a dome over a dance floor. Keep moving, keep busy, wake up in the morning, go to bed at night and occasionally, before you remembered to stop yourself, hope something would appear out of this ratrace that you could believe in.

She pushed the chair back, but as Jacob Levy did not turn his head, she walked around the cot to say goodbye. His eyes were closed and tears had squeezed under his lashes. The pain in his arm was more than he could handle.

How do I know what anyone else thinks or feels or goes through, she accused herself, who am I to stand around laying down the law? I might at least have noticed he's sick. She put her hand over his, on the khaki blanket, and said, "I'm sorry, Jake."

Then she stooped quickly and kissed his hand because his forehead was all bandages. "Jake, believe me, there are enough unhappy women already."

He did not open his eyes or speak. She crossed the room, careful to keep her heels from clicking on the cement floor, and closed the door.

> 27 <

He lay with his good arm across his face as if he were shielding himself. He felt sicker now than he had at the very beginning, from fever and the different pains in his head and in his left arm. They talked to him until he thought he was going crazy. He wanted to shout at them all: *I'd do it again*. But he was too tired and besides they were his friends. No one blamed him so why should he shout at them? They did blame him, only not for what he had done.

Bert said: if it'll make you feel any better I'll go out and shoot some of the sons of bitches myself, but you got to admit, Jake, we'll never get them all. It stands to reason, everybody's been fighting them for more'n five years and there's a lot of them around. The Colonel says that Major's a regular lawyer and he's bound to know what's best when it's a trial. I don't see how it hurts the krauts if you're shut away somewheres. The guys feel bad about it, Jake, they don't want to see you go to jail.

The Colonel said: Major Jarvis knows his business, Levy, you ought to let him decide. We're all sticking with you and I don't care if a steering rod busted and you killed fifty krauts. But it's done and over with and there's no sense being stubborn. It's a hard thing for the Battalion, Levy. You've been with us a long time and it's your outfit too and I know you don't want to foul up the record.

Dotty said: Kathe.

Dotty was right; he knew she was right. Every time he thought of Kathe he stopped himself because he felt it would be like running out on the people in Dachau and in the train if he only missed Kathe and grieved for their life. So he ran out on Kathe: that was what Dotty meant. How could you do what was decent if either way you had to cheat somebody?

He moved a little in the bed but he could not ease his arm. The doctor had been in a hurry, with some guy brought in for an operation, but he said the place where the bone came through was infected and later tonight they would take off the plaster. The infection was what made his face so hot and gave him this empty shaking in his stomach. The doctor's been swell to me, Jacob Levy thought, he agrees with Major Jarvis too.

Kathe, Kathe, he said in silence, I never wanted to spoil your life. I love you. I wouldn't of written you unless I was sure I could build you a home and take care of you. But you see how it is. I have to think of those poor people too. I tried to help them, Kathe, I can't go back on that. Then he thought, suddenly and finally: nobody can give them back their lives. He was too late. He should have tried to help them long ago. Now he was lost again in his confusion.

He knew he would not be able to get it straight, no matter

how often he went over it, because it was too big for him. He would never understand how such a place as Dachau came to be and was allowed to go on for twelve years. Governments decided those things between themselves; governments didn't explain to people what they were really doing. Even if he had known about Dachau all along he didn't see how he could have helped, except he would have volunteered for flame throwers.

They said it wasn't murder but he had intended it to be murder. They called it manslaughter and Major Jarvis said he was certain he could get him free if he would keep his mouth shut but if he pleaded guilty he would go to jail for ten years. You might as well die as go to jail for ten years. What could you do and what would you be, afterwards? You could not offer yourself to Kathe, ruined and dirtied with ten years of jail. And Momma would be there, all that time, trying to hold her head up and maybe dying of it herself.

He had expected the army to hang him because that was the law but he believed what he had done was right. Now he believed what he had done was useless: one man could not teach the krauts to be ashamed. Maybe nobody could if they didn't feel it themselves. He had not helped the people; he had only killed three more krauts. He was not sorry about the krauts and he never would be. Even now, remembering, he hated them as much. They knew what was going on; they lived there; they heard it, saw it, smelled it. If they'd had any human feelings, they'd have pulled the people out of the train; they'd have attacked the barbed wire where it was open to anybody with fields around it, and let the prisoners out. The Nazis would shoot them for trying, but that was when you had to get shot. If you didn't, if you sat in your house and didn't notice or thought Dachau was okay or were too scared, you were filth the way the S.S. guards were, only slimy hiding filth. He would never be sorry about them, though he had not planned to escape himself. It was a fluke he was thrown from the jeep instead of flattening against that tree. If he'd thought at all, he wanted it to be even between them, the same as if he'd killed them with his bare hands. And still it had not helped the people; that was what he came back to. If I had a million dollars I'd take all those poor people and put them on a fine farm, he thought. But he did not have a million dollars and the band was pressing tighter around his forehead and he was not thinking clearly as he needed to.

I don't know, Jacob Levy said to himself, I can't understand it all. He couldn't save the people before and he couldn't look after them now. Once in his life he had done something, of his own will, for nobody he knew, not caring what became of him after, and it was no use. And maybe the reason he didn't tell Major Jarvis please to fix it so he'd be free was because he wouldn't admit that he was wrong, and he might as well sneak out of it the way you always tried to if you'd made an ignorant mistake. Now he had nothing left for himself because his faith was gone. He foundered in this despair, thinking: I should of hit that tree harder.

He lay for a while, given over to pain, and drifted into not sleep but a feverish dozing rest. Then he forced his mind back, saying to himself: I oughtn't to be like this. I can't run out on Kathe. I'm all she's got too. He had to get it straight about Kathe. Even if he couldn't handle the big things, he loved Kathe and he was sure he could make her a home and see that no harm came to her. But was he? It wasn't a question of sure. What happened once could happen again. Look how it was in the war. First the krauts bombed women and children and then we bombed women and children. How could you guarantee there wouldn't be a Dachau again?

The idea came by itself, unexpected and menacing, and he lay still between the sweaty sheets, feeling a new fear. How can you be sure, he asked himself, and it seemed that the voice in his brain was whispering. I'm a Jew, he thought and remembered the faces in the prison, I'll always be a Jew. He was getting cold, underneath the fever, and a weight heavier than plaster pinned him to the bed. He could not move, imagining the world which had grown ugly and strange, after Dachau, change and widen so that all of it, everywhere, was dangerous with a danger you could not see. The danger was poisoned, spreading, and you would not know from what direction it came. The people must have waited in their houses, on their farms, and never known what day they would be called for nor where they would be taken. What happened once could happen again.

The city was silent and there was no sound of nurses walking in the halls or men calling or talking in the wards. The plaster over his ribs was crushing him; he could not get enough air in his lungs. He had discovered something he shouldn't know; he must not speak; he would let no one see he had guessed. He must wait.

But what if you didn't wait? What if no one could make you wait? He lashed his legs, ripping off the blanket. When he tried to sit up the pain seized him and he had to lie back. I'll keep my carbine, he thought; and the room was a trap like a prison cell. I won't take a thing from anybody and if

they come to get me, I'll fight. They'll never get me or anybody of mine in a death transport; they'll never put us behind
barbed wire. I learned a lot in this war; I learned plenty. I
could organize a place so they'd have a rough time coming for
us.

Only Kathe doesn't know. She doesn't know it's not the
same anymore. It isn't the way I thought when I wrote to
her. You don't know, Kathe, you haven't seen it. He had to
get her now quickly and take her away where she would
be safe. But where was safe? There hadn't been any place for
the people to hide. Nowhere was sure but he still had time, at
least for now. He could buy their piece of land, if he hurried,
and fix up the shack with everything she'd want and watch
over her and see she was happy, for as long as he had. But
he couldn't guarantee anything, that was the difference. And
maybe she'd be better off without him. She was just a girl:
alone, no one would trouble her.

I love her, he thought, and now the voice in his brain was
shouting. I love her and she loves me. What can people do
if it's not safe for them to love each other?

You can't get excited, he warned himself, and rubbed the
sweat and the tears from his eyes; that won't do Kathe any
good. I'll explain it to her. I'll tell her it's bad. I'll ask her
if she wants to take a chance with me and I'll show her
it's a big one. I wouldn't want her to get into this unless she
knows what we're up against. I'll tell her about the Dachau
people and how it was with them. And then I'll say: Kathe,
we'll go ahead with our life but if they come for us, I'll fight.
I'm never going to wait any more.

That's the one thing you got to know, Kathe. I'll fight for
you and Momma and Poppa and anybody else they come

after. I don't care if they're not Jews the way Major Jarvis says. It's the same thing, Kathe, I saw it with my own eyes and I'll fight for them too. Kathe darling, I never meant it to be like this. I thought it would be the two of us, with nothing to bother about, there by our stream. You don't have to if you don't want to, Kathe. I'd understand it if you said you couldn't, now it's all different.

He got up, slowed by his weakness, and held to the bed for a moment. Then he walked to the barred window, as he did every night, and looked at the smooth blue evening sky.

"You want to, Kathe?" Jacob Levy said, aloud. "You want to take a chance?"

The air felt cool against his injured body. The city was closed in, under the curfew. It was so quiet you might think you were in the country, the wonderful country of woods and mountains that he remembered and longed to see. She will, he thought, I know she will; and found his hope again.

Afterword

I knew the title of this book before I began to write it; the title has always been the last thing I know about a book. I heard the words in a briefing of Lancaster crews at a British bomber base on a dark cold late afternoon in March 1943. An R.A.F. officer stood by a small table and spoke to rows of young men sitting on benches, like a school class. The officer told them, in a way I failed to understand, where they were going, probably he gave map co-ordinates, and what they were expected to accomplish when they got there. All I really understood was how long they had been doing this, night after night, and how quiet and tired they were. Then he said, "The point of no return is. . . ."

I didn't ask questions of men engaged in the heavy, appalling tasks of war; I listened and watched, and if anyone wanted to explain anything that was fine. Perhaps someone explained then, but I had already taken in what I needed. The point of no return was a specific time limit, stated in hours and minutes. When reached, the pilot must head the plane back or it would have insufficient fuel to stay airborne and land in England. Turn or die; if other causes of death such as anti-aircraft fire or enemy fighters had not supervened.

The time between briefing and take-off was hard; they had accepted that, too, night after night. The young men sat in their cold, scruffy common room and read. The call for departure was matter of fact. The crews were driven to the ungainly black bombers that looked like giant shoe boxes or maybe coffins. The planes climbed into the sky one by one and circled until they had come together in formation, then they disappeared in the dark. The people on the ground waited through the endless, freezing night until they came back, one by one, not as neatly as they had taken off. It was a good night; they all came back though there was a strained silent listening, that lasted for five or ten fearful minutes, until the last two, stragglers, could be seen, black against black. I felt half sick from cold and sadness for the young men and was careful not to show it, while I thought about those powerful, ominous words, "point of no return," a technical phrase concerned with the fuel load of an airplane.

When this novel started to ferment, or whatever novels do, it had its name. And it had Jacob Levy, who suddenly emerged as a complete presence. I saw where he was going but not how he was going to get there. He settled in with me, a good, simple, unthinking young man, hardly a man yet, wonderful looking though he was unconscious of his appearance. He had not looked at himself or at anything much. I figured he was eighteen in the September before Pearl Harbor, in his last year at Soldan High. He was so constant and so real that for an uneasy while he invaded my sleep and I thought I was dreaming his dreams not mine.

I lose what I write. As if my memory were a black hole, information vanishes after the work is done. I am left with floating wisps of disconnected knowledge and snapshots of recall. They say that nothing is lost; everything stays in the memory, but I do not believe it. I feel crippled by this inability to hold on to learned facts and am eaten with envy for people who have organised, timeproof memories.

With Jacob Levy, it was willed forgetting. I wanted him to relieve me of the memory of Dachau. I counted on my proven defect, my black hole memory. If I gave Dachau to Jacob Levy, I would lose it. In 1937, I was told about Dachau by Germans of the 11th International Brigade, Germans who were fighting fascism in Spain since they could not at home. Dachau was not the worst concentration camp; it had the distinction of being the first. It was established in 1933, as soon as Hitler came to power; a pilot project, you might say.

Our official war aims in the Second World War were the Four Freedoms, laudable intentions, but governments' words are only words; wait for the deeds. I doubt that the fighting men were much moved by the Four Freedoms; they had simpler aims, such as getting rid of the enemy and getting home, alive. I was fixed on my private war aim: Dachau, symbol of the horror of Nazi doctrine and practice, the reason the war had to be won. I wanted to see Dachau opened and finished forever. By bumming lifts across Germany, as the Allied troops advanced, I got to Dachau a week after American soldiers discovered the prison camp at the end of the village street. It was a special justice to hear the news of Germany's defeat in the Dachau infirmary.

Having re-read this novel, I marvel at my boldness in writing it. It would have been logical to write a war story based on men in the noble, eccentric, multinational British Eighth Army and on action I had followed for months: the Italian campaign. I knew little about the American Army and nothing about an American infantry battalion because I was denied the right to hang about and listen and watch such a unit, due to the rules of the U.S. Public Relations Officers in London, overlords of the American press.

These officers permitted only one correspondent from a magazine to report in combat zones. As I had taken second place on my magazine, I was forbidden to work where the war was being fought. This was absurd and intolerable; I went AWOL. From D-Day until the war ended, I was on the run from those London desk officers who had threatened to deport me to the U.S. if I again disobeyed their orders as I had by smuggling myself to the Normandy invasion. It was no trouble to move about on my own, but safer to stay away from American positions where I might be noticed. In Nijmegen, at the end of the disastrous Arnhem action, an M.P. of the 82nd Airborne division picked me up, convinced I was a spy because I had no papers to account for myself and was not wearing proper uniform. He took me to the commanding General who laughed and said that if I was fool enough to be there he had not seen me. I fled anyway, after a few days, when a friend sent word that I better hide, the London P.R. office knew where I was. This is the long-winded reason why I had no experience of an American infantry battalion.

But Jacob Levy needed an infantry battalion and needed it in terrain I had only seen for a week during the Battle of the Bulge. So I made it up, for him; Lieutenant Colonel Smithers' battalion, the Colonel and the men in the battalion, their daily life, their combat, and Dotty and Kathe and their lives as well. They all had to come into being because of Jacob Levy, the first invention. I could not now write a sensible paragraph about Lieutenant Colonel Smithers' battalion. Nothing remains; none of my understanding of the time and place and people, none of my small gleaned technical knowledge of the war. Nothing except Dachau, which remains intact.

Clearly, Dachau was Jacob Levy's point of no return; he could never go back to being the simple unthinking young man he was before. He was blasted into a knowledge of evil that he had not known existed in the human species; and so was I. I realise that Dachau has been my own lifelong point of no return. Between the moment when I walked through the gate of that prison, with its infamous motto, *Arbeit Macht Frei,* and when I walked out at the end of a day that had no ordinary scale of hours, I was changed, and how I looked at the human condition, the world we live in, changed. I remember what I felt: frantic, insane fear. I had to get away from Germany at once, no matter how; I could not breathe the air or endure the faces of Germans around me. Years of war had taught me a great deal, but war was nothing like Dachau. Compared to Dachau, war was clean.

More than forty years on, I know that my fear of Dachau was justified. If men could do that there, men could do it again anywhere, when sanctioned by the State. And they have. Various adaptations of Dachau thrive in some ninety countries now. It has been a splendidly successful model: the State declares that crimeless people, any people, are enemies of the State. Then the State locks them up, starves them, tortures them or "disappears" them, the language of our time. The Nazi formula for war has also been copied, in the needless wars, large and small, that have raged every year since 1945. *Schrechlichkeit,* frightfulness. Standard operational procedure nowadays; no rules; anything goes. I see Lieutenant Colonel Smithers' battalion as the last fortunate soldiers.

Long before I finished the book, I told Max Perkins, the great Scribner's editor, its name, *Point of No Return,* and he objected. It was too bleak, too despairing, people would not read a novel with that grim title. If anyone had suggested editing my work, I would have refused with fury. But I caved in on what was fundamental to this book, its name. It must have been a failure of nerve, struggling too long in uncharted country, confidence leaked away. Giving up my true title did not alter the writing or the shape of the story; it simply spoiled the book for me.

When I finished the last chapter, in a rural motel in Florida, I leafed through a Gideon Bible, the only thing at hand for leafing through, and came on "the wine of astonishment" and its surrounding psalm. "Thou hast made the earth to tremble, thou hast broken it; heal the breaches thereof; for it shaketh. Thou hast shewed thy people hard things; thou hast made us drink the wine of astonishment."

For my novel, *The Wine of Astonishment* is a ludicrously wrong title. Hitler, not God, had made the earth to tremble. I would have done better to call the book *Jacob Levy* since I had no other ideas. And I had no other ideas because the only right title was *Point of No Return*. After typing out *The Wine of Astonishment* wearily, and sending the manuscript to New York, I took no further interest in the book. I did not feel it was mine with this makeshift title. I cannot remember anything about its publication, apart from being puffed up (still puffed up now that I think of it) by a letter from *Infantry,* the journal of the U.S. Infantry School, asking for the date and location of my first homemade engagement in the forest, as they had no record of it.

In 1949, a year after my book appeared, J. P. Marquand published his much-acclaimed novel about a New England banker, entitled *Point of No Return.* The moral is: never lose your nerve. Since then, I have come across three novels by widely different writers called *The Wine of Astonishment.* The title, so wrong for me, is not even unique. Through the years, "point of no return" has slipped into commonplace, trivial usage. To me, the words stand as they did when I first heard them; an instruction to men at war, a statement of finality.

My novel has been out of print longer than most Americans have been alive. In this new re-issue, I am reclaiming my original, true title, *Point of No Return,* and thus reclaiming the book for myself.

Martha Gellhorn
Kilgwrrwg, Wales
December 1988